praise for michael guillebeau and
MAD Librarian

"This book is truly every librarian's dream come true. After fighting budget battles over and over again, librarian Serenity has lost her library funding. What's a librarian gonna do? . . . **A funny, moving story of our most precious institutions under threat.**"

—*Cayocosta72 Reviews*

"The hilarious patchwork of characters who run the Maddington Public Library (aka the MAD) take the perennial matter of budget cuts into their own hands. Irreverent and boisterous, this book is for anyone who believes in the power of books and libraries."

—Gina Sheridan, Author of
I Work in a Public Library

"Billed as Breaking Bad—The Library Edition and one would have to agree. Just think, as a book lover, how far would you go to save the library and the books that you love?"

—Joanne Cook

"A great adventure in the fed-up world of librarians! Funny, exciting, and realistic."

—Aimee Meuchel, Librarian

"*Mad Librarian* is for anyone who loves books, libraries, and cracking good writing. Guillebeau sheds light on our struggling library system with clever, quirky prose and a perfect balance of humor and darkness."

—Jaden Terrell, Author of
the Jared McKean mysteries

"*MAD Librarian* lives up to the pun of its title—MAD characters, MAD Library location, and MAD humor. Guillebeau has created a character in MAD librarian Serenity, who not only pays tribute to all librarians, but is exactly the one you hope works at your community library. A fun easy read."

—Debra Goldstein, Author of
Should Have Played Poker and Maze in Blue

"Great story! Loved the characters and the flow of the story. Librarians that know what they want and how to get it."

—Lisa Einwich, Librarian

"The librarians of MAD fight the good fight, say the things we are all thinking, then do the things that none of us actually do when we are wide awake. I was happy to go along for the ride."

—Rosann Goldblatt, Librarian

". . . You are taken down a crazy, MAD road of murder, corruption and . . . The passion of books and what they can do for an individual, a town, a community."

—J. Fearnley

"... Pair angst and social dismay with a wide-ranging story that offers dashes of something for everyone and you have an original production recommended for readers unafraid of chick-lit stories laced with social observation as a pillar of the community decides enough is enough."

—Diane Donovan, Midwest Reviews

"... nothing less than a powerful love story between a woman, Serenity Hammer, and the people of the city she serves as their librarian. I will never look at libraries or librarians the same way again ..."

—Kathleen Cosgrove, Author of
Entangled and *Engulfed*

praise for Michael Guillebeau's **Josh Whoever**
"... the collection of oddball minor characters and surprise twists deepen an already strong story. An engrossing debut. Mystery Debut of the Month."

—*Library Journal*

praise for Michael Guillebeau's **A Study in Detail**
"Sharp dialog, peculiar but fleshed out characters, an absorbing story, and finally, a depth of understanding of human complexities, desires, and foibles. . . Five well-deserved stars."

—Heather Haven, award-winning author of the Alvarez Family Murder Mysteries

thanks from the Awesome Librarians

HALF OF ALL of the income from *MAD Librarian* goes to the Awesome Foundation for Innovation in Libraries fund. The Innovation in Libraries Chapter was created by a small working group of passionate librarians within Library Pipeline who wanted to provide a catalyst for prototyping both technical and non-technical library innovations that embody the principles of diversity, inclusivity, creativity, and risk-taking. Naturally, we embedded these principles into the grant selection guidelines. For more information go to http://www.awesomefoundation.org/en/chapters/libraries.

MAD
Librarian

Michael Guillebeau

Madison Press
Madison, Alabama

Published by Madison Press
Madison, Alabama
madisonpresspublishing@gmail.com

Book Layout © 2017 BookDesignTemplates.com
Cover Design by Artrocity.
Author Photo by Randall Bachmeyer.
PRE01102017

MAD Librarian/ Michael Guillebeau. -- 1st ed.
ISBN: 978-0-9972055-2-7

dedication

THIS IS A BOOK of fantasy. But it is about a race of fantastic creatures who actually inhabit some of the most underfunded and overworked places in our often dirty real world.

They're called librarians, and, more and more, they're called on to shoulder any burden the rest of us don't want. They sign up to work with books, and wind up looking after kids dropped off for day care from moms who can't find anything else, caring for homeless men who can't find anywhere else, providing medical and legal advice, and helping people find jobs. The list stretches to infinity. The resources don't.

But what if they did? What if a librarian had all the power and money she needed?

This book is dedicated to the librarians who should have more but who always, always find a way to do more.

one

little pricks

SERENITY TRIED.

She tried to be a model librarian: professional, polite and as gentle-spoken on the outside as she could possibly be.

Her library was America at its best. In its public spaces, the MAD—as the librarians called the Maddington Public Library, from the abbreviation stamped on its books—was the eminently normal center of an eminently normal small Southern city. No matter what else was going on in the city outside: failing schools, drugs in the street, too few good jobs, teen-aged boys wearing their pants too low and homeless men with no pants at all—the city fathers expected Head Librarian Serenity Hammer to keep the MAD a calm oasis of normalcy as proof that the city fathers themselves were actually doing their jobs. And, they expected her to do that whether they did anything themselves or even supplied the library with actual support.

Serenity tried to live up to that, too.

That was why on a hot August morning, she was locked alone in a children's reading room with a coffee cup of rum for fortitude, a rat named Faulkner for company, a copy of Harper Lee's *To Kill a Mockingbird* for guidance, and a highly illegal choice before her.

Serenity Hammer was a librarian. And Serenity was mad.

• • •

TWO DAYS BEFORE she wrestled with moral dilemma, Serenity threw open the library's glass doors on a hot Wednesday morning in August. She smiled as patrons flowed past on their way to her books.

She picked up a handful of books from the "to be shelved" cart and turned to the stacks. She ran her finger along the spine of one, inhaled the paper-and-ink smell, and smiled again.

Someone screamed, "Damned stupid computers." She put the books back on the cart.

Maybe later.

She then walked up to a worn-out older woman who was slapping a worn-out library computer like it had stole from her. Serenity took the woman's hands away from the computer and held them.

"I knowed this was a bad idea," the woman said. "I told my councilman I needed a job and he said they had to close the employment office and he told me to go to the library.

But your damned computer just tells me what books you got here. Don't want a book; want a job."

The woman tried to pull her hands away but Serenity held on. The woman's jaw was still jutting out but her eyes were full of fear and shame.

Serenity put the woman's hands in her lap and pulled up a chair. "Then let's find you a job. What can you do?"

"Not a goddamned thing. Forty years looking after my husband and he died. Now I don't know what to do and they ain't nobody to ask that won't charge more money than I got and I just feel like everybody's letting me get torn to pieces."

"So, what have you been doing in those forty years?"

"Cooking and cleaning and raising kids and—"

"There. Know much about baking?"

"Well, of course. Who do you think made all them cupcakes the kids took to school?"

"Good." The woman slid over and Serenity brought up a web page. "There's a bakery out on Segers Road. They specialize in making treats for people who have special dietary needs. They were in here yesterday looking for a book on hiring folks."

The woman shook her finger at the screen. "They better be careful. My husband Christopher was a diabetic. There's some stuff you got to know if you're cooking for diabetics."

Serenity touched her on the shoulder. "You're just what they need. But you'll need a resume." Serenity slid back and turned the keyboard to the woman. "You type, and I'll help you."

A few minutes later, a warm sheet of paper slid out of the printer, and Serenity handed it to the woman. "Take that to Stacey out at Liberated Specialty Foods, see if you can help each other."

The woman's tears were gone, "What would we do if the library wasn't here?"

Serenity said, "My library will always—"

A blue-haired woman grabbed her elbow.

"This thing ain't got nothing in it."

She shoved a book in Serenity's hands and Serenity smiled. The woman was the wife of the Church of Christ's choir director. She had joined the Romance Book Club so she could condemn immorality. Flipping through the pages, Serenity handed the book back and pointed to the middle of a page. "Here."

The choir director's wife bobbed her head up and down like a nervous bird, studying the page and popping up to make sure no one saw her. She raised her head one last time with her mouth open.

"Praise Jesus. This is terrible."

Anything to keep them coming in.

Serenity headed for her office door. A twenty-something woman with books clutched to her chest and a librarian's badge blocked her path.

Fine. She didn't want to face what was waiting behind that door anyway.

"Ms. Hammer, he's back."

"Who?"

Amanda Doom pulled one hand from under her books and slowly raised her index finger until it was straight up. "Do you want me to get security?"

Serenity looked over at the high school boy who had volunteered to wear the red "Security" tee shirt today.

"No."

"I can call the police."

"Take them a half-hour to get here," Serenity said. "Besides, he's cousin to the wife of the district attorney. We'll just wind up in a long discussion about his constitutional rights, again. No, we need to end this once and for all. We're a library. Our power is books."

She pulled out the biggest atlas she could carry. "Keep his attention so he won't see me coming."

Serenity weaved through the stacks until she heard two teen-aged girls giggling.

"Smaller than I thought it would be," said one. More giggles.

Serenity peeked through a gap in the books and saw the back of a 1940's style trench coat. She eased her way around behind him and stepped into his aisle.

Doom was standing in front of the man as requested, looking shocked, but now she smiled at Serenity and the surprise was gone. The trench coat spun toward her. Move fast. She opened the atlas and took one giant step forward.

The opening of the trench coat rotated into view followed by the man's grinning face and his . . . pride.

Serenity slammed the heavy book shut on the man with a vengeance. He jumped and screamed and she yanked the book away with a nasty jerk.

He fell back against the stacks and put his hands over himself. "My rights."

She held the book up in both hands like Moses handing down the commandments. "Freedom of the press trumps freedom of expression." Shook it at him. "By. The. Book."

She shoved him aside.

"Come back again, Cy, and I'm going for the unabridged dictionary." The teenaged girls giggled at "dictionary." She held the book out to Doom and the girl took it like she was accepting a dead rat.

"Shelve this, please." Serenity looked back at Cy and said, "I'm tired of wasting my big books on you little pricks."

two

little cash

I NEED ARMOR.

Serenity looked at her office door and knew that the real battle lay inside, but she didn't have the heart to face it yet.

So, she called in support.

She picked up a book at random from the shelving cart, glanced at the spine (Paula Brackston's *The Midnight Witch*), and headed into the stacks.

Other people have horoscopes and morning prayers to predict their future. Librarians have books. Shelves and shelves of books. This was the tiny part of her day that she fought for. Moments with the smell and look and touch of thousands of books, walking among them, imagining a child reading a book and learning what it was like to be a man, an old woman reading another book and feeling the wonder of being a child again. *Pride and Prejudice, Catcher in the Rye, The Jungle*—books that had changed her life, and the world's. She took a deep breath and inhaled as much of the dust of paper and ink as she could and wished she could disappear into the two-dimensional world forever.

Carl Sagan said we are all made of stardust; she was made of book dust. And, like every day, she would take her omen for the day from the book dust. She slid *The Midnight Witch* into its home and looked at the next book on the right to see an omen of what the day would bring. The book was Ray Bradbury's *Something Wicked This Way Comes.*

That can't be right.

She studied the shelf and found a reprieve. Someone had carelessly shelved *Something Wicked This Way Comes* ahead of *The Illustrated Man.* She swapped the books.

Better.

"An illuminating day ahead," she said to the books. Encouraged by the random promise of her books, she went into her office to face all the bills, paperwork and accounting books it took to keep her books alive one more day. She sat down at her desk, just her alone against the world.

Almost. Something scampered through the stack of books on her work table. She jumped up and stared at a small, beady pair of rat eyes that were staring back at her. The rat waddled out from the pile, a tiny ball of fur afeared of neither God nor man. He stood up on his hind legs and studied her. They both stared, waiting for the other to run away. Neither ran.

"Hope you've got your library card," said Serenity, "'cause I sure as hell don't have money to pay an exterminator."

The rat didn't seem impressed. She studied him and tried to find some meaning here.

"Karma. I'm going to be kind to you and share my office, and the universe will be kind to my library." She looked back at the rat. "You can stay, but you'd better deliver."

She flopped down at her desk and picked up a half-empty cup of cold coffee from the top of a stack of paperwork. Then she reached into the left-side drawer and pulled out an almost-full bottle of Myers's rum that she had taken off a gaggle of teenagers who were drinking in the stacks. She looked at the clock. Ten A.M.

When she acquired the rum, her rule had been one taste at the end of the day. Then she decided to put her drinking in God's hands and only drink after he had handed her the first crazy crisis of the day. Cy and his itty-bitty problem qualified.

Who am I to defy the Almighty?

She gulped the cold coffee to get rid of it, made a face, poured the rum, had the first taste, and made a better face. Then she thought about it and poured a little in a bottle cap and put it as close to the rat as she could without scaring him and his good karma away.

She put the bottle back and studied the stacks of books, unpaid invoices, and paperwork that overflowed her office. She fired up her ancient computer and brought up the library's accounting program. She had enough cash on hand to maybe buy a free Jehovah's Witness handout, and no more money coming in anytime soon. She swiveled to the stack of bills and picked up the top one. It was from the library's internet provider. Overdue. She picked up the phone and dialed.

"Janice?" she said. "Tell me you've got some good karma for me there."

There was a long, awkward pause. "I hope this is about lunch, Serenity. I'd love to do lunch with you. But if this is about the library's bill, I can't do anything about that. Today is turn off day for the library. Four o'clock, and you know it."

Serenity studied the rat, and the broken shelf on the wall behind him. "Janice, we're the library, for Christ's sake. We can make do without a lot, but we can't function without internet. The day we lose our internet is the day we close our doors."

"And internet providers can't function without money. Serenity, don't do this to me. Look, why don't you put out a collection jar, ask for donations?"

"If you'll accept whatever I collect today as partial payment, I'll bring the money to you personally."

Janice paused. "No, sorry. I just looked at the account. You owe a lot more than any collection or donor can come up with. And my boss is insisting on full payment this time." She sighed. "Serenity, you know I support the library, but I've got a boss, just like you do. I've got to give him something. Now."

"C'mon, Janice. You know that's not fair, we're the library. I know for a fact that you let TLA Aerospace slide a lot longer."

"Yeah. And while TLA didn't have enough money to pay their bills, they still found money to contribute to every local politician—and get a tax credit for it to boot. And their president plays golf with my boss. They got connections. You don't."

Serenity looked at a set of dog-eared blueprints pinned to the wall, starting to yellow. "Yeah. Been told."

There was silence, then Janice said, "Have you tried short skirts and push-up bras?"

"Only on Joe. How long have we got, really?"

Long silence. "Don't do this to me. Four o'clock. My boss will be knocking on my door at four-fifteen for confirmation that I've cut you off."

Serenity took a deep breath. "But he would rather have money. What if I could promise you that the bill will be paid in full by Friday?"

There was a long pause. "I'd laugh at anybody else who said that, Serenity. But you and Joe are the only people left in town famous for being absolutely honest. If I guarantee my boss that payment is coming, then my ass is on the line. And yours. If you don't come through, I'll be in trouble and nobody will let the library slide on anything ever again—and the library always needs to slide on almost everything. You are absolutely, positively sure you can do this?"

Serenity looked at the screen and saw the string of ze-roes that represented her projected income. Then she looked at the rat, who was exploring his rum. He looked up at her and she took his head bob as encouragement. Maybe karma really could work by Friday. She downed the rest of the rum.

"I absolutely, positively promise."

She didn't feel illuminated.

three

little women

TWO SKINNY WOMEN DRIFTED into Serenity's office, just as they did every day at eleven o'clock.

Doom—nobody called her Amanda with a last name like that—was a model-thin young black woman with coffee-and-cream skin, and a taste for tight superhero t-shirts and tighter jeans. Joy Quexnt—nobody called her Quexnt with a last name like that—was as old as Doom was young, and skinny even compared to Doom. She peeled off a white oxford shirt. The Grateful Dead tank top underneath showed her skeletal white arms covered with blue tattoos.

"Remember," Serenity said. "Keep the shirt on out on the floor. Our city council doesn't like tattoos."

Joy gave her a terse nod. Doom tried to sit on the edge of a crooked wooden chair that was in the corner by the door. The chair cracked and settled half way down and Doom jumped and balanced half on the chair and half in the air. Joy ignored this and slumped into the one functional visitor's chair and studied a fresh patch of blue ink on one of her skinny arms.

"This place is a dump," she said. "Broke chairs, broke toilets, a headless tin man in the playground from where kids were throwing rocks at him. And slow Wi-Fi." Her tattoo seemed to pass some test and she dropped her arm into her lap, right next to her other white-skinned blue-tattooed snake of an arm.

Serenity watched Doom's chair to see if it was done adjusting itself. Satisfied that it was as stable as anything else in the room, she sat relaxed in her chair and sipped her Myers's. "What it is, is the best we can do with what we've got. This city needs us and our books, whether it knows it or not. Until the city figures that out, we've got to keep the public areas working as best we can. That includes rotating the broken-down furniture from the public spaces into the offices and being careful how we sit."

The rat scampered out from his home in the books, took a long leap onto Serenity's desk, climbed up on her coffee cup, and took a long whiz there. All three of the humans stared at the desk, as horrified as the rat was unconcerned.

The big, brown-and-gray-and-dirt colored Alabama Roof Rat (Rattus Alexandrinus Geoffroy—you could find his picture in 598.097, *Peterson Field Guide to Mammals of North America*, on Shelf 37) stared back at them and seemed to grin.

Doom snatched a book from the nearest stack and hurled herself straight up in the air, the book poised over her head like a sword of vengeance from the graphic novels she lived for. She screamed at the top of her arc then crashed down to smash the rat and the cup. Brown liquid, rat pee, and pottery shards exploded like a small mushroom cloud and settled all over the messy stacks of papers, cards, books, CDs, pink message forms, invoices, yellow post-its and leftover food on Serenity's desk. In the end, the rat lay motionless on his back with his feet sticking up in the air.

"Jesus Christ, Doom." Serenity dug a handful of paper napkins from yesterday's half-eaten Wendy's lunch and wiped down a now-stained book. Then she held it up and shook it at Doom. "Look at this. That's a review copy from a local author. What am I supposed to tell Mike?"

Joy glanced up sideways from studying her fingernails and said, "Tell him the rat gave him his first honest review."

Serenity glared and sopped up liquid.

"Ms. Hammer, he was peeing in your coffee," said Doom. "He's a rat."

"He was our rat. We protect things around here." In the middle of the mess, she poked the dead rat. The rat flipped over, hissed at her, and ran back into the clutter.

"Thank God Faulkner's all right," Serenity said.

Doom said, "He's got a name?"

"He's good luck, and we need all the luck we can get."

Doom wasn't convinced. Serenity looked at her. "I let you keep your good-luck spike. I've got my rat."

"My spike is an actual library spike, a sharp hand-made nail from Colonial times set in a wooden base. It's from

America's original library in Philadelphia, probably used by Ben Franklin himself to keep track of important papers by spiking them. That's where the phrase, 'spiking a story' came from with newspapers—"

"Yeah, I know, I've heard it," Serenity said. "I know spikes like yours used to be important in libraries and newspapers. But now they're just a hazard to children—and others. I told you, you could keep it, as long as it stays high on the shelf behind your desk, where it can't hurt anybody."

"It does. I use it to keep notes on great chapters from my murder book club. I read about a great way to kill somebody and *bam*! It goes on the spike."

"Jesus," Serenity rolled her eyes. "This is supposed to be a library, not murder for hire."

"What it is, is a dump," said Joy.

"You said that already." Serenity stuffed the wet napkins in the trash and sat down. "Let's get back to budgets." She pulled up a coffee-and-rat-pee-stained sheet and squinted at it.

"Rat should have peed on the budgets," said Joy.

Serenity shook liquid off the paper. "Thanks to Doom, he did. Like everybody else."

"How bad?" said Doom.

"Bad. The council is divided between our backers, who think that, since we're already one of the best small libraries in the South—" Joy snorted and Serenity glared at her "—we don't need more money."

"And then there is the Evil One," said Doom.

"Councilman Bentley's not evil," said Serenity. "He just wants to zero out the library budget and give everyone in the city Amazon discounts."

"Evil."

Serenity stared at the numbers floating on the brown-stained paper. "Maybe. He couldn't convince the council to de-fund us completely, but he got them to slash our budget to the bone for next year. And they've given us nothing for right now. Even if I can find a way to pay our bills over the next few days, I don't see a way out long term. Either we cut back on buying books or cut salaries. Or close. And that's a real possibility if we don't do something."

Doom jumped up and clenched her fist in the air. "We don't cut books. Books are our power."

Serenity said, "Well, look around you. We're the only three full-time paid employees left. We're each doing two jobs, and the volunteers and part-time kids out there are doing more than their share. We are barely keeping up with getting books to people as it is. And it's getting worse. Because we're so short-handed, we get more complaints. If we can't do something soon, we won't have time to do anything but handle complaints."

Doom stabbed a set of dog-eared blueprints that covered one wall. "That's why we've got to push hard for a better future. What does their precious budget say about the library expansion we all know this city needs?"

Serenity closed her eyes. "Not happening this year. Same words that we heard last year. While the last mayor found the money two years ago to clear the land next door and pour the slab for the expansion, current conditions—that's their phrase—do not permit us to complete the project at this time."

Doom slapped the blueprints. "No tutoring area for kids and teachers?"

"No."

Doom slapped them harder. "No incubator for writers and entrepreneurs, small creators who can use the library to form the creative core of the city?"

"No."

Joy mumbled. "Not even the coffee shop?"

Serenity opened her eyes but couldn't look at either Joy or Doom. "Maybe next year. You know how it goes. Every year, I go back and beg the council. Sometimes I get some money; sometimes not. It's the way the game's played."

Doom uttered an un-library-like expletive and dropped herself back into her chair. "Screw the game. We're not giving up books. Cut my salary."

"Not mine," said Joy. "Got a spot on my stomach just itching for skin art of the Last Supper with the masters of rock and roll as disciples."

"I'm not cutting anybody's salary. You two are all we've got. It's my job to get my ass out there and beg for a little more. Enough to keep us alive."

Doom had her arms folded. "I will not give up. You said we were going to build something new, starting right here in Maddington. A place where, when people had questions, they got answers. When people needed help, they got help. A city of books; a city built on knowledge and its power. You said that. Was that just talk?"

Serenity looked at the ceiling. "Yes, it was."

four

jiminy damn cricket

THE WOMEN LEFT. Serenity reached over to the table and picked up a blue mug with the words SHE BLINDED ME WITH LIBRARY SCIENCE on it. Then she took out the Myers's for reinforcement. Halfway through pouring, she looked up and saw Joy slouching at the door, pulling her long-sleeved shirt on.

"That's not coffee," Joy said.

Serenity took a long sip and the smooth, sweet burn took her away to a Florida Panhandle beach with white sands and gentle waves.

"Ain't rat pee either," she said.

"Good point."

Joy was studying her arm. "You need something, Joy?"

"No. But you do." Joy looked up from her arm. "Here's the thing. If you keep eating shit, all they'll do is let you—and the library and the city—eat more shit. That's the game they've got you playing."

"Who's they?"

"The rulers of the world, particularly here in sweet little Maddington. The big dogs and the big crooks and the big corporations that run this city like their own personal trough."

"Joy."

"Really, did you not see *The Matrix*? Whole movie was based on the idea that everything we think we see is just an illusion created by the evil real world to keep us asleep and happy, while the masters rip off the world and take what they want and leave us with crumbs. Everybody liked that movie because, deep down, they knew it was the model for their own little city."

"I think some of your tattoo ink went to your brain."

"Can't you hear the masters laughing behind your back while you're begging for scraps?" Joy asked. "Then they take all the good stuff for themselves and dare the world to stop them. Don't you know how to read those polite rejection letters they send you?"

"Of course I know how to read," said Serenity.

"No, you know how to read nice things, like an RSVP to a tea party. The real world ain't no tea party—particularly here in Maddington. You need something to translate nice-speak to real-speak before you read anything else from the masters of the dirty world. Here. Pick up any of the polite letters you've got explaining why rich and powerful people can't contribute to the library."

Serenity rummaged through a stack and came up with a letter written on expensive paper. "Here's a letter from Lois Treland. She's a very nice lady who wanted to help but couldn't."

"Treland?" Joy asked. "The developer who was almost bankrupt until our local congressman told the EPA that the land she wanted to build on wasn't really wetlands, it was just a temporary vacation spot for ducks who could be happily relocated by hunters?"

"Yeah."

"So now Treland's rich. Richer. Okay. I haven't seen the letter, right?"

Serenity nodded.

"Let's read it out loud," Joy said. "Except that, anywhere they say, 'we care deeply,' read, 'we don't give a shit.' Anywhere you see, 'we see the value of your project,' read, 'we don't see how this could possibly give us more hookers or high-quality cocaine.' And any sentence with the word 'nice' in it becomes 'go to hell.' Now read."

Serenity looked down at the paper.

"Out loud, please," said Joy. "I think you need the education."

Serenity grumped but read.

"Dear Ms. Hammer." She raised an eyebrow to Joy to show how polite this was.

"I . . ." Serenity hesitated, but made the change. ". . . don't give a shit about the needs of the city of Maddington. While the Maddington Library is a shining jewel of our community, I . . . do not see how it can supply us with more hookers or high-quality cocaine. Therefore, I must regretfully decline, but be assured that I sincerely wish that you and the library have a nice day." Serenity paused and looked evenly at Joy as she corrected the last sentence.

"I sincerely wish that you and the library would go to hell."

Now Joy raised an eyebrow. "Does that feel about right?"

"Yes. No. I don't know. Somedays. In any case, thanks for your input. It's good for us to have an ex-cop in here. Little different attitude than most librarians."

Joy laughed. "Yeah, I'm the MAD Jiminy Damn Cricket. And you don't want to know the translation for 'thanks for your input.'"

"No, I mean it, Ms. Cricket," said Serenity. "Thanks. But what difference does it make? They've still got everything we need."

"That's because they've got everything they can steal, and lawyers and political action committees to see that they don't go to jail. And, they know that nice people like you will be satisfied begging for rat pee."

"Begging is all I've got."

Just then the phone rang, and Serenity punched the speaker button.

"Maddington Library. Serenity Hammer speaking."

"Lie-brarian Hammer, I want you in my office in ten minutes."

"Councilman Bentley."

"Councilman Doctor Bentley. My office manager said you wanted to waste some of my time. I've got time in ten minutes. After that, I'm booked all week."

"I'll be there."

"Hurry up."

"Yes, sir." She took a sip of rum and looked over at Joy. "And Councilman?"

"What?"

Serenity purred. "Have a very nice day."

five

rectal thermometer

COUNCILMAN DOCTOR BENTLEY was a pediatrician popular with every parent in Maddington who wanted someone to be tough on their kids. That left him plenty of time to be a city councilman who was tough on the city and the money-wasting bureaucrats who worked for it.

Serenity had been sitting alone in Doctor Bentley's waiting room for thirty minutes, reading three-year-old *Highlights* magazines and an ageless *Bible Stories in Pictures*. She looked at the receptionist behind her Plexiglas window and smiled. Sharon smiled back, so Serenity stood up and walked over, if only for the change.

Sharon slid the window open.

"Sharon, Doctor Bentley said he was in a hurry for me to get here. Can you check to see what he's doing?"

A shake of the head. "Be careful. He gets mad if you just call him 'Doctor' anymore. It's 'Councilman Doctor Bentley.' And he's doing the same thing he's always doing.

Reading political magazines and fishing magazines. We've only had two appointments this entire afternoon. I'm bored out of my head, like most days."

"Then why—"

"He likes to make everyone wait at least twenty minutes, so they know he's important." She looked at the clock and smiled hopefully at Serenity. "Shouldn't be much longer."

Serenity went back to her plastic chair and picked up a fishing magazine stuck among the children's literature. After a few more minutes, something buzzed on Sharon's desk and she showed Serenity back to an exam room.

Serenity tried to take a chair.

"Oh, no," said Sharon. "You sit up there. On the table. The doctor likes all visitors to sit on the exam table."

"Really? The children's exam table?"

"Really."

Serenity looked for an easy way to climb up on the table in a short skirt and high heels.

"I can give you a gown, if that will help," Sharon said. Serenity glared at her and Sharon added, "He actually prefers that you wear the gown. The drug reps have learned to just go along."

"Well, I haven't." Serenity turned around and backed up to the table until her butt touched it. Then she jumped, pushed back, and landed on the table with as much decorum as she could muster. She thought she had salvaged a shred of her dignity until she heard the table's paper cover crackling under her butt.

Recovering her patient smile, she said, "We'll be fine."

Sharon left her alone. After a few more minutes, the door opened and Bentley stepped into the room wearing a long white lab coat with a pocket full of pens and instruments. Serenity forced an even bigger smile and started to say hi as Bentley looked down at his clipboard and yelled over his shoulder. "Sharon! Tell our next young patient he will have to wait while I deal with more government bureaucracy."

Then he closed the door and glowered down at Serenity.

Still smiling, she said, "Councilman Doctor, I wanted to discuss ways we can both fulfill our shared desire of making lives better for the people of this city we both love so much." It sounded even cheesier now than when she had rehearsed it.

"Lie-brarian." He waved a finger at Serenity's face. "I know why you're here. You're just a lie-brarian, telling any lie to keep your feather-bedding government job."

Serenity thought about telling him what he could do with her job, thought for the millionth time about giving up and going south to the beach. At forty-five, she still had the legs to get a cocktail waitress job on the Panhandle, fight off old men at night and bake her troubles away on the hot sand during the day. It would probably pay more than the library, and be a hell of a lot more fun.

She had just the right comment for Bentley on the tip of her tongue and opened her mouth, ready to let the words fly like cannonballs. Then she thought how quickly Bentley would find a TV news camera. On screen, he would turn into a kindly grandfather, shocked at what the librarian had said to him. He would use her comment to tear down her library. She could run away to the beach, but her books could not.

"I don't care about my job," she said. "I care about making Maddington a city built on books and knowledge and the power of information. And you'll see that the budget I'm submitting complies with everything the council has directed me to—"

"Lies! Lies! Serenity girl, you sat there in the council chambers and promised that this expansion was cancelled."

"No, sir. The council suspended expansion funding for this year, along with most other funding—at your demand. You'll see that the only token funding keeping the expansion alive for later is our Special Projects fund, which comes from donations. And the Special Projects fund has no taxpayer money—"

"Lies. Who do you think makes those donations? Taxpayers. Taxpayers who are sick and tired of your begging and your bake sales and car washes and fundraisers."

True. If she had a dime for every neighbor and relative who'd told her they were sick of fundraisers—well, she'd have enough dimes to pay for internet. Which reminded her.

"Councilman, all we need right now is a small advance for this week only, from the funding scheduled for next quarter. Not an increase in funding. Just a small accounting juggle, really."

"Ha! Ha! So you're in trouble. I knew it." He waved his finger in her face again and Serenity dreamed of reaching out and breaking it off. "One more failing government operation that we're going to close to save the people of this city money."

"There is plenty of money for the library in Maddington, Councilman. Maddington is a thriving tech center. Look at all the money those companies in Research Park bring in. We only—"

"You only want to rob those businesses of money they've rightfully earned. Business is the lifeblood of Maddington. They generously give us a little money for our city, and for civic organizations like yours to play with, as long as you stay out of their way." He leaned forward. "Your job is to take as little of their money as you can. And that is why we are going to reduce your government-boondoggle library until it's small enough to drown in a bathtub."

She hopped off the table and waved a finger in his face. "Maddington's books are never going to be drowned." Then she remembered to be polite and added, "Sir."

"How dare you talk back to a representative of the people?" He scrawled his name at the bottom of a form and shoved it at her. "Pay your deductible on the way out."

Serenity scanned the paper and looked back at him. "You're billing this as an office visit?"

"Only way I can get paid. Everything has a price, dear."

Serenity opened her mouth to object but he pulled a rectal thermometer out of his pocket.

"What?" he said. "You want me to take your temperature?"

lovin' joe

SEEING THE WATER ALWAYS brought Serenity comfort. Their small house on the lake felt rooted in the wild-
violet-covered hill that slanted down and connected to the
lake, and the lake connected to . . . Well, Serenity was not
sure what it connected to, but when she was home, she felt
connected to the house and the land and the water and to
whatever it was that she felt a need to be a part of.

She stepped into the kitchen from the garage and
dropped her keys into the bowl her son had made at Camp
McDowell so many years ago. Then she looked out through
the French doors at Joe, who was next to the grill on their
weathered gray deck. The lake was in the distance. Joe still
looked like Waylon Jennings, she thought. Shaggy brown
hair, scruffy beard, wide shoulders. The reading glasses that
were a new addition last year had slid down to the tip of his
nose and he was doing something with his hands that she
couldn't see.

Joe turned back to a cookbook on a rack and she saw that his big hands were kneading a dry rub into a white slab of fish. She watched the rhythm: hard, soft, smooth, working the flavor in. She remembered what she had thought the first time she felt those hands, back when she was young and had foolish thoughts.

Yeah, she told herself, like those thoughts were gone now. She stood there a minute, enjoying the watching and dreaming, then opened the refrigerator and took out two Rocket Republic brews.

She sneaked up on him. "Babe," she said as she kissed the back of his neck.

"Sweetblossom," he said without turning.

"How'd you guess?"

"I'm a detective, ma'am," he turned to give her his little-boy grin, "paid by the City of Maddington to deduce these sorts of things."

"Hey, deduce this." She waved his bottle at him and set it on the table. "And don't use that name in front of anybody else."

He held his dirty hands away from her and leaned over to kiss the side of her neck in an awkward gesture.

Awkward, but effective.

"I hate that name," she said. "But you, sir, can call me that anytime. As long as we're alone."

"Sweetblossom. Sweetblossom," he whispered into her neck and kissed her again, then straightened up and washed his hands in the outdoor sink next to the grill.

"Take a load off, darling," he said. His drawl was half-real, half-act.

"After what I was just threatened with," she said, "sitting down doesn't sound good."

He shook the water off his hands and looked at her while she told him about her meeting with Bentley.

Joe said, "Bentley's the same guy who cut the police budget and wants us to buy our own bullets, at least for practice. Said the city would still pay for any bullets that actually killed someone and accomplished something. Said teachers were glad to buy their own supplies, and we should be proud to support the city, too."

Serenity took a long pull of her beer. "Hell, I'd be glad to pay for a big grilling fork like the one you've got there, heat it up over the grill, and take Bentley's temperature by shoving—"

He put a finger on her lips like he was stopping her, but she knew it was just an excuse to touch her.

He looked into her eyes and said softly, "You never used to be so mean."

"Who's to blame for that? You're the one who made me a Hammer. Before that, I was Serenity Sweetblossom, born in the back of a VW microbus and named by two of the most clueless old hippies who ever lit a joint."

"I like your parents. They are who they are."

"I like them, too. I just don't want to be them. I used to dream of marrying somebody normal named Jones or Smith, maybe change Serenity to Sheila and fade away to a quiet white, picket fence life—a quiet life like a small-town librarian. Instead, I wound up a Hammer and spend my life fighting losing battles."

"Aw, darling, you were always a hammer. Way your momma tells it, you were such a terror as a child, they had to change communes every six months. I just gave you the name."

"When I was young," she paused several seconds and he gave her space, "I didn't give up, didn't give in, didn't put up with crap, and I didn't suffer fools gladly. I rebelled against everything in their hippie world and kept threatening to run away to the 'normal' world. Now that I've been in the normal world for twenty years and should be some kind of pillar of the community, it seems all I do is smile and pretend and take crap to keep my books alive. Smile and take crap. Even that's not enough anymore." She leaned into him. "Here at home is the only place I can get away and be with somebody I can always be honest with. So, what you got for me tonight?"

"Grouper steaks, with a Mojo rub I'm trying with a little Slap Yo Mamma added. Black beans and heart-of-palm salad. All for my Sweetblossom."

She put her arms around his neck, her bottle resting on his back. "You don't do the cooking to impress me. You cook because your favorite detective hero, Spencer, was always cooking."

"Always honest, Serenity," he said. "But Spencer was from Boston, and he cooked. In Alabama, men grill. For their womenfolk." He kissed her and she had to pull away when she got hot and bothered.

"That's one reason I'm proud of my sweet home Alabama. I'm also glad to have a husband who's always honest with me." She hesitated. "I've got to tell you something, though. I'm not sure how honest I was about something today."

He raised an eyebrow.

"No, I didn't lie to you. I've always been honest with you. Somebody else. But we've always made a big deal about our honesty. If I'm going to start telling lies, it's going to affect your reputation, too."

His eyebrow stayed up.

"You know Janice at the internet provider? I absolutely promised her I would have full payment to her by Friday. I've got no idea how to do it."

He exhaled. "Oh, honey, you always find a way to make these things work. The Hammers have a way of doing things right."

"Law and Order Joe."

"Law and Order Hammers."

"I guess," she said. "I just wish to hell that people would stop patting me on the head and telling me I'll find a way to do the impossible." *Even you.*

"You can always quit and do something else," Joe said. "I always thought you'd be a better cop than a librarian."

"And I could carry a gun and shoot my troubles."

"That's the way it works. Believe me, Serenity. You've got a book of rules to follow in your world. I've got another book in mine, and mine is much dirtier. Stay where you are in the nice little library world."

"Yeah," she said. "Stay where you are, little girl. Play by the nice normal book, and beg for scraps. Think I heard a stronger version of that earlier today."

"For right here, right now, let's play by our own book."

She looked far away, then blinked and nodded.

They chattered, teased, and bantered while Joe cooked. Then they ate standing up at the bar at the railing, watching a blue heron circle the lake. When the eating was done, Serenity said, "That was the best thing I've had all day."

"Maybe we can make it second best," said Joe. "You tired of standing?"

"Oh," said Serenity. "You think I'm ready to sit down?"

"Oh," said Joe. "I wasn't thinking of sitting."

Later, she propped herself up on one elbow and watched Joe snore. In a world where nothing else seemed right, there were still some things the two of them could make work. She studied the lines in his face. Yes. Still Waylon Jennings, she thought. Maybe with a touch of a graying Clint Eastwood.

doom goes to hell

IT WAS THURSDAY MORNING, and Serenity had Doom in her office. Amanda Doom, actually, who was so mad that she was shaking.

What a start for a Thursday morning.

Doom was standing with her feet apart in a superhero pose she had probably picked up from the manga stack. One hand was on the hip of her skinny, black designer jeans. She wore them today with a tight blue Superman jersey with the big red "S", dressing with as much power as she could muster. She dropped the other hand that had been pointing at Serenity like a loaded gun.

"Ms. Hammer," Doom said, still shaking. "I worship you and I know you're my boss."

Serenity took a sip of her coffee and thought it might already be time to switch to rum. "Why do I always know that, when you start like that, I'm about to catch righteous bloody hell?"

"It's not right," she said. "Our mission here is to work for books and readers. You told me that when you hired me."

"I know I told you that, but the city is right in that we work for them."

Serenity tried to wave Doom silent but keeping Doom silent today would take more than a hand wave. "Bentley is behind this. Any man who's trying to imprison books is wrong about everything." She threw her head back and yelled. "Freeee-doom."

Serenity studied her. "You came in ready to fight today."

"Ready to fight after this." She waved a wadded-up piece of paper at Serenity. "We are not going to do this."

"I got the same memo and I hate it as much as you do. But they're right. We're city employees. If the city wants you in the computer room,—"

"You mean the children's reading room."

"—which the city made us convert to hold the city's computer servers . . . Well, as long as the servers are here, and as long as you bragged about having a computer science minor, the city cancelled the contract for maintaining their software and wants you to do the maintenance in-house. In your spare time." She paused. "And me. Because I've got a minor in accounting, they've put me on the city accounts. Actually, because they've laid off everyone who can tell the difference between accounting software and actual accounting, we're both on everything. And expected to do everything."

"And you're just going to give in to them?"

Serenity picked up her coffee mug and took a long sip. "Almost all of our funding comes from the city. I work for them, you work for me. And, maybe, by being cooperative, we can get some funding from them to keep us alive. Doom, you don't know how bad things are and how little time we've got. I'm fighting to save the books, the city, the library, and your job. If we have to eat a little shit to do it, so be it."

Doom waved her hand at the closed door to the outer library. "Look, I turned down jobs at bigger libraries than this. You promised me a grand crusade for the Holy Grail, that we were going to turn Maddington into a city built on books. I treat this place like a temple. Did I tell you that I lost my virginity here?"

Serenity shut her eyes. "God, no, Doom, I don't need to hear this."

"Yes, you do. You need to know what this place means to me. First day at work here, I found a stash of condoms in the back stacks, left there by teenagers, I guess."

"Not the first time we've found condoms, sometimes even in the books. Sometimes used." Serenity looked at the clock and tried to convince herself it was late enough for rum. Shouldn't have to listen to this sober.

"I figured the condoms were a sign the books were trying to give me. So, the first night that I was the one closing up by myself, I had a boy come in. We went back and arranged Jane Austen and J.D. Salinger and an original X-Men graphic novel around us and—"

"Enough. I really need to pretend that didn't happen."

"Well, I can't. Every time I come to work I smile, proud that I became a woman in this library. My self-image will take a terrific blow if I find out I gave my virginity to an accounting program."

Serenity shook her head. "Who was the boy? I didn't even know you were dating anybody seriously."

"I don't remember. Just some guy."

"You remember the books around you but not the boy?"

"You made a promise to me: here, we will build lives around books, and we will lead Maddington to greatness. You promised me, and I took you at your word."

Serenity took an even longer pull of her coffee and stood up. "Doom, I don't know. I don't lie to anybody about anything." She thought for a second and then added, "Well, I try not to. I made those promises about making Maddington something special when the old mayor was here and supported our vision. But things are different today. For today, we have to give in and you have to get your ass out to the computer room. Now."

Doom drew herself up into her full superhero pose, fists clenched and skinny arms tense at her side, like she was going to destroy a small building with her hands. Then she slumped and dragged herself out.

"Bentley's right about you," she said at the door. "Lie-brarian."

eight

little man with a big hat

IT WAS HARD for Serenity to take this seriously.

The mayor looked like the round little man in the Monopoly game, the one with the drooping white mustache and the top hat and tails—but without the top hat and tails today.

He was sitting behind a massive walnut desk in an office bigger than the whole adult fiction section of her library. It was hard to take a meeting with this man seriously, except that the library's future depended on it.

"Mayor Johnson, the city needs your help. By Friday."

"Absolutely." He beamed across his desk with a big, baby-kissing smile. "Would you like some coffee?"

"No, thanks."

He yelled past her. "Miss Henson, would you bring Mrs. Hammer a cup of coffee?" He returned to beaming at her. "How would you like it?"

"I don't—black, I guess."

"Any way you want it. This is your city and your office."
He furrowed his brow and gave her a grave look. "I'm so
glad you stopped by. I have a question that I need your
unique expertise on."

Serenity breathed a sigh of relief. "Thank you, sir. It's so
good to be taken seriously. As the librarian, I've got a
unique vantage point on our community and I think we can
use the library to make Maddington a great—"

"As a woman, what do you think about how I've decorated my office?"

She paused. "It's—fine. I guess. It looks like any government bureaucrat's office. Big desk, pictures of you with
important people—"

"That's me with the governor there."

"I see that."

He put on a serious expression and locked eyes with her.
"The opinion of women voters is very important to me.
There are many areas where women are much more qualified than men. I want you to know that I take your opinions
on office decoration very, very serious."

"Seriously," corrected Serenity.

He nodded solemnly.

"The polls show that I'm trailing with women voters. I
want you to tell your friends that I listened to you and that I
was very seriously."

"Serious."

He looked peeved. "Well, which is it?"

"It's an adverb when—never mind. I think this is a very nice office for a government bureaucrat."

"Statesman." He sat up proudly.

Serenity saw an opening. "And the people of Maddington have a crying need for a real statesman, starting at tonight's city council meeting."

"I'm your man. Our city can count on me to give the very best. I have always been at the forefront when it comes to leading our city forward."

Serenity tried a salesman's smile but it felt forced. "Yes, sir. You've done so much. Maddington is one of the finest cities in Alabama—progressive, educated—"

"Don't forget friendly."

"Yes, that too. However, our leadership is at grave risk."

The mayor stood up. Standing, he was about five feet high and five feet around. "We will not stand for that. Whatever my city needs, I'll give."

"Sir, our library is the cultural center of Maddington. We need to expand the library and make it the focus for better educational opportunities, and an incubator for creativity and job growth. But, instead of that bright future, because of a lack of funds, we may soon have to close our doors."

He set his jaw. "How can I help? Are we going to do a bake sale or a car wash? The mayor himself will wash the first car!"

Or eat the first cupcake, thought Serenity. Not the time for that. "No, sir. We've had car washes, and bake sales, and book drives, and donation nights at restaurants and bars, and NPR fund appeals, and every kind of fundraiser imaginable until people are sick of them. We need more."

He tugged at his chin and paced back and forth. "Your mayor will have to think of something. Perhaps you could talk to Paul Molcut. He seems to have a lot of luck in getting corporations to donate stuff."

"I have, sir. Mr. Molcut certainly seems to have the ear of businesses and civic organizations in North Alabama. But Mr. Molcut feels that the businesses in Maddington have been as generous as they can be. What we need, sir, is for the city to restore our previous funding level, and fund the expansion. Without city funding, there is no way for us to keep our doors open."

He stopped and looked at her. "City money?"

"Yes, sir. Last year, the city generously funded the library at a level of—"

"But that was before Councilman Bentley organized his group to punish politicians who spend money."

"Yes, sir, but the library provides far more value than the small amount of funding we ask."

"But Councilman Bentley will withdraw his endorsement if I push for more spending. You do know that this is an election year? Statewide, almost all offices are up for grabs in just a few months. Governor, congressmen. Me."

"Maybe he'll stand by you, sir." Serenity swallowed hard. "Surely Councilman Bentley knows what a fine statesman you are for the city of Maddington. I think he'll respect your leadership." She swallowed again. "The people certainly do."

The mayor struck a visionary pose. "Mayor Johnson is the man to lead Maddington into a proud future."

Serenity brightened. "So, if we request that the council restore full funding for the library, we have your support?"

"Absolutely. As long as it doesn't cost any money."

"Well, sir, the original budget had a little more than the proposed budget has. Really, just a little more."

He beamed. "That's the beauty of Maddington democracy under Mayor Weatherford Johnson. Any citizen can propose anything they like, tonight at the council meeting. If the council approves, why, I'll be all behind it."

"But you won't speak in support, sir."

The smile took on a crocodile quality. "You don't need my help."

"Uh, thank you, I guess, sir. There is one other small thing. We'd like to propose a small, no-cost accounting juggle to help the library get past a short-term problem. You can do it without the council's approval."

"Certainly. As long as Councilman Bentley doesn't oppose it."

Serenity stood up and slumped to the door. With her hand on the knob, she turned back and thought she might as well be talking to the Monopoly man. "Sir, have you ever considered wearing a black top hat?"

The mayor beamed. "You think it would make me look like Lincoln?"

how do you shelve an ak-47?

SERENITY STARED at the blank page.

How the hell do politicians do this?

She sat at her desk working on her speech for that night's city council meeting. Every word counted.

Of course, that meant that no words would come to mind. The notepad in front of her was still blank after an hour.

Start with anything. She remembered Natalie Goldberg's first rule for writing and sex: Keep your hand moving.

"Ladies and gentlemen," she wrote.

Then she scratched that out. There were no women on the present council.

"Gentlemen."

Well, hell, there would be women in the audience. Leaving them out was just plain rude, so she scratched that line out, too.

Back to "Ladies and gentlemen."

Is it reverse sexist to put women first? Scratched that out.

Faulkner was perched on the table at her elbow, twitching his whiskers.

"What the hell are you looking at?" she said. He didn't budge.

"Arrogant bastard," she muttered. Then she threw her arms at him and screamed, "Aargh!"

He still didn't budge. But, the man standing in her doorway squeaked.

She looked up to see a man in full camo gear. He was an older man, with a white ponytail and a Vietnam Veteran ball cap with small holly branches attached to it, presumably for more camouflage.

"I'm sorry," she said. "Can I help you?"

He jerked his chin at the nameplate by the door. "You the librarian?"

"Yes, sir."

"The head librarian?"

"Yes, sir."

"Don't want to talk to nobody but the head librarian."

"That'd be me, sir."

He stepped in and closed the door behind him. She opened her mouth to stop him but decided, what the hell.

He looked at Faulkner. "You got a mascot."

"Appears that way."

"Pets are good."

She nodded. "How can I help you, sir?"

He swung a duffel bag off his back and reached in. When he withdrew his hand, at first it looked like he had a black pipe in his hand, but then Serenity recognized it as an automatic rifle.

"Holy shit!" She froze. Stay calm. Stay calm. Stay calm.

He stood there with the gun in his hand and a crazy look in his eye and said, "Think the library can help me, ma'am?"

She forced herself to stop staring. Her eyes fell on a mug with the words KEEP CALM AND ASK A LIBRARIAN.

"We help everyone, sir. You've come to the right place." Silently, she wondered if they had a book on how to disarm a maniac. If not, she needed to order one, for next time. If there was a next time.

"That's what I heard. People say this library handles everything."

He shifted the rifle and Serenity looked for something to throw but he set the weapon down on her desk before she could move. Then he stepped back, his back straight in a remembered posture from fifty years ago. "AK. Took it off a dead Viet Cong. Now that we're friends with those little yellow bastards, I thought it would be right to try to give it back to his owner. Or at least his family."

He reached for the rifle. Serenity jumped up and pinned it with both hands.

"Here." He touched the barrel. "Some kind of gook writing. And a number. Somebody, somewhere ought to be able to tell who it was issued to. I know this ain't exactly a book of Shakespeare, but I don't know where else to go and you're—"

Serenity finished, "The librarian. Yeah."

"So, I thought I'd let you write down the numbers and shit, see what you could find."

Serenity looked into his tired, crazy eyes and pressed down harder on the rifle. "I need to hold onto this, sir. To find the owner."

He thought about it a minute and nodded. "Tired of carrying the damned thing around for fifty years."

He disappeared from the doorway and was gone.

Serenity picked up the rifle and held it in front of Faulkner.

"Maybe I need to take this to the council meeting tonight. Maybe this will be my rectal thermometer."

For lack of any better place, she shoved it behind a filing cabinet. Then she looked back at Faulkner. "What? I'll tell Joe about it tonight and get MPD to come get it. I don't have time to deal with this now. And it's not like you know where to shelve an AK-47."

big man cowering

THEY RODE in Joe's city-supplied car, a vicious-looking black Charger with a police bubble on the dash, and the radio and computer separating him and Serenity. Serenity was muttering to herself and fidgeting with the button to roll the window up and down. The hot summer evening air would roar in for a moment and turn the car into a sauna. Then the window would go up and the full-blast air conditioner would freeze them.

Joe said nothing, which was probably a good thing, but it didn't protect him.

Serenity left the window up and turned on him. "What the hell is wrong with you men?"

He said nothing and it still didn't help him.

"I mean, you either want to screw us all, either literally with a rectal thermometer or figuratively with your politics. Or, you are completely clueless and not worth the time it takes to talk to you."

Since silence wasn't working, Joe said, "In fairness, it's not just men. Remember Councilwoman Margaret Wardzinski? Ever try to talk to her?"

"Yeah. All she wanted to talk about was how I was wasting every minute of my life that wasn't spent evangelizing for Jesus."

"The captain asked her one time, trying to be friendly, how much time she spent reading her Bible every day. She gave him a horrified look and said, 'Think of the souls I might save in the time I'd waste reading.'"

"Good thing she broke into a Catholic mass and demanded they all convert to 'real Christianity.' Losing the Catholic vote cost her the election, particularly since the mass was on TV and on the internet—and then network news."

Joe smiled to himself, thinking he had escaped.

"Okay then, what the hell is wrong with people?" Serenity turned on Joe like it was still his fault.

"You're asking a cop that? Too much leniency for repeat offenders. No criminal penalties for citizens who don't report crimes. A system that's inherently corrupt and won't touch the powerful. Too—"

"All right, Dirty Harry, it was a rhetorical question. You know what I mean. Can't this council see good sense? If they approve this budget tonight with almost no library funding, I don't know how to keep our doors open. I've told them and told them and they just smile and say, 'You'll find a way, Serenity.' And I'm supposed to keep my mouth shut and say 'Yes, sir,' and 'No, sir' and make chicken salad out of chicken shit?"

"In fairness, you can't keep your mouth shut and at the same time say 'Yes, sir.' For the record, I don't see you doing much of either. And we're on our way to speak at the council meeting where you will probably say a lot more than that."

She glared. "You know what I mean. I'm tired of making something out of nothing." She paused. "And I'm scared shitless to have to stand up and give a speech tonight with this city's future riding on it."

"You'll be fine. Finding a way to make things work is what you do best."

She thrust herself across the computer at him. "Do you know what a piece of bullshit that is? It's like one of those things from Joy's nice-to-real translation book. What it really means is, 'Don't expect any help from us. We'll dump problems on you any way we see fit, and expect you to clean up the mess.' I don't know which is worse: my friends who are sure that I can fix this quietly so they won't have to stand up to Bentley, or Bentley's gang who will be happy when I can't, and the library goes out of business."

Joe thought about asking about that translation book but said nothing.

She poked a finger into the side of his face. "Is that what you want? Law-and-order Joe is going to sit there and watch people get away with practically murdering his own wife?"

She looked at Joe cowering in his seat. He reminded her of a cartoon elephant who was afraid of a mouse. "Just don't leave me tonight, babe."

"You know I won't," he said.

"I know. Just keep your gun handy if things get out of hand."

"Do I need to shoot them, or you?"

"Doesn't matter, so long as one of us gets some relief. Probably do me a favor if you just shoot me now. I'm so scared of speaking in front of everybody, I'm shaking and afraid I'm going to throw up."

"Just pretend you're talking to me. Besides, you've got your notes."

She looked at the stack of index cards in her hand. "I'm sweating so much I'll probably soak the cards too much to be able to read them."

They pulled into the municipal complex and parked. She cracked the door open and hesitated on the edge of her seat. "Joe, this has got to work. They can't have my library."

"You'll find a way," he said. Then he smiled. "Just don't rob a bank or I'll have to arrest you."

She tried to smile back, but it faded. "Yeah. Do things the nice, right way."

He reached over and touched her thigh and she pushed away and looked out into the still-humid Alabama air. The Maddington Municipal Center was a modern brick building that tried to combine a spire with traditional Southern architecture. The results looked good if you squinted at it in the right way, not so good if you didn't. Serenity usually was able to find the harmony in the building, but tonight she just saw a war between the two themes.

Maddington had been both a high-tech center with businesses built on genetics research and NASA contracts, and a deeply conservative old Southern country town. The former mayor had forged a partnership between the two cultures and grown jobs and services. But he moved to California and the council appointed Mayor Johnson, and he was . . . well, charitably, he was not the same, and the city spent more time fighting than progressing. The high-tech jobs and businesses and workers were drifting back to the larger city of Jericho next door, leaving Maddington increasingly filled with empty storefronts and hollow-eyed people coming into the library for help.

Serenity stared at a small knot of people marching into the building from the other side of the parking lot, all of them two steps behind Bentley, like warriors following their chief.

"Honey," said Joe, coming out of the car, "Don't be afraid of them. Politicians get to strut and pose and pretend, but they don't run anything."

Serenity waved her hands at Bentley's entourage. "I sure as hell don't see anybody telling them what to do."

"You won't see the people who tell them what to do here. Wouldn't recognize them if you did. It's the big companies and the crooks. No, scratch that. It's what's behind the corporations and the crooks. Even here in little Maddington, it's like Vegas with its big hotels and showoffs strutting around, all for show. Somewhere in a back room in Vegas is a little man who takes a trivial one percent from every bet, every drug deal, every hamburger sold—and takes it every day. Those guys sit back and laugh at the rest of the world. There's less glitter in Maddington, but the same spiders exist here. And, you never know who they are until their names come up in a police investigation and someone high up taps you on the shoulder and says, 'you don't need to look at him.'"

"You and Joy ought to get together and form a Paranoids Anonymous chapter," Serenity said. "And maybe I should go to your shadow bosses for money."

"Those guys take, they don't give. And they set up useless politicians to keep people like you and me from getting to them."

"Well, tell them to stop trampling my library."

"Yes, ma'am."

Serenity quick-stepped to get ahead of Bentley's group and Joe hurried to catch up. She marched in and claimed two seats in the front row, sitting with her back straight and her eyes straight ahead. She would get it right this time.

Then she felt a tap on her arm. Joe said, "Just don't overreact this time, honey."

She gave him a nasty look and he slumped down in the chair and pulled his hat down over his eyes. From under the hat came the words, "Please, Jesus."

gone with the windbags

THE LOCAL big-haired Baptist minister opened the council meeting with a prayer while Serenity said her own silent one. The mayor started to read the agenda but Bentley leaned into his microphone so his voice boomed with the authority of God.

"We don't need all that, Weatherford. We're just here to approve the budget we talked about last time." He smiled at his crowd and leaned back into the mic. "Let's get this government business over so we can get home in time for the Braves game on TV tonight." There was polite applause from a few of his people.

"Well." Mayor Johnson looked around to the other council members. All were seated behind a walnut dais set three feet higher than the common people. He got no objection and heard a couple of "C'mon, c'mons." The mayor looked out at the crowd. "I guess that'd be all right. I guess, if there's no objections, we can vote."

Serenity got to her feet and wiped her sweating palms on her dress.

"Mr. Mayor." She cleared her throat. "I'd like to speak on the point."

Bentley rolled his eyes. "Serenity, girl, I explained this to you in my office this afternoon."

"Yes, sir. You did. I'd just like the opportunity to present a few points to the council as a whole."

Mayor Johnson looked at Bentley. Bentley waved his hand like he was swatting a fly.

"Make it fast. Game starts in thirty minutes."

"Yes, sir." She held her index cards up and tried to focus, but her hands were shaking.

"Ladies and gentlemen. Under this proposed budget, our library will have to close its doors. We can't—"

She tried to shuffle to the next card and the stack got loose and exploded out of her hands and fluttered down to the carpet like a white cloud of wayward birds. She gasped and dropped to her knees and tried to scrape the cards together.

Bentley's voice boomed over the loudspeaker. "Let me help you, Serenity. If your library is unable to support itself, then we can take the funding we allocated last year, and use it to open our citizens up to the biggest library of all—the internet. A place with more books than any library can ever have. Our citizens can have discounts at sites like Amazon and iTunes. Every citizen will have his own library in his own living room."

She gave up on the cards, stood up, and pointed at the cards.

"The internet is like those cards on the floor: lots of information, and no accountability. When your children go to the internet, they may find what they need. They may not. Or, as our police will tell you, they may find much, much worse. And when they are discouraged or hurt or lost, the internet does not care, and does not help.

"Our library—your library—is the only place where anyone, anytime can consult with a professional for free. We have knowledgeable professionals hired by the city to help; and they are accountable to help and inspire all of us.

"Maddington is in a battle with other cities for high-tech firms and startups that are too small to afford a full-time research staff. That battle is between the forces of knowledge and the forces of rumor and guesswork."

She turned to one of the council.

"Councilman Jacobs, you're our lead recruiter for new businesses. What would it mean to you if you could take potential businesses to the new library and tell them that Maddington is a city built on books and knowledge, tell them that when they have questions—technical questions, legal questions, business questions—they can come to the library and have professionals research answers in minutes?"

"We would kick ass," Jacobs sighed. "I get tired of being asked what's special about Maddington, having to tell them we've got a Walmart and a Burger King."

A couple of the councilmen nodded. Jacobs looked at the nodding heads and said, "You know, the funding Ms. Hammer requested is really not that much. Not for what we get."

Bentley shook his head. "Low taxes. That's what companies want."

Jacobs said, "We're talking pennies here, Mr. Bentley."

Bentley's voice boomed. "That's how it starts, a penny here and a penny there."

Jacobs said, "You know, we do have another unannounced project. Maybe we could divert some of that funding."

Bentley pulled back from the microphone and hissed at Jacobs. "That money is earmarked. And off the books."

Bentley nodded to his crowd. A man stood up and yelled, "No more spending." Others took up the chant.

The two nodding councilmen stopped nodding.

Bentley smiled sweetly. "Serenity, girl, we don't need to waste the people's money on books when we have the internet. Books don't matter to people anymore."

"Books don't matter?" Serenity shouted at Bentley. "Where do you think all these ideas you think are so original came from? Books are our connection to all the wisdom of the world. Books let people from hundreds of years ago and a thousand miles away enrich our lives.

"Books. Books and people. And that's all our library is. A junior high school boy, sitting next to volumes of Shakespeare and Hemingway, writing his first story—that's our library. A girl reading a book on electronics and a book on music and coming up with a new component for the music industry—that's our library. Books and people—libraries— keep this city alive. I beg of you, don't take our library away from our city."

Jacobs said, "I move that we restore the library funding requested by Ms. Hammer."

Bentley shook his head. "We will punish any politician who tries to increase spending."

His crowd chanted. "No new spending."

The motion never received a second.

Serenity stood there, alone and awkward. Then she looked at the crowd and shook a finger. "I will never let you take away our library."

"Ms. Hammer," Bentley smiled down on her like a father lecturing a wayward child. "We aren't the ones taking your precious plaything away from you. Your library—and all of these so-called community programs—are in danger of dying because people like you act like government bureaucrats, and insist on running your toys by your government bureaucrat rules. Your rules are what's killing you." He pointed a finger. "Someday soon, in typical government bureaucrat fashion, the pot of money that you have mismanaged will run out, and you will find a bill that you cannot pay. You will come back to us and beg, like the bureaucrat that you are, for more money. And on that day, we will shut your outdated library down and sell your precious books by the pound."

Serenity turned her back on them and stomped out. Let them have it. Let them have it all and take their precious city to the hell it deserved. If they don't care, I don't care.

Joe followed her out to the lobby. "Honey, you can only fight so much. I think that's probably the best way to end it."

She swung at the air violently, missed and hit Joe in the face.

"Oh, honey," she said and reached out to apologize. He was standing hard and still as stone, pretending it didn't happen or didn't hurt or didn't something,. So, she respected his macho and pulled back and blamed his swelling eye on the men inside, along with everything else. She stomped back into the council chambers. From the back of the hall she shouted: *"You. Will. Not. Take. Our. Library!"*

twelve

maybe i can shoot somebody

SUNRISE ALWAYS FELT like a new book to Serenity, ready to be opened so all the good words could spill out.

Friday morning, all she wanted to do was keep this book shut.

She had been sitting on the darkened deck since she got home, curled up on the glider in her Crimson Tide sweats and wrapped in a blanket. Next to her was a notebook for ideas.

The page was blank.

The door opened and Joe came out and sat two coffee cups on the glider arms and sat down beside her. She scooted to her side and pulled the covers around her tighter.

He studied her. "Today, right?"

She ignored him but picked up the cup and took a sip.

"Pretty sunrise," he said.

"If you like sunrises."

"I'm guessing you've got no ideas?"

She turned quickly and sloshed coffee. "None."

"What can I do to help?"

"Mr. Law-and-Order Cowboy?" She snorted. "Shoot somebody, maybe."

"Tell me who."

"You don't have enough bullets."

"Maybe you can be a books-only library with no internet and almost no money."

"Kind of like a one-legged man running a marathon," she said. "Half the people will have questions we won't be able to answer, and they'll have nowhere else to go. And, the city council will shut us down as soon as they find out."

She drank more coffee. "I'm going in to work. I want to spend every minute I can there on the last day that it will be a real library."

She leaned down and kissed him. She looked at his purple-and-black eye that was almost swollen shut. "Sorry."

"I'm thinking of calling it a fashion statement. No big deal."

"You didn't deserve it."

"You couldn't hit the people who did. You think you could give me one of your 'MAD' stickers to put over it? Maybe make it say 'MAD Kicks Ass.' I can walk around city hall and make sure the council gets the message."

"I think MAD's ass-kicking days were over before they really began." She looked at his eye. "Maybe you could tell people you got it during a bust."

She stood up. "Maybe I'll come by the station later. Talk to you and the chief about a job down there."

"That's the thing about our having a good reputation for doing things the right way," Joe said. "People know they can trust you with something like being a cop." He laughed. "Good day for it, with me being a walking billboard for your punch." He paused. "Ironic. In modern times, the library's become the place where everything that falls through the cracks winds up. Folks who don't have anywhere to go turn to the library. Without it, they'll just crash and burn and become police problems. At the police station you might be doing the same things with the same people."

"But with guns and prison sentences instead of books."

"Well," he said, "there's that."

thirteen

into the dark

THE LIBRARY WAS DARK and early-morning cool when Serenity unlocked the door. She went to her desk and poured herself a full cup of Myers's. Faulkner climbed up on a stack of books and twitched his whiskers.

She took her first sip. "I don't know what to tell you. Eviction day's coming, for me and you both." Another sip. "They'll probably convert this place to another Walmart Mini-Mart. So watch out, they'll probably douse the whole place in rat and insect poison—after they throw out the books."

She stood up. "C'mon. I'm going to take you outside and set you free before they destroy this place. If I can't save anything else, I'll save one rat."

She reached for his tail but he jumped a foot to the left. He didn't run away, though. She reached for him again and he did the same little jump-and-stick thing.

"Suit yourself," she said. "You want to stay and go down with the ship, I'll admire your courage. More than I've got."

She sat back down and he returned to the book he was sitting on. "What you got there?"

She stood up and Faulkner moved away. She picked up the book.

"*To Kill a Mockingbird?*"

She thumbed to the first page and sat down and read. One of the great things about being a librarian was being able to read tons of books. And one of the great things about reading tons of books was that they each lived in you long after you put the book down, until, finally, a librarian's brain felt like a small city of characters wise and silly, evil and noble, all waiting to be called up at any moment.

One page in and she recalled the whole book. Closed it.

"Atticus Finch," she said. "One of the greatest heroes ever. A whole town doing wrong and he still does the right thing."

Faulkner stood up on his hind legs.

She looked at him.

"So what?"

But he kept standing.

fourteen

short ugly words

NINE A.M. Serenity had been wallowing in self-pity for hours. Time to go out and be a real librarian, if only for today. She put her hand on her office door and tried to prepare herself for anything.

She wasn't prepared for the searing hot musty air that boiled from the stacks and slapped her back into her office. She forced herself to open the door again and pushed her way into the heat.

Joy was slouched behind the counter. She pointed at a man in a blue service uniform sitting at a table by the door. He looked up at Serenity and smiled.

"Compressor, ma'am. AC's dead in all the public areas. Good news is that the offices are on a separate system, so your office should still be okay. I was just about to bring you your estimate."

The sheet had a long column of numbers. A really long column of numbers.

"Looks like this baby hasn't been maintained in years," the man said. "Disaster waiting to happen. I already called the office to get the parts lined up because I figured you'd want us to get this done ASAP. These buildings weren't made for occupation in Alabama in August without AC; you don't even have any windows that open. It'll be 120 degrees in here by noon. Office said they'll need payment up front. They said you'd understand, but you can call them if you want."

Serenity stomped off to her office with the estimate in her hand, swearing to herself and glaring at anyone who dared to make eye contact. She looked at the estimate and the spreadsheet on her computer. The number on the sheet was well into five figures. Her spreadsheet barely made it to the left of the decimal point.

Well, she wouldn't have to worry about the internet bill. Her library was dead right now.

It was a relief, actually. She could call Janice and say, "I would have had your payment, but . . ." She could recover her honesty, and be blameless. Blameless when she called the mayor's office. Blameless when she called the staff together and hung the sign on the door. Maybe she could even feel blameless when she looked at a book someday and thought of all the books mildewing in the oven that had once been a sanctuary that she swore to protect.

She had done her best. When she was a girl, hadn't they told her that was all you could do? Do your best, then smile and shrug when the world went up in flames. She pulled

Mockingbird off the shelf. "Atticus Finch," she said, "you fought the good fight. You always did the right thing. And when it wasn't enough, you told Scout that you had done your best and held your head high."

She put the book back. "Here's to all us noble losers." Then she thought of a Sheryl Crow song and paraphrased it. "If it makes you proud, why the hell am I so damned sad?"

She uttered a short ugly word. Then a whole string of them.

fifteen

atticus finch was wrong

SERENITY FELT like she needed to cry or scream or apologize. Apologize to anybody, for anything. Anything but losing the library. She wasn't ready to talk about that yet.

She avoided the AC man, sitting patiently with a hopeful smile, and went looking for Doom in the computer room.

"Children's reading room," corrected Doom when Serenity called it the computer room.

"At least it's cool in here. This and a couple of other offices are the only places with AC today."

"Bentley kept the air conditioning on for his precious computers," said Doom.

"That's just chance. Bentley didn't cause this."

"You don't know that."

Serenity pulled her hand up to take a big gulp and found that she had picked up Mockingbird instead of her coffee/rum cup. She'd probably had enough anyway. She looked at the tiny children's desks and chairs, now piled like discarded toys in the corner to make room for the servers. She felt old and tired and beaten—and a little drunk, but not drunk enough to tell Doom what was going on yet. "Look, Doom I came here to—"

"Amanda. I want to be called Amanda if I'm just a computer jockey instead of the goddess of the books. Going to get me a button-down oxford shirt and a pair of nerd glasses and—"

"Amanda. I came in here to apologize for snapping at you yesterday. And for—everything."

Doom was slumped over the one functioning desk in the middle of the room, her hands on the keyboard and her red-rimmed eyes locked on the monitor, refusing to look Serenity in the eye. "No need, Mistress Hammer. I am your slave. I get it."

"Oh, for crying out loud. Dealing with you is like dealing with a teenager. You're nobody's slave. It's just a job, not a mission from God. If libraries are folding all over the country, you can still have a good job and a good life doing stuff like this. Keeping up the city's software is important. The city bills all the utilities and cable TV and internet services through this system."

Doom said, "And a hundred million other little funds and accounts, taxes, and who knows what. There's too much here for anybody to pay attention to most of it. Most of what they've got me doing isn't even software development, just low-level accounting crap. None of this is worth even one of those books out there."

"C'mon."

Doom stabbed the screen. "Look at what I'm working on right now: a fraction of a cent. You've taken me away from Jane Austen and put me to work justifying pennies. Less than pennies. See, this person owes the city one hundred seventy-five dollars and thirty-four cents for their electricity last month. Actually, they owe 34.12 cents. So, the city bills them for thirty-five cents, and passes thirty-four cents on to the electric company. At the end of the day, those pennies get swept into a fund called 'Residuals' and that account has to have a justification written at the end of the month explaining where the money came from, since it really isn't owed to the city and it comes from no specific source.

"It doesn't matter what you write for the justification, because nobody ever cares enough to look at it or look at this account at all. So, instead of protecting books that people want to read, I'm fabricating paragraphs that no one will ever read."

Serenity waved her finger at Doom. "Young lady, you don't realize how lucky you are to have a job and a skill. Even after the library's gone—"

She looked at the screen and stopped with her mouth open and her finger hanging in midair. Then she dragged a child's chair over and sat next to Doom. She looked at Doom, looked back at the screen, then looked back at Doom. "That's it. Our power is books. They don't control the books. We do. We rule the books. Even these books."

"Ha. Ha," said Doom. "You've said that a million times. It was inspiring when you promised me Shakespeare and the Bronte sisters, but now you just give me the city's accounting books. Very funny."

"No. Really. Our power is books."

Serenity drummed Mockingbird against Doom's desk while she studied the figures and tried to get a thought out of her head.

The AC bill had five figures next to it. The Residuals fund had five figures next to it. High five figures.

And nobody cared.

Doom tried to say something but Serenity cut her off and shoved her aside. "Get your ass out there and open all the inner office doors that you can. Except for this one. Get as much AC out of the offices and into the public areas. Give me every minute you can. I'll take over here."

"I don't know how much good just opening doors is going to do," Doom said. "And really, Ms. Hammer, you don't know how to do this stuff here."

"Out. Now. Give me every minute you can. And lock this door behind you."

Doom went "mpft" and stomped out of the room.

Serenity heard the door slam and click at her back. She logged Doom out, then logged in as herself. A few taps, and the Residuals fund was on the left side of the screen, the Library Special Projects fund on the right. There was a line of action buttons in the middle. One read, ONE-TIME TRANSFER.

No one would ever know.

She looked at the box next to the actions that read AU-THORIZATION. Telling herself it was just curiosity, she tapped the pull-down and looked at the list: City Council President, City Financial Director, Mayor. Not Librarian.

Good. Can't do this. Even if I wanted to.

More curiosity. She selected "Mayor." A box popped up with PASSWORD beside it. She thought of the mayor, giggled, and entered "Password."

The authorization box disappeared, replaced by a single word, AUTHORIZED.

Serenity sat back and looked down at the book in her hand. Atticus Finch's stern face stared out at her. She imagined his finger coming out of the cover to shake at her.

"You always fought fair, Atticus Finch," she said. "Fought by the nice book."

She looked again at the numbers on the screen.

"You fought fair, and you were always honest and righteous. You won respect. And Tom Robinson—the man who trusted you with his life—died in prison while you played fair, you son of a bitch."

The book flew out of her hand and slammed against the wall.

She pushed the button.

sixteen

thirty seconds over maddington

"THIRTY SECONDS," said Serenity. "If I can have you a check in thirty seconds, when can you have us up and running?"

The HVAC guy looked up. "Lunch time. Maybe sooner, if we can get the parts out here fast. We'll do the compressor as soon as it gets here and do the maintenance work tonight when its cooler."

"Get that compressor moving. I want to see it in the parking lot before I hear another complaint."

He saluted.

Joy was slowly checking out a stack of books to a woman with five kids, all of them sweating and the kids were whining. Serenity scooped up the books and dumped them on the woman.

"Book freedom day," she said. She looked at the line of nice people waiting politely to check out books. "Don't take the time to check things out in this heat. Take what you need, bring them back when you're done. This is your library, and we trust you."

She snatched Joy up by one elbow and dragged her, complaining, to the front door. "Find something to prop these doors open. It's hotter in here than it is outside. Greet people as they're coming in. Explain the situation to them, tell them to get what they need and get out without taking the time to check out."

"You can't just—"

"We can and we are. We're not closing these doors, and we're doing everything to stop complaints. Now go. I've got a check to cut."

She sprinted to her office. Cool air poured out when she opened the door. She grabbed a stack of brochures and used them to prop the door open, then went to her computer and opened up the accounting program and sent a check to her printer. While it was printing, she picked up the phone.

"Janice?" she said. "Give me a price now, and I mean right now. Everything we owe you, plus enough to cover the next year."

"Well, I can talk to the boss and see if we can get you a discount for—"

"Too slow. Give me full price right now."

She gave her a number.

"Good. Get down to the library in the next fifteen minutes, pick up this check, and take it straight to the bank."

"Serenity, is this check hot?"

"Everything down here is hot as hell today, and I mean everything. You want your money?"

"I'm walking out to my car."

Serenity sent the second check to the printer. When she looked at the balance, it was almost gone. Good. If they caught her, there would be less for them to take back. She grabbed the checks and ran out. The HVAC man was standing in the doorway, smiling.

"Truck's pulling into the lot now. I told them to hustle."

"Thanks." She handed him the check. "When the driver has unloaded the compressor, tell him to take this back to the office, and deposit it today."

He looked at her but took the check. "Sure."

Serenity next caught Joy and handed her the other check. "Janice is going to be here any minute. Don't let her even get out of her car. Give her this and get her on her way. I don't have time to talk to her right now."

She marched through the main room and ignored the chaos as the nice people of Maddington fought over books that had always been free anyway as if they were designer dresses at a penny-a-dress sale. Serenity patted a little girl who was running with a stack of Seuss books as tall as her head.

"Read them all, dear," she said.

Serenity then had to separate the garden club president and the Baptist minister's wife who were fighting over a DVD of *The Untouchables*.

"Dears, this is too violent for either of you. You want, hmm . . ." She rummaged through a pile of books now on the floor and came up with one of Debra Webb's steamiest romances and handed it to the garden club president, "this." She dove into the pile again. "And you, dearie, you really need this." She handed the Baptist minister's wife a copy of *The Electric Kool-Aid Acid Test*. "Now go on out."

She found Doom throwing doors open. "When you finish with that, find every volunteer you can. Get them to stand by the front door. They can take everybody who comes in by the hand, help them find what they need and get them back out quickly."

"Ms. Hammer, people are going crazy. This is crazier than Christmas Eve at Belk's Department Store."

"Great, isn't it? And we really aren't doing anything we haven't always done. Books have always been free. But by reminding them that it's their library, and their books, we've turned our polite customers into an enthusiastic mob."

She looked at the chaos of people fighting over books. Then she put her fingers in her mouth and whistled. Heads popped up and froze, like groundhogs caught in the crosshairs.

"This, ladies and gentlemen, is what our library is going to be from now on. Welcome to the MAD."

seventeen

howl

THE NEW COMPRESSOR CELEBRATED its birth with a satisfying cry and a blast of cold air. Serenity waved to Doom and Joy. "C'mon."

She herded them outside and closed the front glass doors to keep the precious cool air inside the library. "Let the volunteers handle things for a bit. We need some fresh air."

They walked to the bench out front with the statue of children reading.

Doom said, "We smell like wet dogs."

"Victorious wet dogs, Miss Doom. Victorious big, wet dogs."

They stood there in the hot breeze and watched the crowd. A couple of girls were bragging to each other about what they had snatched. One squealed. Behind them, their mothers were swapping books.

Serenity pointed. "That. Right there. That is what I want the MAD to be."

Joy plopped down on the bench next to the statue. "A bunch of hot smelly women fighting over books?"

Serenity sat down on the other side of the bronze children.

"Yes—well, I mean no, we've fixed the AC so maybe the hot and smelly will fade. But a mob fighting for what we've got to offer? Yes. A place where people come for whatever they need? Yes. And we're going to find a way to do it."

Joy nodded. "This is the most fun I've had since I've been here. I had one woman come up to me and whisper that there was a book she'd wanted to get for years, but was afraid someone might see her checking it out and report her to her church."

Doom said, "Another customer for *Fifty Shades of Grey?*"

"Worse. She wanted *How to Join the Democratic Party.*"

"They'll not only kick you out of some churches around here for that," said Serenity, "but burn you as a witch on the way out, and sell tickets. I hope you put the book in a plain brown wrapper."

"Better. I swapped covers with a Ronald Reagan biography. But look, here's the point: yesterday, she wouldn't ask because she thought our library was what everybody had always told her a library should be: quiet, timid, and following a ton of rules. Today, the MAD was a place to help her grow." Joy smiled. "Kind of like a police officer turning her body into art."

Serenity smiled back. "I see you ditched your shirt for the tank top. The Quext art gallery on display for all to see."

"It was hot. I'll follow the rules and put my shirt back on as soon as I cool off."

"Be who you are. We're done timidly pretending so we don't offend anyone. Hell, who knows? Maybe we'll open a tattoo parlor on the side, to go with the tutoring areas and business incubators we're going to have. I don't just want a library anymore; I want a MAD. A no-rules knowledge center for a city built on books. For as long as we can. Show them what they could have."

Doom ran to the slab beside the library. "Here's where we planned our expansion. Are we going to do this?"

Serenity looked at the bright young face and said, "I hope so. I hope we can do more. Someday."

Joy said, "Like maybe provide medical help? I don't mean medical care or a clinic, but resources to help people connect with those things. A woman came in the other day and wanted to know about thyroids. She couldn't afford to ask a doctor. I found her a book, but what if we had a real medical expert to get her started and point her to the clinics and doctors and any choices she could afford? And a legal expert, too."

Doom waved out at the field. "Dream, ladies, dream. We'll never do it unless we dream it first, without worrying about the how. We need a library where a guy with an idea can get help building a business plan and marketing and . . ." She waved her hand at the field. "Presto. Medical and legal clinics, there, maybe on the second floor above the stacks. And there, third floor is the business center. Work space for startups, and knowledge resources for everything they could need. What city can compete with Maddington for new jobs if we have all that?"

Doom said, "With maker spaces with three-D printers and fabrication centers so entrepreneurs can build prototypes without spending thousands of dollars on equipment, then walk next door and get real help in starting their business."

Yes!" Joy said, "And you know what? It may be because I'm old and cranky, but I get tired of people dropping off their kids for hours at a time and expecting me to look after them. I mean, look at me. How desperate does a parent have to be to trust their kids to me?

"But they're right, too. It's like everything else. The library is the only place you can get a professional for free. So, if a woman can't afford day care, she drops her kids at the library. We can complain all we want, but it's going to happen. Might as well make it happen right." She waved her hand. "Day care, fourth floor."

Doom pointed her finger at the field and said, "*Bam*! Next time a woman comes in and says she needs to work but can't find a job and nobody will watch her kids, we don't have to send her away with a pamphlet. We'll tell her to go to our clinic, and our business center, and our day care. *Bam*! One less unemployed woman in Maddington.

"And," she continued, "one less business that's under-performing because it can't find employees. Knowledge. Better connections to knowledge will give us new businesses and jobs. You want knowledge, come to the library."

Joy said, "Oh! And the fifth floor will be tutoring—"

Serenity held up her hand. "Dream, ladies, dream. But we've just gotten a one-time . . . gift. Just enough to get us through the week. And no more money coming behind it. But for now, let's start with what we found works today. Doom, do you know any way we can have people check out their own books, like we're doing right now? I don't want our librarians spending their time checking out books, when they can be revolutionaries blowing up their city with knowledge."

"Sure. We can put RFID tags in the books and on the patron's library cards. Maybe—"

"I don't care. Just do it."

Doom pulled out her phone. "I've got to call some of my geek friends."

Serenity waved her away. Joy, however, didn't leave, and instead studied Serenity. "Going to be interesting to see how you're going to ask Bentley to give you money for all this."

Serenity looked toward the empty slab next door.

"We're not. That's the only thing I'm sure of. I found money in the books today to keep us alive, maybe for just a few days. I think it's a sign. I'm going to do my best to make all of those dreams come true. I don't give a damn what I have to do to find the money, but we're not begging any-more. Let them stop the library big dogs if they can."

Then she threw her head back and howled.

trouble in paradise

"PRETTY GOOD SHOOTING, Marshall Dillon," Serenity said. She was on the verge of falling asleep with Joe wrapped around her, and both of them wrapped up inside the after-sex glow. Safe. Warm. Happy.

Joe's voice was sleepy-sexy, breathing soft in her ear. "We've got you to thank for that," he said.

She giggled but it sounded more like a purr. "Not entirely. If I recall, there was a hand that wasn't mine, and a mouth, and—"

"And they were all exactly where you said to put them, and exactly when. If you had played all prim-and-proper coy, you would have been asleep ten minutes ago."

"And I would have missed out on number two, and number three, and—oh, number four was something special."

The slow deep voice rumbled in her ear. "But who's counting?"

She wiggled her hand onto him and purred. "They all count for me."

"Again, you did it. We did it. Moments like these are the rewards we get for being honest and direct with each other."

"Always honest," she said, on the verge of slipping away to her dreams. "The one thing the Hammers and the Sweetblossoms had in common."

Joe whispered, "You build on the right things, you get the rewards."

"I like the rewards."

She felt her eyes closing, a small smile on her face. Joe shifted and she knew he wasn't quite as close to drifting off as she was.

He kissed her neck and laughed.

"All that energy tonight, Sweetblossum. What got into you?" He laughed again, lazy. "Other than . . ."

She mumbled her standard answer. "Another day." It was usually enough to satisfy Joe. Joe's cases—the ones he could talk about—were usually more interesting for them to discuss than anything that happened at the library.

But as she remembered her day, her eyes opened.

"Joe?" She felt safe and warm. "There's something I need to get your opinion on. And some ideas. I kind of committed myself without knowing how to do some things."

"Good time to ask. Right now, you know my answer to anything you want is going to be 'yes.'"

"Well, maybe," she said. "You spend all your time trying to catch people who do something wrong—at least wrong in the nice world of books. But some things are wrong, but not really wrong."

Joe laughed. "I hear that from everybody I arrest. All the way from 'pot should be legal' to 'he needed killing.'"

"I guess. But I'm not interested in that right now. The ones you don't catch—how do they get away with it?"

There was a long silence. "You mean like, you want to know how to get away with murder?"

"No, not murder. Just—never mind. This wasn't a good idea. I just kind of need to talk to my best friend Joe without other parts of him hearing."

There was a shift and she heard his reading light click on. She buried her head into the pillow to shield her eyes.

"What's that supposed to mean?" he said.

She came out of her refuge and saw tightness around his mouth. "No, it's like—never mind." She snuggled up to his naked chest. "Let's just go to sleep."

He sat up straight and she slid off of him. "Which part of me do you want to go to sleep?" he asked. "The one you wanted to talk to, but now you don't? Or the one you don't want to talk to at all? You think I'm just supposed to roll over after that, and not even wonder what part of me you want to keep secrets from?"

She sat up now, feeling too vulnerable and naked to have this talk. She jumped out of bed and felt her breasts bounce in a way that would have felt sexy five minutes ago but felt exposed now. She pulled an Alabama football jersey out from under her pillow and stood on her side of the bed as she slid it over her head.

"Nothing," she said. "There was nothing important I wanted to talk to you about. Just—shelves. At the library, I want to put up some shelves."

"So you wanted to speak to the carpenter in me, but not the electrician?"

"Oh, for crying out loud, Joe. You get so—judgmental. I wanted to ask you one little thing without having to hear from Mr. Right and Wrong."

Joe slid a tee shirt over his head, picked up a Michael Connelly book and waved it at her.

"The cop in this book says, 'Everybody matters or nobody matters.' It's the same thing with right and wrong. All of it matters, or none of it matters. Right and wrong are all a man's got—at least, it's all this man's got."

"Damn your right and wrong."

He tried to smile. It was weak, but it was an honest attempt. "Right and wrong, and my Sweetblossom. That's all I've got, and I'm not giving up on any of them. We'll work this out. Right now, I'm going to go sit out on the deck and read for a while."

Then he was gone, and Serenity was standing by the bed, shaking.

perchance to dream

SERENITY WAS DREAMING.

Her body wasn't sleeping and her eyes were wide open, but her head was filled with dreams that she couldn't shut off as she lay there, alone, in her bed.

She was running through the woods with Robin Hood and the Merry Librarians. With them, Bonnie and Clyde (the cool movie ones, not the nasty real ones) were robbing banks to fund Texas libraries.

Freedom fighter Serenity.

But her brain was awake enough to know she was dreaming. Only in books can you find that kind of weirdness.

In the darkness, she looked at the other side of the bed. No Joe-sized lump. And, if there had been, the chances were good that she wouldn't be able to keep from sharing her secret with him.

Despite her dreams of glory, what did she have to share? A brief hour where she had hoped to make her library something more, something great? And for one hour, had the power to do a little of it, along with a promise she would do more.

And it was, you know, technically, illegal, which was why she hadn't asked Joe to come back to bed.

She got up and looked at the clock. Three A.M. Saturday morning. She was too wired to sleep in her bed at home alone, too unsure of herself to try to find where Joe was.

She showered and drove to the library, puttered in the darkened stacks for a while, and then lay down on the three-legged couch in the storeroom/lounge and spent an hour tossing and turning. When she went back to her office she tried to work, but couldn't focus.

Faulkner came out.

"Yeah, sure," said Serenity. "What a joke. I find money to keep the old rattletrap open a little longer and I'm dreaming of—what? A library palace? More likely I'll be running the prison library. At least there I'll probably have a bigger budget."

She looked at her favorite rat. Faulkner wasn't laughing.

"You're right." She took out the rum and filled his bottle cap and her mug. "Hell, just barely sunrise out there now." She toasted him. "More fun to be fired for being a drunk than for being a thief. And both are probably better than being a pathetic failure to my library." She took a sip. "God, I'm tired of self-pity."

There was a crash outside in the stacks.

Serenity looked around her office and grabbed the biggest book she could find for protection. She looked at the title. If I hit them with this, at least they won't be the first person put to sleep by Joyce's *Ulysses*.

She stuck her head out and looked out at the front door.

The MAD was being invaded by Will Shakespeare himself.

twenty

even a horse's ass can buck

WHAT'S MORE, the noise was Will Shakespeare dropping his rocket launcher as it caught on the door coming in.

Never seen that in the stacks before. Serenity lowered the heavy book.

Shakespeare bent down to pick up his weapon and Darth Vader crashed into him and they fell to the floor. Will saw Serenity and looked panicked.

Scarlett O'Hara stepped over both of them.

"Honestly, you boys," she said, "I do declare."

Serenity recognized the accent and then the face. "Doom?"

"Why, Ms. Hammer, I am so flattered that you recognized little ole me."

Serenity shook her head. A horse (Black Beauty, she guessed) was stumbling in. Or rather, the front half of the horse was.

"Lord a' mighty," said Serenity. "To what do we owe the pleasure of this unannounced and probably totally inappropriate visit?"

Doom/Scarlett put her hands on her hips in a gesture that would have worked for either identity. "It was inappropriate yesterday, when this was the library. But now, this is the MAD. It's our place. Everybody's place for everything. All the time."

"Yeah," said Serenity, maybe we need to go slow on that idea. It's just kind of a dream right now."

Doom gave an un-Scarlett squeal as several boys in football uniforms squeezed past them. "*It is*. It *is* a dream, but we're actually doing this. I mean, you're doing this, and we're helping." She took Serenity's hand. "So I was working with this theater group. We were doing the dress rehearsal for our play, which explores the idea that all great literature is basically the same. We open tonight, if you want tickets."

"Thanks."

"But I'll warn you that it may not be very good. It's all improv."

Serenity watched Snow White sweep in, followed by three guys walking on kneepads, presumably to stay in character as dwarves. "Imagine that."

"Our rehearsal was really, really bad. So we went to a bar and kept rehearsing. Rehearsing and drinking. They threw us out after a while, claiming we were loud, and we went to another bar. They decided to close early. We went to an after-hours club, but then they closed. Can you believe all these places closing right after we got there? We were buying a lot of drinks, too. And I mean a lot."

King Lear stumbled in, leaning on Sam Spade.

Serenity said, "I can see that."

"Then the sun came up and we couldn't get into the theater and we couldn't get into a bar. I said, 'I know what Serenity Hammer would want us to do.' So here we are, the place for everything the people of Maddington need. All MAD, all the time."

"All MAD," Serenity agreed.

Doom gave her a drunken hug and bounced off.

The rear end of the horse came in bringing up, well, the rear. "Serenity!" came a cry from within the folds of black cloth. The half-horse came up to Serenity and pulled the cloth back.

"Jolene," said Serenity. "My favorite drama teacher."

"Former drama teacher. The school board cut out the drama department last year. All schools. Serenity, thanks so much for opening up the library to us."

Serenity laughed, "I'm not sure I did, but—"

Jolene grabbed Serenity's arm. "You don't know how bad it is. It's getting hard to find a place anymore. No place, no money. Soon, there will be nothing but reality TV to spur people's imagination."

"No wonder we're so brain-dead."

Jolene wouldn't let go of her arm. "And poor. That's the really stupid thing of all this. By not spending money, we're costing ourselves jobs and even bigger money. Georgia,

Florida and other states are funding film and TV centers. Guess where Hollywood goes to spend millions of dollars making movies? Guess where the big buildings housing hundreds of people working on TV news networks are?"

"Not here."

"Not here is goddamned right. Doom tells me you're going to change that. She says you're building a new library here that will have a place for all this. A place where kids can get the experience and training they need. A place that can do things faster and better than the schools do. So that, maybe, for once, Alabama will be ahead of the world."

Serenity pulled her arm away and looked at Jolene. The dark horse fabric covered everything except two sad, human eyes, staring, pleading with Serenity. Behind her, Doom had most of her troops ready to start. She tapped her watch and looked at Serenity.

"Jolene, you know I'll do what I can, but, there's so little I can do. Really, Doom gets carried away—"

"Serenity, you're all we've got. You've got to find a way."

"I'm not Robin Hood, Jolene. I'm not a savior. I'm just a small-time librarian. And lately, not even a very good one at that. I can't—"

Doom yelled at them.

"Hey, we need that horse's ass *now!*"

the chirping of a single drunken cricket

MID-AFTERNOON. A head peeked around the corner of Serenity's office and then ducked back. There was giggling. The empty doorway filled with a double bouquet of roses, followed by a teen-aged girl.

"From Mr. Hammer," she said. "Honestly, he is so dreamy." Serenity pushed papers aside and motioned for the volunteer to put the vase on the side table where Faulkner lived. The girl stood there with a big grin, like she'd found herself in the middle of her own personal romance novel.

Serenity looked at the girl and wondered if the word "dreamy" was cool again, or if this sweet, clueless girl was just sweet and clueless. She also knew that until she could get enough paid staff, she was dependent on volunteers like her to keep it running, even if they thought books with a Dewey Decimal System number on them should be filed under "Math" because they had numbers.

Serenity smiled at the girl, if not at the flowers, and went back to studying the stack of invoices along with the dwindling balance in the Special Projects fund.

The girl was still there when she looked up, still giggling.

"He's waiting," she said. "He said he would stand in the lobby all day for an answer. Really, if you need time to fix your hair or makeup, I can go back out to the desk and stare at him. He's just so—"

"Dreamy. Yeah, I get it." Serenity noticed there was a note attached to the flowers. She ripped it off and the vase teetered, and the girl held her breath until it stabilized.

The note read, STILL FRIENDS? MORE? I DIDN'T LIKE THE WAY WE LEFT THINGS LAST NIGHT. CAN I MEET YOU FOR DINNER AT THE CAFÉ AND MAKE IT UP TO YOU? SIX?

Serenity thought about how Joe probably looked in the lobby. Most likely, he was leaning back against the door-jamb, cowboy hat still on and tilted lazily over his eyes, looking like he would wait there forever for her. He knew how to play the part of a romance hero.

Not going to work today. Not yet.

"Tell him six-thirty. Maybe seven."

"You aren't going to tell him yourself?"

"You tell him. I've got work to do."

"But he's standing there waiting with those kissable lips and—"

Well, that answered the question of whether "dreamy" was back in the teen lexicon, or whether this girl spent too much time in the romance stacks.

"You tell him. And stay away from those lips."

The girl left and Serenity put her head down on Hemingway's *For Whom the Bell Tolls* and prayed the inspiration in it would seep through. You can't win, but you can be brave. Inspiring. But not a how-to book.

She wondered what Hemingway himself might do. She pulled her head up and looked for her cup. You can't win, but you can stay drunk. She fished the bottle out and held it over her mug.

Joy slunk into Serenity's office and dropped herself into the good chair.

"Some show this morning," she said. "Got any more of that?"

Serenity poured, passed the mug to Joy, and found the STAY CALM AND ASK A LIBRARIAN mug and filled that one for herself.

"Best part of my day," Serenity said, "was when you came in to work early at seven A.M. and stumbled into the middle of Doom's play. You said, 'What the hell?' and they added you and your line to the play."

Joy turned her right arm sideways, almost spilling her rum. "Yeah. Now I've got to get up on a stage tonight, deliver the line I'll probably have carved on my gravestone, and walk off into the night." She studied the arm. "You think I ought to get Sneaky Pete to touch up the red on this before tonight?"

"I think you'll stand out just fine without a touch up. It still raises the question: what the hell were you doing here at that time of morning? You always bitch when I ask you to open at nine."

"You know how, in a really big rock anthem, there's always that big chord? That barely-restrained thrum-thrum-thrum that sets your soul on fire, tells you something big is coming?"

Serenity took a sip of her rum. "You have a soul?"

"Yeah. Tattooed on my ass. Want to see? Anyway, I never felt that when I was coming to work in a library. MAD, on the other hand . . ."

Serenity said, "Joy, I don't know how much longer we can—"

"Besides," said Joy. "I have an idea for tonight. You'll have to get here early tomorrow morning if you want to see it."

Serenity nodded slowly. "You know, you might want to run ideas by the head librarian first."

"Not after yesterday. Our MAD. My MAD. Your job is to keep it running for all of us. Reminds me, I need to borrow a pickup truck tonight."

Serenity raised her eyebrows. "I don't suppose I should ask you why?"

"No."

"Okay. That I can do. Talk to the guys at the glass shop on Main Street. We give them enough business with kids knocking out windows, they ought to be glad to loan you one."

"Thanks. May need more for this project eventually."

"Good luck," Serenity said, "I lay awake most of the night dreaming of ways to come up with more. Look, this was a one-time kind of thing. Now that I've shot my mouth off, I don't know how to keep this going. We may be back to being just Maddington Public Library soon. If that."

"Hell, no. Hell, no. Did you see the look on Doom's face this morning? This isn't just her job anymore; this is her life. Hell, you've even got a seventy-year-old burnout dreaming of what she's going to do with her MAD, now that you've promised her one."

"Joy, I have no idea where to look for what we need. Other than the truck."

Joy said, "But we know you can work wonders. We've seen you—" She stopped to stare at Serenity. "Serenity, I'm sorry."

Serenity dabbed at her watering eyes and forced a laugh. "No, I'm sorry. No big deal. I just can't do all this." She raised her mug and Joy reached out and pushed the cup down. "Enough of that. You need this now. You need MAD as much as we all do."

Even the effort of pushing Joy's hand away seemed too much so she sat there and dissolved.

"It's just . . ."

Joy kept her hand on hers. "I know. Let it out."

After a few minutes, Serenity said, "I made so many promises to all of you. To myself. And I can't do it. I've got to find a way to put the money back. Apologize to Joe. Go back to being . . ."

"Don't worry about us," said Joy. "We were asking a lot of you, and we shouldn't have. I don't know where you came up with the money you have so far. Or the inspiration."

"I really wanted us to be something more. All of us."

"We can still do a little. Maybe we can't do everything we wanted, but we can do more than we settled for. We can continue to do every little thing we can, as long as we can, until they stop us. Even if it's not for long. You changed us with just that little sliver of a dream. Made us MAD women, if only for a day or so."

The tears were gone. "I'm glad you had that day. Glad we all had it. But without money it's going to die, and I can't get the money.

"I'm just a lie-brarian, after all."

twenty-two

beware of rabbits bearing gifts

EVERYTHING ABOUT JOE made her mad. Serenity stood in the doorway of The Café and watched the waitress swooning and chatting up Joe while he sat at their favorite table, smiling back sleepy-eyed. She wanted to march over and tell the waitress that those aw-shucks looks in that big man's body made promises that they couldn't keep. Well, she guessed they kept those promises. Maybe she didn't want to say that to the waitress, but she did have things to say to Joe.

"You!" She bore down on his table. Joe looked up at the sound of her voice, his soft brown eyes coming into view from under his hat and his welcoming smile blooming before he had a chance to take in her expression.

"You!" She stopped in front of him and put her hands on her hips. "You are a fraud. Pretend to invite a girl to dinner and you bring her to a jail."

Joe's smile withered. "It's one of your favorite places," he said. "Sure, it's a café built in the old city jail, but you always thought that was cool and—"

"It is still a jail. And I don't like that you intentionally brought me to a place where people used to get tortured by people like you until they told their secrets, and then you people locked them up for having secrets."

"Do you want to go somewhere else?" asked Joe.

Serenity pulled out a chair and sat down. "No," she said, "this is fine."

She looked up at the waitress, who was still standing there with a fixed smile on her mouth and her eyes wide.

"Let me have Charisse's Quinoa Salad. And unsweet tea."

Joe said, "No rabbit food for me. Cops eat cheeseburgers. Rare."

"Yes, sir."

When the waitress left, Joe put his hand over hers. Surrounding, warming, protecting. It was a safe place for her hand to be. She looked at their hands while Joe studied her expression and seemed to wonder if he had stepped on another land mine today.

But she didn't pull away.

"You know," she said, looking at their hands. "That's kind of what we are. What we've always been. The lawman and the lawman's wife. The fierce moral code and the little woman wrapped up in it. Dodge City."

He smiled, a bit weakly, and she kept her eyes averted, studying their hands, not wanting to be charmed by his smile right now.

"Miss Kitty," he said, "you want me to build you a saloon, just say the word. Me and Festus will be over at first light and commence to hammering and nailing."

"No, I mean—I don't know. I'm having a hard time explaining this, but I really need you to understand. What if I want to build the saloon myself? What if the saloon I want to build is so big that it won't fit within the limits of those big hands of yours?"

Joe was trying to keep his smile.

Serenity said, "You know—without trying to get too bawdy here—in one literal sense men live their lives inside women. In our bodies, in the homes we make. But it goes the other way, too. I always wanted something normal and warm and safe, and you wrapped me up in those big old arms and gave me just what I wanted. And just like our hands—while it's true that you've always lived in me—it's also true that I've always lived inside you, and your world and your rules."

He squeezed her hand and smiled. "We've always made a happy home for each other."

She pulled her hand away. "But there are things I have to do outside of your world. And I need your support, even if you may not think it's right."

He studied her face. "Honey, we build our life on what's right. Do the right thing, and move on. And I support you in all of that."

She snatched her hand away. "But that's you and this is not about you. Why do you always think that every blessed thing is about you, and what you've done, and I'm just here to settle the dust?"

She stood up. "I'm not hungry. I've got work to do, thanks to you and your goddamned prison of right-and-wrong."

The waitress was returning with two plates in her hand and the same confused look on her face.

"Do you want your salad?" she said.

"Tell him to eat the salad. See what it feels like to be a rabbit instead of a hunter."

chariots of the lesser gods

SIX O'CLOCK IN THE MORNING and she was in the middle of a dream. Serenity's dreams—unfortunately—didn't include kissing Valentino by a crystal-blue Italian stream. No, she had people begging her to do what she should, and Joe had handcuffs because she had done what she shouldn't. And it was all the same thing.

Nor had her night included much sleep, or anything else, as she and Joe spent the night pulling the covers from each other and complaining about it. At some point she realized that Joe had won the last battle and she was coverless.

"I am tired of you always thinking you can win just because you're Joe and you're right." She jumped out of bed. "I'm going into work."

"Good. Maybe I can get some sleep." Joe yanked the covers one more time for dramatic effect.

In the bathroom, she looked into her eyes in the mirror. Christ.

Cleaned up, dressed up, made up, she looked at Joe one last time before she left. He looked good, and she resented that. She grabbed the covers and yanked them off of him.

"Jesus," he said.

"No. Just me. The woman who used to count on you for support."

He said something to her back as she was leaving but she didn't stop to hear it.

When she got there, the outside lights were on at the MAD and the inside lights were dimmed. She was fumbling with her keys when she saw something moving inside and pushed on the door. Unlocked. She stepped inside.

Her eyes adjusted by degrees. First, she saw an enormous four-poster bed with motorcycle wheels at each corner. It was almost blocking the door. Then, there were three guys under one quilt, snoring in harmony like a scene from a Three Stooges movie—if the Stooges had been played by the guys in ZZ Top. One beard was carefully spread on top of the covers, one tucked underneath. I guess there's no real answer to that old question.

She jumped when she realized someone was standing next to her with a gun.

"Joy," she said when she realized who it was.

"Shh." Joy put her Glock back in its holster. "Don't wake our patrons."

Now that she could see, Serenity surveyed the library. Scratch that. Serenity surveyed the flophouse. Behind the four-poster with motorcycle wheels was what looked like a baby's crib with lawnmower wheels. It contained a man with his feet hanging over the end. On the other side, a plywood mockup of a '57 Chevy with a mattress for a cab held two more. It went on like that for as far as she could see on both sides.

"Lost Boys," said Joy.

"That makes you Wendy?"

"Yeah."

"You know you can't have a gun in the library?"

"Can't have beds or people sleeping, either. The library has to be empty and useless at night. Made me think of the way these guys feel, and I put two and two together. Thought about what you said about doing as much as we could for as long as we could."

"I thought you said that."

"Well, you inspired it."

"Whatever," Serenity said. "Looks like two and two added up to about twenty."

"Eighteen."

"Where'd you get these beds? If that's what you call them."

"Remember that bedstead race they have every year on Founder's Day, where people have to push a bed down the street? Most people break their beds down and take them back home. Some don't. The city keeps them in a storage shed," she pointed out the window, "about a quarter of a mile that way. We got the key—don't ask how—and rolled them out. Now that the sun's coming up, we're going to roll them back and clean things up. I told the boys: one scrap of paper, one table not moved back, and they'll be back at the interstate underpasses again."

"Good work. This is illegal, immoral—and fine with me."

"Thanks. But I didn't ask. My MAD." She pushed the light switch up. "Everybody up. Let's get this four-wheeler cattle drive rolling."

As old men grumbled out of beds, Serenity said, "Leave me one. That one, the single cot with bicycle wheels. I need to get some rest. We can keep it in my office." Then she thought about it. "I'll bring my own sheets from home. Maybe a plastic cover, too."

"You want to move it in, I won't stop you."

"And get the gun out of here. My MAD, too."

Serenity pushed the cot in behind her visitors' chairs and laid down. Different dreams here. She dreamed of a buzzing library full of people getting what they needed. A city growing and prosperous. A city of books.

A thump at the door eventually shook her out of her dream. The light was streaming in now: mid-morning. She sat up, shook her head, and reached over to open the door.

Doom said, "We need something."

"Of course."

"This is Levi Buffett," Doom said, and stepped aside. A tall young Asian man with dreadlocks nodded. "Mr. Buffett's got a business idea that he needs help with."

He nodded. "I've got an electronics device that we think can revolutionize the automotive industry. I've put together investors. But the problem is this: to assemble it here in Maddington, we need to buy components from China. And eventually, we'll want to sell our products to Asia and Europe, as well as the US. We think we have the markets and suppliers lined up, but the regulations are killing us. We want to spend our money on development and marketing, not import/export lawyers. If we had a set of the import/export regulations here, I could do the homework myself."

"I remember you," said Serenity. "You played basketball at the high school, and then at the university."

"Yes, ma'am," he said, "and a couple of years pro in Europe. Now I'm back home. I want to take the money that I made over there and build something here. But if I can't get the support I need here, I may have to go to Silicon Valley."

"We don't want that. How much are a set of these regs?"

"Two thousand dollars."

Serenity nodded. "Expensive, for a library whose account is back down to zero. We can barely afford to buy a Hardy Boys book. Used." She thought about how much money she already had to repay.

What's another two grand? "How about a trade? We find a way to get the regs, you study up on them, and become our designated volunteer. When other folks come in who need help with this stuff, we'll call you in."

He grinned. "Teamwork. Like that."

"OK. I'll find . . . something."

Doom and the man were gone, and Serenity wished she could go back to sleep and dream again. Dream up some more dollars.

arguing with the gods

THE BOOK FOR THE DAY turned out to be Hemingway's *For Whom the Bell Tolls*. She yanked it off the shelf, went around the corner and locked herself in the server room. Just her and the evil Maddington computers. The sad children's desks stacked in the corner bore witness.

She pulled up the chair and logged in. Friday had been a one-time thing. But it had worked. One time. Now she had to put it back.

She looked at the book.

Yeah, I get it. The bell tolls for me. Ha ha. Library gods.

It was time to end her brief foray into crime. She looked at the sheet in her other hand that held her retirement fund account number and balance. She could put the money back before she got caught, talk to Joe, and explain that she'd have to work a few years longer than they'd planned before they retired to the beach. She'd make it up to him somehow.

But she couldn't make it up to the people who needed her library. Next crisis, and Bentley would close them down.

Sorry. I can't win this fight.

She looked at the screen. The Residuals fund was back to almost where it was when she had transferred it. It made no sense that the city was stealing that much a penny at a time, but she didn't care. Now she was looking at the other transfer options. She imagined that she saw one at the bottom: TRANSFER SERENITY TO JAIL. Seemed right. Maybe inevitable.

Maybe not so bad, though. Real prison couldn't be worse than the prison of giving in and going along.

She blinked and saw the option to transfer money into the account. Reaching for the paper, she knocked the book to the floor. It landed upside down, with Papa Hemingway's picture staring up at her.

"No," she clearly heard him say. "You didn't hear what I said. What did every English teacher you ever had tell you about my books? You can sum them all up in a single sentence: 'You can't win, but you can be brave.'"

Out loud, she added, "And mad."

The screen had the same list of actions as yesterday. Below the ONE-TIME TRANSFER was a button labelled TRANSFER DAILY. She set up the accounts and hit the button.

"How can you argue with the gods?"

twenty-five

stealing jokes from richard nixon

SERENITY WALKED OUT the door and said to Joy. "I'm going to Rocket Republic Brewery. I've got to get drunk before I come to my senses."

She was sitting on a stool wondering what kind of beer they might serve in jail when Doom slid in next to her.

David the bartender jerked his chin at Serenity and said to Doom, "You going to give her a ride home?"

Doom nodded back.

"Then I'll give her that fourth Mach 1 she's been asking for." He poured a glass and put it in front of Serenity. Doom tapped the bar and he poured her one, too.

Doom picked up her glass and looked at the workers who were busy in the brewery in the back. "It won't work."

Deny. Deny. Deny. "What? I didn't do anything."

"You transferred the Residuals fund."

"No, that would be—might be, uh . . ."

"Magnificent. Revolutionary. Although it wouldn't have worked," Doom said.

"What do you mean? It did work—if I did anything."

"You set it up as a daily transfer. That would have caused a daily trail that people would have monitored." Doom drained her glass. "I—or the mayor and I, if you want to be picky—fused the accounts permanently. Locked the account for anyone but us. It will look like it's always been that way. And the same people who didn't care still won't care."

Serenity stood up. "No. Doom, I don't want your fingerprints on any of this. Get back in there and change your name to mine on all of this. Even if the mayor technically authorized things, I don't want anyone to see you were logged in at the time. If anyone ever sees anything."

"I want my name on all of this."

"Absolutely not. If anyone goes to jail for—I don't know, embezzlement, maybe fraud—it's going to be me."

Joy slid in on the other side of Serenity.

Doom said, "Jail? They should give you a medal. That's the most wonderful and heroic thing I've ever seen anyone do. A city of books! And I know the book I'm moving to the front of the library tomorrow. *Robin Hood!* The city does not have a right to even one cent of that money. They stole it. Not you, but them. All you did—all we've done—is take it back for the people. We've done nothing wrong."

"Theft, misuse of government funds—"

"No," said Doom. "Joy, you used to be a cop, right?"

"Yeah, 'til they fired me for accidentally setting a body on fire."

"Yeah, yeah," said Doom. "I really want to hear that story—again—sometime. Right now, though, we need legal advice. If a little of that money went to a different city account, like to the library Special Projects fund, it wouldn't be embezzling?"

"Maybe not."

"It would be like un-embezzling. The city's embezzling from the people now. We're just giving it back to the people. We're un-embezzling."

Serenity brightened. "Yeah. That's it."

Joy thought about it. "No crime against un-embezzling that I know of. And, even if there is, the city will not going to want to admit they were taking this money in the first place."

Doom shot her fist into the air. "I told you. It's not a crime, it's a revolutionary act. Free-Doom. We're heroes of the people."

Serenity thought about it and said, "A narrow-minded prosecutor might take a different view."

"But suppose he didn't know?" said Doom. "This is outside of the usual accounts. Anything mandated by law—like a tax—has to be audited. I don't see any sign that anyone audits this."

"And I can testify that our judgment was impaired when we decided to do it." Joy turned up her beer, chugged it, and tapped the bar for another.

"Let's be clear, Serenity said. "All of us. This is me. I did this. You didn't. Particularly not you, Doom. Or you either, Joy. My name goes on everything."

Joy picked up her glass. "Jail don't scare me. Truth be told, it was a blessing in disguise when the police fired me. I always had more friends among the crooks than I ever did with the cops." She set the glass down. "Besides, I'm almost seventy, living in a little room and shelving books. I can do the same thing in prison, and get them to pay for the knee replacement I can't afford." She looked at Serenity. "I can pay the price, if you can."

David put another beer in front of Joy and she picked it up. "But just you and me. The kid can't go to jail. Wherever we're going, we're going together," she said, "but we protect the kid. Anything we do, we protect the kid."

Serenity nodded.

Doom shoved a book down the bar to Serenity. "Have you read this?"

Serenity turned the book over. *Fifty Ways to Kill Your Lovers and Other Enemies*. "I never should have put you in charge of the Noir Book Club."

"No, you don't understand. This guy finds the fifty people who most need killing, and finds an original way to kill each of them. The point is, what he does is a heroic act even if it's against the rules, and even against the law, technically."

"Technically? Doom, the book leaves out the part where the protagonist kills people and goes to jail. And a lot of other things. I'm not sure that's the interpretation we want you to bring to the book club. Or to anything else."

Doom took the book back. "You two can treat me like a little girl if you want, but I'm going to be fearless. We have a vision, it's a worthy vision, and I am going to protect it." She raised the book over her head and waved it at Serenity the same way that Serenity had waved the atlas when she ran Cy out of the library. "By any means necessary."

Serenity threw up her hands. "Joy, tell her."

Joy looked up from her tattoo. "Yes, child, murder is illegal and not a proper hobby for a young lady like yourself." She turned to Serenity. "But, as a cop, I also saw a lot of times where the big guys used the law to keep little guys in line. By the time I left the force, I was tired of arresting Robin Hoods who the sheriff had caught violating some little rule that offended the princes. I think we're on the line here, but I think a good attorney could spin this in our favor. And, while I don't want to get all civic-minded, I think this library—this MAD—is worth fighting for—as long as we keep the kid out of jail. And safe." She waved a finger at Serenity. "That means you don't tell your husband."

Serenity looked at her glass. "Agreed. If we do this right, by the time they catch us—catch me—we will have the expansion underway and it will be too big for anyone to shut down. Maybe some will say this is wrong, and they will have the law on their side. Maybe someone will have to pay a price. And that's got to be me."

Joy raised her glass and said, "Damn the law. Let's be heroes."

Joy and Doom clinked their glasses together and looked at Serenity.

After a long second, Serenity touched her glass to theirs and said, "In the words of our immortal president, Richard Nixon, we could do this, but it would be wrong."

They paused, then all three of them laughed harder than they had laughed in a long time.

two thieves don't make a right

SERENITY WAS TOO DRUNK to go home and explain it to Joe, so she left him a message about a night meeting and went to the MAD for the night.

"Keep your paws off of my spare cot, lady," the scruffy man sitting on his rolling cot in the library said as Serenity hesitated in front of the empty cot next to his.

Joy yelled from her cot behind the circulation desk. "Get nice or get out, Josh. You can always go back to San Francisco. You know the rules."

Joy unfolded herself and walked slowly to Serenity. "You want a cot out here, Serenity, we've got a free one in the women's area, over in the children's section."

"So you've got women now?"

"Women and children. We've got a twenty-five-year-old girl from Ivy Green. She was thrown out by her husband last night with her five-year-old. The women's shelter closed last year when they took away its funding. She heard about us. Tomorrow, I'm going to get one of our other women—Chakira—to watch the kid while the mom and I find her a job and a place to live." Joy looked at Serenity. "I'm paying Chakira as a jill-of-all-trades day worker in the library. It may take some library money to get the Ivy Green girl started. Hope I'm playing the new MAD game right."

"Looks like you've got it exactly right," Serenity said. "What's the woman's name?"

"How the hell would I know? She's not my friend. Just somebody the library needs to help. My job."

Joy started to walk away as Serenity said, "I think you enjoy the job more than you let on."

Joy stiffened. "Wendy. Girl's name is Wendy." Then she walked away.

Serenity went to the break room and got a pack of peanut butter crackers and a Diet Coke, and took them to the server room.

Doom's workstation and the server's rack were shoved into the back corner. The rest of the room was filled with children's desks and chairs, as Doom was setting up a reading workshop for tomorrow.

Serenity sat down at the desk and logged in as herself. She then searched for anything connected with either the Special Projects fund or the Residuals account that had Doom's name on it. Each time she methodically changed the name to Hammer. She finished both the crackers and the work, leaned back and stretched. Then she looked at the clock and saw both hands straight up. It was midnight.

Just then the Residuals account flashed red. Serenity leaned forward. Someone had tried to access the account, and their transaction had failed. Moreover, they had tried to withdraw money, but the money was now residing in the Library Special Projects fund, with only a few thousand dollars left in the Residuals account.

The transaction bounced, so the people who had come for their money had to know. Trembling, she looked up the code for the organization that was just now realizing their money wasn't where they expected it to be. It wasn't one of the authorized users she had seen, and wasn't anything she recognized. This code was just "GG." She looked up the contacts table for GG. No such entry. Looked in the history. No history. No description.

She looked at the destination code for the transfer. MYOB. Someone's idea of a joke. Again, no record anywhere.

Serenity pulled up the raw transfer account and found a bank ID code and account number associated with it. She switched to a web browser and spent a few nervous minutes tracking down both the bank and account.

Bank of the Bahamas, a private numbered account.

But there was more. Some programmer, years ago, in an effort to be thorough, had included the trail of the last successful money transfers in the failure block. A MAD withdrawal was the last withdrawal. But right under it was the record for the last successful deposit. Nothing but an account number.

Serenity recognized the routing part of the account number as a bank in the nearby city of Jericho. And she had the account number of the account that had made the deposit.

money gusher

THERE WASN'T MUCH SLEEP to be had in Serenity's office Sunday night. She spent most of the night talking things over with Faulkner, who surprisingly, offered no answers. When the sun came up, she went to the Waffle House for breakfast and woke up sometime later with her head on the table next to a half-eaten plate of eggs.

"Ms. Hammer, I thought I'd just let you sleep." The waitress smiled at her. "Reckon I spent enough of my days growing up with my head down on a desk at the library, while Momma worked at one no-count job after another."

Serenity looked at the sun, which was high over the horizon. Then she looked at her watch. "Oh, God, I've got to go."

"You want some coffee to go?"

"God, yes."

Sam the Squatter met Serenity at the library door Monday morning with a big smile. Like he did a lot of mornings.

"Sam, the answer is still no."

The smile didn't fade. "I keep asking. I figure I spend most of my days here anyway. If we were married, I could probably sleep here, too."

"Talk to that woman," she pointed to Joy, "about that. No need to try to game the system anymore, Sam. We're coming to you." Serenity laughed. "Though it is good for a girl to know where her charm lies."

"You are charming, Ms. Hammer. And kind. And beautiful. And I brought you a token of my love." He held out a half-eaten blueberry muffin, probably rescued from the dumpster behind the corner bakery on his way to the library.

"Aw, Sam," she said. "That is so sweet, but I'm dieting. You eat it for me."

"Oh, Ms. Hammer, you're the last woman on earth who needs to diet."

She patted him on the shoulder and walked away. Joe better watch out. One more night like the last few and she might say yes.

Ten feet from her office, she stopped. She could hear Doom's voice coming out of her open office door.

"We are going to make Maddington a city built on books, and we are going to honor the woman who gave us the vision and determination to do it. The cornerstone is going to read, 'Serenity Hammer Annex.' People are going to know who did this."

Then a man came out of her office. It was Seth Burroughs, the general contractor who had been selected for the expansion before the expansion stalled. He walked up to Serenity with his hand out.

"Congratulations to all of us, Serenity," he said. "I don't know how you made it happen, but this city needs this." He laughed and jerked his chin toward the door. "I don't know how you created that firebrand, either. That's a fine little Serenity Hammer you've got in there."

He moved on, tucking a sheet of paper into his clipboard.

Serenity turned the corner. Doom had her back to the door, hands on her hips, studying a set of blueprints spread out on Serenity's desk.

"Busy?" said Serenity.

Doom jumped and spun in the air. "Oh, Ms. Hammer." She threw her arms around Serenity and almost lifted her from the floor. "You should see what we're doing. I just signed the contract with Burroughs for him to start work on the expansion."

"You signed?"

"I signed your signature for you." She plucked a pink page off the top of a stack of papers. "I know I don't have the authority. Technically."

Serenity looked at the signature, SSHammer, with the two S's like lightning bolts. "Technically, no, you don't," Serenity said. "And, my signature doesn't look like something from the Nazis. More than that, I don't want my signature done by you. You can get fired for that. Hell, I ought to fire you for that."

"You wouldn't fire me."

"Well, you can go to jail, and I won't be able to stop that. This is fraud, and what's going to happen when the checks bounce? Even with the residuals, we don't have nearly enough to start this."

Doom smiled. "We do. Here's the best part. You took the wrong account. What you transferred was the daily—as in the Residuals for yesterday only. And it was only a small part of yesterday, because of when you made the transfer. The total Residual fund, the one that no one has ever accessed or checked on, is huge, like millions of dollars every week."

"Can't be. From residuals?"

Doom shrugged. "I don't know either. But it is. And I've locked it to the library. Permanently."

Serenity raised an eyebrow.

"Yes," said Doom. "I did it under your login."

"Good. It will get me to jail sooner."

"It's huge, Ms. Hammer. That's why I came in here this morning. I wanted to surprise you by getting a start on fixing things up."

Serenity picked up the next sheet on the stack.

"Plumber?"

"Yeah. Got a guy to fix those toilets in the front women's room that have been broken forever. He's working on them now."

Serenity looked at the signature on the sheet. "Yeah. I can see that I told him to do that."

Doom beamed a proud smile. "I'm only doing what I knew Serenity Hammer would do. But that's the tip of the iceberg here. The Residual fund has more than we can spend, and more coming in faster than I can count. Since it's being transferred automatically, that means the Special Projects fund has more money than we can spend." She smiled a smug little smile. "So, I authorized the start of the expansion. But we've still got to find more ways to spend money. A lot of money, fast. The Special Projects fund has a cap, and it does get audited if it ever goes over the cap. If we don't spend money—lots of it—we'll be in trouble."

"How much?"

Doom pointed her to the screen.

Serenity looked past Doom to the display on her computer. "Doom, that's bigger than a few pennies off of everybody's cable bill. That's more than . . ." As she was calculating in her head the balance jumped again. "Doom, we'll never get away with this. This isn't just nickels and dimes. This is millions of dollars. God knows where this is coming from, but they'll want it back."

Doom drew herself up. "Then we have to spend the money before they come for it, and before the Special Projects fund gets too big to hide. We're doing the right thing here, and I'm proud of it. We won't back down. No matter what we have to do to protect this."

Serenity looked at her. "Doom, there's a line we're not going to cross."

Doom's smile came back. "But what we're doing is right. And we won't get caught."

Serenity thought of all the books on the shelves that started with that sentence.

my little friend

SERENITY SAT AT HER DESK, trying to arrange all the contracts and work orders that Doom had signed into some kind of order, and feeling like she needed to be just a librarian again, if only for a few minutes.

She stood up and Faulkner scooted away. "Oh, big baby. I'm just going to go empty the drive-up returns box, do one librarian thing, then fire up my computer and get back to playing master criminal."

She found Joy was wrestling a cardboard box the size of a desk in front of what used to be the checkout box.

"I got this from the moving company. Even though we just declared free books at the MAD on Friday, by Monday morning, we have more returns coming in than we ever had with the old system. Got books that aren't even ours, people bringing in anything they think someone might want to read."

"Don't throw them out," said Serenity. "If they want them in their library, we want them here, too. Get—what's the name of that know-it-all woman, the one who comes to every book club and has read twice as much as anyone else?"

"Ms. Pethel?"

"Yeah, that's her. Get her down here to sort through what we can take and what we can't. Pay her, too. But not by the page."

Serenity shivered as she went out the door to the drive-up return box. She hadn't expected a cold breeze on a mid-August morning, but there it was. She touched her hand to the metal and felt a chill go through her. Then she took out the key and opened the door, which gave a screech that old metal usually made. She scooped the pile of books and DVDs into a stack and carried them to the check-in desk. One DVD had a yellow post-it on it. She slid the Scarface DVD from the pile and read the writing.

LIBRARIAN,

GIVE OUR MONEY BACK, OR SAY HELLO TO MY LITTLE FRIEND.

She looked at the cover, which featured Al Pacino cast as pure evil and pure meanness, his face twisted into a grimace as he fired his automatic weapon at someone below him. So this was who she was robbing. Not small-city bureaucrats pretending to be big dogs, but real monsters.

Good. Let's be real heroes.

It was still a losing game. But, before she lost, she could add a book, a room, a library—and steal a few more bullets from the little friend of the snarling man on the DVD cover. And protect girls like Doom, she told herself.

Four days ago, she was weak-kneed at speaking to bureaucrats. Now, the thought of real monsters made her stronger. The things you do when you get mad.

men at work

SERENITY STOOD UP from her desk and waved her pen at Faulkner. "They can say hello to my little friend."

She stepped out into the stacks looking for anything that could be kick-started with money, right now. Through the window, she saw Seth Burroughs' crew sitting around drinking coffee and laughing. It looked as if they had drawn a few chalk doodles on the concrete and spent the rest of the morning hammering a couple of boards into a makeshift table with a couple of benches, which they were putting to good use.

Maybe she couldn't kick-start this with money, but there was clearly some kicking to be done.

Head down, arms flailing, she marched up to Burroughs. He turned with a condescending smile and his men snickered.

Serenity said, "What the hell do you think you're doing?"

"Working." The men laughed. Laughed even harder when Serenity gave them a dirty look.

"Get your asses up and get this expansion built, now. This isn't the kind of work I'm paying for."

"Yeah, it is," Burroughs said. "Let me explain to you how the world works. This is what balls-to-the-walls work looks like. We're going as fast as we can." A couple of men snickered. "Really. See, here's the thing. Because this slab is more than one year old, the city inspector has to re-approve it before building starts. Even though the slab was actually over-engineered to hold twice as much weight as originally planned, the slab hasn't changed and the plans haven't changed. So, he'll come out and tap on a few places to verify that, yes, the concrete is still strong enough. Take him ten minutes, but it can't be done until his schedule lets him get out here. And then we'll have to wait for more inspections at every step. Sorry."

"Hurry up and wait," said a man behind Burroughs. "Like the army. But I wouldn't guess that a little girl like you would understand that."

Serenity glared at the man. "I understand why men want to make everything seem as hard as they can possibly can. It's called overcompensation. Don't you guys have a better way of proving you've got a dick?"

The man shut up but Burroughs didn't. "I'd love to prove it to you by throwing up this building in record time. If it'll make you feel better, we can run around like crazy to show you we're working as hard as we can."

He paused, daring Serenity to challenge him.

"We'll have everything done before the inspector gets here. Even if he gets here on time, which he never does."

Serenity threw up her hands. "This needs to be done in like a month, tops. Any way we can."

The men laughed, but Burroughs didn't. "I'd love to. You can't believe how much I'd like to finish a project and stand back and say, 'We did the best that could be done here' instead of feeling beat-down and useless at the end, ashamed of all the compromises, bribes, and double-dealing I had to stomach to get a project done even half-assed and late."

He waved at the men behind him. "What do you think it would do to these guys, too, the real workers who get things done in this city? Right now, they go home. The wife asks about their day, and they say, 'Another day, another damned dollar.' Suppose they could go home and brag about what they did, tell their family there were people cheering them on because they were putting up a library faster and better than anyone ever had? What kind of city you think that would be?"

"Then do it. We need to get this built before . . . before the weather turns. Think how it would feel to build a library in a month or so. You'd be proud forever."

He shrugged. "Partly, you're right with what you first said. Too many guys have to prove how big their dick is by slowing things down. There are too many pointless rules, and too many men sick of enforcing little rules but doing it because it's the only paycheck they've got. And, of course, money. You can do anything with money."

"If I can get you all the money you need, can you do this in a month?"

"If and if and if. There was a group in China that built a thirty-story skyscraper in fifteen days. Imagine that."

He looked off and thought about that for a moment. Then the thought must have turned sour, as he turned and spat.

"What the hell," he said "What the hell are we talking about? This is here and not China or some other fairy land. Only a drunken fool would think we could even get an inspector out here today to approve the layout."

Serenity looked at him. "You get to work on something productive—anything. I'll get the inspector. Then we'll both get drunk."

hair, money, and government

SHE FOUND city planner Ron Powell sitting at a picnic table in Kidland Park sharing a pizza with his daughter. As they chewed, they watched two kids hammer away at a wooden tower with two sticks. Built by volunteers, the park was tough enough to stand up to even a bureaucrat's grandchildren.

Powell was a wiry, intense black man who had been a Maddington High School baseball player, and had a few years in the minors when he was younger. He came back home and ran a sports bar until people wearied of hearing stories of his glory days. Then he ran for elected office as the city's planning director. Former fans immediately saw the connection between baseball, beer, and city planning. He was swept into office overwhelmingly, and had been there for a decade, growing old and cranky without daily training.

Serenity held her hand up and smelled her breath. Her head was starting to show the effects of too much morning rum. She hoped her breath wasn't showing it, too. She vowed to throw out the demon rum as soon as she got back. This was too much.

She popped a mint to be sure and teetered across the mulch-covered playground on her high heels.

Smile, girl, smile, she told herself.

"Director Powell," she said. He turned slowly and she caught a glimpse of a tired, angry old man before he recognized her and put on a big campaign smile.

"Slugger," he said. "Call me Slugger. And you're that librarian that kindly hosted a reelection event for me the last time I ran."

"So glad you remember me, sir." Actually, the event was a children's reading festival with games and fuzzy mascots. Powell showed up and gave a ten-minute speech on his glory days and the need to vote for him, while the grade-school children and mascots looked at each other and tried to make sense of it, and Serenity tried to figure out how to get him to leave.

Whatever.

"I'm up for reelection again, you know."

"Yes, sir. And I have a pressing problem facing our city. I'm sure that if you help us, a grateful city will sweep you back into the office where we both know you belong."

His smile faded a little. "You think the way to get reelected is to serve the people?"

"Isn't that the way it's supposed to work?"

He laughed, tired. "Maybe. We just hired a consultant who's telling me that I'm in trouble this election. People have forgotten what I've done for them. Guy running against me looks like a Hollywood movie star, one of the ones that went on to a big career in politics—and he's got money." He laughed again. "Consultant's telling me that's what this election's going to come down to: hair and cash." He rubbed his hand over his balding head. "Ain't got much of either." He clapped his hands on his legs. "Enough about me. Let's see what we can get done for you in the time I've got left. What you need, young lady?"

Serenity took a deep breath. "It's not what I need. Maddington needs a library expansion. We've found money for it, but now we're held up waiting for inspections."

"I'll see if I can get somebody out there next week. No promises, but I'll try."

"Actually, sir, we need them today. And the problem is going to get worse going forward. My contractor tells me that there are a ton of inspections coming up."

"He's got that right. We want to be sure things are done right, but that doesn't mean we can't push a few things. My office sees itself as an enabler, helping to make Maddington something special. Tell you what. I'll try to get somebody out today, and you let me know whenever you need help."

"Thank you, sir. We really want to get this expansion done in a month."

He paused. Serenity waited. He paused longer. "There is very little, young lady, that can be done in a month. I'm sorry."

She thought about the Chinese skyscraper, and thought about all the answers he'd have to that.

"Well, I thank you for any help you can give us. By the way, I might know a source that could contribute generously to your reelection."

He brightened. Then he looked carefully left and right. "Maybe we should continue this talk in my office."

They both stood up. He ran his hand over his head again and laughed. "Might even get myself a wig."

Serenity said, "Might not need it."

seven stories in seven days

RON POWELL'S OFFICE WAS DECORATED in a style best called Twenty-First Century Jock. Pictures of a young Powell shaking hands with Chipper Jones. A crowd at the old Maddington Stadium cheering as Powell rounded third, charging home with fire in his eyes. And behind the desk, a life-sized picture of a young Ron Powell—with hair—finishing a swing and looking skyward.

Powell took a seat behind the desk and motioned Serenity to a wooden bench in front of his desk.

"Took that out of the old Maddington Stadium, back when Maddington was just a little country town."

She sat, and tried to avoid splinters.

"Yes, sir."

He waited. She waited. He smiled and she nodded. "Sir, we have a donor who's funding our library expansion. It's important to him that the library do something big, and do it fast. If we can get the library done in a month, I think he would also be very supportive of the reelection of the man who helped make it possible."

He looked sad. "I don't know if I can do that. I thought this was just maybe you offering a hundred dollars. I'd try to get you up to a thousand, buy enough campaign signs to keep this crappy little job for another four years."

He stood up and walked to a framed flow chart on the back wall and beckoned to Serenity to join him. It looked like someone had covered the wall with spaghetti and sticky notes.

"Inspect and approve a building in a month? Let me show you what you're talking about." He pointed. "See that? That's what we're looking at, young lady. I'd love to take your donor's money, but I don't make promises I can't keep."

He went back and sat down on the bench and hung his head. Serenity took a seat beside him.

He said, "It may be time to bow out of this job anyway. I'm tired of doing nothing but chicken shit stuff every day."

She started to object, but he pointed to the batting poster. "See that? That was me. Home run 100. First man ever to hit 100 for the old Stars Double-A baseball team. Only made the majors once, for a week. But I set that record, will always be the man who did it. See that old man in the crowd, face looks like he just took a big bite of a turd pie? That's my father. Bet me I couldn't make my first high school team. Rode me every day of my life, told me I'd never be anything but chicken shit."

He took a deep breath. "Maybe he was right. But, for that one moment, I was a god. A god who never made a real dent in the pros, but a god all the same."

He glanced at Serenity and a smile flickered. Then it was gone. "That's life, ain't it? Technically, I was a loser in baseball, never made the show for long, but I felt like a winner ' cause every swing of the bat was mine. After baseball, I lived my life like they told me to. Ran a business and made money. Won elections. Won, and felt like a loser when I had to do what I was supposed to every day."

He looked at her. "Sorry. What I'm supposed to do today—what I have to do today—is tell you that we can't approve your little building in a month."

Serenity looked at the poster of Powell swinging for the fences, catching the one rare pitch that would lead to glory. "What if it wasn't a little building? What if we went bigger? Much bigger." She pointed at the picture and held her gesture until he looked up and followed. "What would it take to feel that way again?"

"I'm an old man."

"We're all old men and old women. And we're still children at the same time. Scared, and then sad because we gave in to our fears. What if we didn't? What if we got crazier than ever? Crazier than you felt when you went out to that first tryout, not sure if you could do any of it? How would that feel?"

"Good. Until we crashed."

"Good enough to be worth the crash?"

"Maybe."

He sighed. "All we're talking about is approving a building?"

"Maybe more. What would it take to make something a hell of a lot bigger happen?"

"I don't know. Yes, I do. Same thing that always makes things happen: Money. Overtime for inspectors. Money to rush everything."

She took a deep breath, stood up straight and tried to look like she was giving a serious, thought-out presentation. "Mr. Powell, I heard that somewhere in China they put up a thirty-story skyscraper in fifteen days. What if we did a seven-story building in seven days? It would put Maddington on the map, just for trying. After a week, we'd have a library to build a city around, with services and job creation beyond our imagination. What would it feel like, to stand there on the day when the doors opened, and know you did it?"

He pointed at the baseball picture. "It would feel like that. But the Chinese could only do something like that because they can spend all the money they want. And, because one guy can control all the bureaucracy."

"I've got the money," Serenity said, "if you've got the bureaucrat."

Powell stood up slowly. Looked at Serenity like she was as crazy as she was. Looked at the victorious man on the wall. He crossed behind his desk and pulled out a quart jar of clear liquid and two glasses.

"I'm a Baptist." He poured both glasses. "We don't drink. This is country courage. Moonshine. Doesn't count as alcohol because you don't have to go to the liquor store to buy it."

Serenity took her glass. He held his up to toast but then paused. "We're probably going to crash and burn."

"Possibly."

He looked back at the young Powell. "Sometimes, it's better to die trying than to live giving up."

"And we might even succeed."

He looked at her for a long time and took an even longer sip.

"No. But let's die trying." He studied her face carefully. "All in?"

He raised his glass to her.

Serenity clinked his glass.

"All in."

She felt drunk before the first sip burned down her throat.

rectal redux

SERENITY'S HEAD WAS POUNDING. She sat at her desk looking at her empty rum/coffee cup and thinking what she had been pouring in was weak compared to what Powell had. Doom was standing in the doorway talking passionately about something that Serenity was having trouble following. Doom saw something out into the lobby and stopped mid-sentence.

"Oh, this is so perfect." Doom skipped away and Councilman Doctor Bentley filled Serenity's door behind her.

"Councilman Doctor. What a surprise."

"I'm billing this as a house call."

She leaned back. "Does your office even know how to bill for a house call?"

Bentley frowned.

"Councilman Doctor Bentley, I'm sorry, but I've got a lot to get done. Why don't you have a seat and tell me what's on your mind?"

She pointed emphatically at her broken visitor's chair, and he sat down gently.

"Serenity, girl," he said. "I heard you were writing some big checks yesterday. I come down here and find Seth Burroughs in the side lot yelling orders and men unloading equipment."

"The expansion's coming. Fast."

"We killed that."

"I told you, all the funding for the expansion comes from the Special Projects fund."

Bentley fidgeted and stared at her hard.

"You're telling me that you're paying for all this with a bunch of little contributions from ordinary citizens?"

"Absolutely."

He studied her face.

"I'm good at smelling rats, and I smell a big one here."

She pointed at the bookcase next to Bentley's shoulder. He turned and found himself eye-to-eye with Faulkner. He squealed and jumped.

"Oh, for crying out loud," she said. "That's just Faulkner, our library rat. He's not costing you a dime."

He shook his finger at her. "There's something worse than a rat here."

Serenity started to say something but was interrupted by a knock at the door. She looked up and Doom walked in. She handed Bentley a long box.

"Councilman Bentley," she said, "after your last meeting with our librarian, some of us here wanted to present you with this. Something for just your personal use."

"What is it?"

He opened the top and saw a long metal tube.

Doom said, "Cattle thermometer."

He dropped the box and shrieked. The chair collapsed and he was dumped on the ground. Doom giggled and helped him up. After he was safely upright, he pushed her away and waved a finger at Serenity. "I'm going to get to the bottom of this."

Doom picked up the box and held it out to him. She opened her mouth to say something but Serenity pointed at her and said, "Don't."

Bentley waved a finger at Serenity. "We are going to make sure you are doing things by the book."

Serenity smiled sweetly. "Councilman Doctor, we are the ones who keep the books. All of them."

"Something's going on down here, and I'm going to find out what. We're coming for you, Serenity, girl."

As he reached the door, Serenity said, "Councilman Doctor."

He turned around.

"Call me Hammer."

angels wake up and fly out of your butt

SERENITY PUT HER HAND on the doorknob and took a deep breath. The whole building was empty, dark, and cold like almost every city building was at night. Dark, except for the light coming out from under the door to the planning board's conference room. She exhaled, opened the door and stepped in to a room full of men sitting around a long table. They all turned and glared.

Seth Burroughs said, "Who calls a meeting for goddamn midnight? Should at least have had cots instead of chairs."

There were no cots in the planning board's conference room. Just office chairs around a table and a glassed wall with the darkened city behind it. The room had that eerie, dissipated energy that seems to permeate spaces like theaters and schools in the dark hours when they sit empty, useless and waiting.

"Blame me if you want to, Seth. I called this meeting to get this train rolling," Powell nodded at the Maddington City Architect sitting next to him. "Or, blame Steve Breaney here. I tried to make it for six, but he asked that I give him a few hours to do his homework."

Burroughs snorted. "Could have saved us all some time and sleep. Won't take ten minutes to bury this bat-shit crazy idea." He hesitated and looked at Serenity. "Although I wish it were real, Ms. Hammer."

Serenity was pacing. "Seth, not ten hours ago you were telling me how much you wanted to do something big."

"My ex-wife wanted angels to fly out of my butt, but that never happened, either."

"Angels would be asleep now anyway," Powell said.

There was a thump at the open door. A dark-haired woman with an apron that read LIBERATED BAKERY was holding a big pot of coffee and kicking the doorjamb with her foot. "Maybe this'll convince the angels to wake up."

Seth stood and walked slowly to the side table where the woman was setting down the pot. "First good idea I've heard all day." He took one of the Styrofoam cups off the top, filled it, took a sip, and made a mock horrified look.

"That's high-test," he said, "but damned good."

"Everything we do at Liberated is damned good," the woman said. "No point in second best. Expect you boys to finally do the same thing here."

"Guys, meet Stacey," Serenity said, "She agreed to bring us coffee to keep us going."

Stacey brushed back a wisp of hair. "Serenity promised me that we were going to do something big in our sleepy little town. About time. I promised to supply the food and coffee."

"Fine." Burroughs walked back to his seat. "Let's do something big. Get your one-story library expansion done in a month. Give your kiddies a new place to read Doctor Seuss." He took another sip, then said, "Damned good. But this plan—hell, this ain't even a plan—ain't got a chance in hell of ending with anything but seven stories of shit piled up next to your library. Even if we can build it—and we can't—nobody would be crazy enough to set foot in it." He nodded at the architect. "You tell them, Steve."

Breaney had been scribbling on a legal pad in the middle of a pile of printed pages and scrawled notes. "Actually, Seth, I told Ron the same thing when he first called me. Ron said, 'seven floors' and I said, 'seven ways crazy.' By the way, Ms. Hammer, how did you come up with the number seven?"

She hesitated, "Well, if we're going to build Maddington around the library, we can justify a lot of space."

They waited.

"Okay, I pulled it out of my butt. Seven stories in seven days. Who knows? But I guarantee you we'll use every square foot."

Powell said, "I thought it was because the biggest building in Maddington right now is six stories. Give us a way to do something bigger than ever."

"Yeah. That was it."

"Whatever," said Breaney. "A few hours ago I'd have said it was six floors too many, and six months too few. I looked at the current expansion plans. There's no way to turn that into seven floors.

"Then I called the guy in China who did the thirty-stories-in-fifteen-days building. Wouldn't give me the time of day."

Burroughs said, "Don't blame him. We're done here."

"Should be," Breaney said, "but that's where we got lucky. You know how the world has changed in the last fifty years, and we used to rely on places like China for cheap components that we could use our brainpower to make into something great? Well, now the Chinese get their stuff from us. And, they use our engineering." He turned to Seth. "You know where the components for these modular skyscrapers come from?"

"Vietnam?"

"More of a third-world backwater than that. Jasper, Alabama. One hour away." He looked at Serenity. "And that is the only reason this is possible. Barely. Maybe. I talked to them with rough numbers. First the guy grumbled that there wasn't enough money in the world to get all this done. I told him we had money and lots of it." He looked at Powell. "That's what you told me."

Powell nodded and sipped his coffee.

"So the man got quiet, and then he told me the back story," said Breaney. "This technology was developed right here at the Army Corps of Engineers in Jericho, as replacement buildings after a natural disaster. It's all metal and glass and plastic boxes the size of rail cars, designed to be snapped together like Legos, all with AC and power and Ethernet conduits. Because it might be used in an area prone to earthquakes, it's stronger and lighter than conventional buildings. Our army developed it, but the US never exploited it. The Chinese did."

"So how long will it take them to build these modules?" Serenity asked.

Breaney actually grinned, which was hard to do at midnight. "That's where we got lucky. The army keeps a stash of these in Jasper for when they need them."

Powell said, "Yeah, but will the current slab support it?"

"I know the answer to that," Burroughs said. "Back when we laid the slab, the concrete supplier was the congressman's brother-in-law. Somehow the slab was specced to hold two floors rather than one, and we poured even more concrete than needed for that. King Kong could dance on that slab."

Breaney looked around the room. "He's right. Gentlemen, the punchline is this: if we can have plans to the Jasper plant by six A.M.—and money up front and use components he already has available—he can have the first floor components here by eight, along with engineers who know how to do this."

He looked around the table. Everyone was silent.

Serenity said, "Stacey, we're going to need a lot of coffee."

"I'll call Lynnea for another pot now, and food."

Burroughs hoisted his cup. "That's just the start. If we're going to work three full shifts, we'll need a tanker of this rocket fuel every day."

"I'll pay for it," said Serenity.

Stacey drained her cup. "Hell, no. This is my town, too. I'll get the coffee and food. I'll get every restaurant and bakery owner in Maddington out of bed. If Jasper, Alabama can get steel here by eight, we can get food here by seven. Your crews will eat better than they've ever eaten in their lives. They'll beg to work in Maddington."

Powell looked at his watch. "We've got to make an announcement to the press. It's too late to wake the mayor. Even if he listened, he wouldn't remember anything I told him. We'll shoot for a press conference at ten."

"Wake the mayor at seven, and hold the press conference at eight," Serenity said. "Have the cameras there with the trucks rolling in behind his back."

Powell smiled. "One advantage to that is we'll have to write the mayor's speech and give it to him just before he speaks. Won't give him time to recycle his same old bullshit. If we promise him reelection cash, he'll say whatever we want."

"We're done with the same old bullshit," said Serenity.

"Then let's stop BS-ing now," said Burroughs. "I got to hire a bunch of men. Maybe I can get some crews from Birmingham and Atlanta here by morning."

"No," said Serenity. "Locals first. Maddington's going to build the MAD. Go outside if you have to after that."

"Where the hell am I going to find all those workers?" Burroughs said.

Serenity leaned over and looked at Burroughs' backside. "Maybe you can hire some of those angels I see flying out."

the mayor throws his hat in

THEY WERE STANDING on a half-finished wooden platform in front of the slab for the library expansion, huddled on the front four boards. Carpenters laid down the other planks behind them and a crowd was gathering in front of them. Ron Powell lowered his cell and leaned toward Serenity. "Trucks are coming through Decatur now, and the mayor just left his house."

"Make sure he doesn't stop. We want his speech to end just as the trucks pull in."

"I've got a friend driving him. I promised the mayor that after this speech, he can run for any office he wants in the state and get it."

In front of them a knot of press people were grumpily setting up cameras and mics. A grizzled old man, trying to look younger in a bad wig, a Channel 10 blazer and a hot young blonde beside him, broke away from the pack.

"Serenity," he said, "you got us news professionals out of bed early for a library event?"

"Won't be the last, Gary. Get used to it. Going to be a lot of library events from now on, and you won't want to miss any of them."

"Really?" The blonde elbowed him aside. "You have burned a silver bullet for what, a crappy little library expansion? You told the station manager that he couldn't just send a reporter, he had to send the two most popular anchors in North Alabama."

The man rolled his eyes at her.

"Shut up, Gary," she said. "Our viewers may not like you anymore, but they like me. And I'm the one who had to get up earlier to get her hair and makeup just right. All you had to do was put that dead rat on your head." She turned back to Serenity. "A library expansion ain't big news, sister. Welcome to the real world. This is the last time you'll see us."

The woman pivoted on her heel and marched back to the newsmen.

Gary looked at Serenity. "She appeals to the younger demographic." Then he followed her back to the pack.

Powell nodded at an SUV coming onto the lot. "He's here."

The mayor had found a black stovepipe hat. The stubble on his chin looked like he was trying to start a Lincolnian beard, but could only get three whiskers to volunteer for the job. He bounced up onto the stage.

"Brief me," he said to Serenity.

Powell was putting his phone away. "Actually, we don't have time. The trucks are turning onto Maddington Boulevard. You've got three minutes. If you want the speech to end with the trucks barreling in, mayor, you take the microphone now. Serenity, you stand behind the mayor. I want you to look like you're beaming up at him, but I want you to whisper his speech in his ear. Mayor, you just repeat what Serenity says and you'll be a hero."

The mayor beamed at Serenity. "I trust you, sweetie. I've already taken your advice on one thing." He tapped his hat and smiled. "And look at how well that turned out."

"Yes, sir."

He turned to Powell. "Seriously, Ron. I'm told this is really big. Can we do it?"

"We can. And, if you want to get credit for the biggest event in fifty years, you need to give this speech right now."

The mayor said, "I'm in."

Powell took the cell from his ear and said, "You guys need to get started *now*."

The mayor stepped to the mic, and Serenity stepped up behind him and whispered, "Thank them all for coming. Then tell them that we stand in front of bare concrete to announce the most audacious and important event in Maddington's history."

"Good line," the mayor said under his breath, and then said to the crowd, "Thank you all for coming today. You know, I remember when I was a small boy—"

Serenity hissed, "No hamming. We don't have time."

He nodded as if lost in his memory and said, "Today, we stand in an empty field to announce one of the most audacious and important events in Maddington's history."

He added, "And I want to remind our voters that this is the kind of boldness and service that they expected when they elected Mayor Weatherford Johnson as their mayor. And—"

"Stick to the script," said Serenity.

The mayor waved his hands for a cheer that never came.

Serenity whispered, "For too long, all of us have settled for second-best."

The mayor said, "For too long, we have settled for second-best—until we elected Weatherford Johnson as our mayor."

Serenity rolled her eyes. "The library has always been the first stop for people looking to better themselves."

"Under this administration, the library has been the first stop for people looking to better themselves," paraphrased the mayor.

"And they've come because they knew the library was the one place that wouldn't turn them away," Serenity said. "No matter how far afield the request, a librarian would smile and say, 'Let's see what we can find out.'"

The mayor went two-for-two on getting things mostly right.

Serenity grew bold. "It hasn't been enough. They've come with questions, but because we didn't have resources, too often they left with their needs—and the needs of the city of Maddington—unfulfilled. People have lost opportunities, businesses have gone unopened, existing businesses have folded, and people have died, because people have come to the library looking for help that they could not find anywhere else, and our library has only been able to offer a Band-Aid. No more."

The mayor was getting into it. He said the lines with real emotion, and shouted "no more" at the top of his lungs.

Powell sidled up to Serenity and whispered, "Trucks are passing Kroger. Wrap it up."

She whispered, "What if someone had the courage to end that?"

Serenity looked down the street and saw the first eighteen-wheeler coming and whispered in his ear.

He shouted, "Here, in Maddington, today, *we do.*"

A few people in the crowd cheered.

Serenity whispered, "Thanks to an innovative public/private funding partnership, which I am personally leading, today we begin the most ambitious building project in American history, here in Maddington, by the people of Maddington, and for the people of Maddington."

The mayor shouted the line and turned to her for more.

She said, "As we speak, trucks are arriving with the first material for a project impossible anywhere but a city as ambitious as Maddington. And when it's done, we will have a MAD that will do all of those things, and more."

The mayor repeated.

Serenity said, "With the whole city pulling together, we will build a seven-story library in seven days."

The mayor turned to her. With the mic still on, he said, "What the heck? They didn't tell me seven stories."

Serenity yanked the mic from him. "This city—my city—will build a new seven-story library in seven days. Starting . . ." She paused and looked at the back of the field, away from the crowd. The first truck bounced over the curb with a crash and rolled into the field behind her with more trucks lined up as far as she could see. They came with a roar and a giant dusty storm that blew over them all—and covered the blonde newsgirl with a thick coat of Madding-ton red clay.

Serenity didn't need the mic to yell.

"*Now*! Welcome to the MAD!"

Then she took the mayor's hat off and sailed it out into the crowd.

to the guest room

"THAT'S ALL GOOD," said Serenity, "but it's not solving anything."

She was lying under the covers, naked, in the dark. Joe had woken her up in the middle of the night, touching her in a special way that usually brought fireworks. Tonight, it just interrupted her nightmare of mafia thugs with bent noses, and the squads of ninja police officers invading her library to get their money back. The man doing the touching and waking her up was himself a police officer, if not a ninja.

Joe pulled away, snatching the covers in the process. "Didn't seem to be hurting anything either," he said.

Serenity snatched back her share of the covers—and then some—and lay there in the dark with her eyes wide open and her mind at the library. Every moment was a step on a tight wire, exhilarating because of the progress to a

goal on the other side, but terrifying because the chasm below was so deep.

But if she was a tight rope walker these days, higher in
the air than she'd ever been, she desperately needed her balancing pole beside her, the one who had always been in her
corner.

She thought of the other sense of Joe's pole. Yes, she
needed that, too. She and Joe had always been clear about
the wondrous, uplifting, balancing, spiritual importance of
good sex. But, as much as her body wanted her to, it was
hard for her to take that sense of Joe's pole while she was
mad at him for not being there as the balancing part of the
terrifying, exhilarating life she was now living.

"Whatever," she said to the mixed metaphor in her head.

Joe lay beside her, probably cold now that she had all the
covers, but lying there silently, patiently.

"We're going to have to talk about all this someday,
Sweetblossom."

"Nothing to talk about. Just not in the mood."

"I know you've got a lot going on at the library these
days, but there's something more. The last couple of days, I
don't know what your mood is. You're more excited and
energetic than I've ever seen you, but I can't get you to talk
to me about anything. Or focus on lovemaking."

"Maybe you just don't know how to 'talk' to me lately,"
she snapped. She regretted it, but there, she'd said it.

Joe sighed and got out of bed. "I feel like I don't know
how to do anything right with you these days," he said with

exaggerated calmness. "Used to be, we felt like one soul in two bodies, and the bodies craved to be joined together. Now you're so far away I can't tell what's going on over there. But I can tell there is something going on. You even said last night there was something you couldn't talk to me about. Funny thing about you, Sweetblossom, and one of the things I love about you, is that you won't hesitate to go to war over something, but you are a terrible liar. It's always obvious when you've got something you need to tell—and it's just a matter of time until you do."

"Nothing to tell," Serenity said. "I've changed my mind. Nothing going on over here that concerns you at all." But he was right and she felt the craving. Not just with her body, but with her soul. She needed all the answers and comfort that she knew were waiting for her in her other half.

But not the judgments. If he wanted to send her to jail, fine, and to hell with him. But not Doom. She wasn't going to send an almost-child off to jail.

So this was all his fault.

"There is nothing in my life right now that concerns you one little bit," she said.

"Well," he said, pulling on his shorts, "whether it concerns me or not—or even if it's something that would have concerned me a week ago and doesn't in our brave new world—at least some of it's a good thing. You're walking with a purpose and smiling for no reason at all. I looked at you earlier and you were a million miles away, smiling and talking to yourself. Or talking to somebody who wasn't there. Something, or somebody, has got you smiling. Smiling to yourself and frowning at me."

He slipped back into bed, slid over to get under the edge of the covers she'd left him. When he put one arm around her she felt herself melt.

"I guess this'll have to do," he said. "Half a Sweetblossom is better than none, at least until she's ready."

She wanted to turn into him. It would be so easy to take a little comfort. And then so easy, after, so easy to slip up and say the wrong thing and watch everything come crashing down.

"Why don't you go sleep in the guest room?" she heard herself say.

top hat walking

"THERE'S A DELAY," said the mayor.

"No delays," said Serenity. "Get this done before . . . the weather turns."

The mayor, most of the council, and Serenity were sitting in the picnic area at the MAD the morning after the mayor's inspirational speech. Serenity had bullied a Maddington big-box home improvement store into bringing every picnic table in their inventory down to the MAD. The tables converted the library patio into a food court and viewing area that looked out over the new construction. Local restaurants kept the table stocked with free food 24/7 for the workers, and for anyone who came to watch the new MAD going up in the lot next door. The barbecue stand on Hughes Road had stocked the tables this morning.

Serenity had been surprised at how easy it was to get the owner to volunteer. She had walked in ready to kick ass for the free food, but the owner thanked her as soon as she asked.

She had pointed at the long line to the restaurant, as truck drivers and construction workers on break picked up food at the closest place to the MAD.

"You're going to lose all that business tomorrow when they can get their food for free," she'd said.

"I'll also lose the cost of the food and will have to pay extra workers tomorrow and open up early," John Lawler said. "And my business will do better in the long run than it ever did because I did all that."

She gave him a look and he laughed.

"Don't seem right, does it? We were taught that the way to make money was to hang on to every nickel, don't give even a smile away if you can't make money off it. Tomorrow, I'll give away more food than I've ever sold in a week. And, I'll get a hundred new customers who have never tried my food—and a hundred more who are just grateful for what I did." He laughed again. "And another thousand more who come to the new MAD. Sometimes, Serenity, the best way to make money is to give things away for free. 'Cast your bread on the water,' as a pretty smart business-man said two thousand years ago. Thanks for the opportunity. We'll have those tables covered tomorrow."

So, the tables were covered with food today, and the benches were covered with workers grabbing a quick bite so they could get back to work, homeless men getting a good meal, and moms bringing their kids out to see their future going up before their eyes.

There was a small wooden platform on the edge of the new MAD that was set up so kids could hammer a nail or turn a wrench, and get their picture taken showing them helping build the MAD.

That is, when the kids could elbow their way past the city fathers and every state politician and wannabe from three states that were getting their pictures taken at the table, usually wearing hard hats to show they were working. Pictures taken, and then gathering around the tables for free food.

"Y'all coming back for lunch?" asked Bentley, ignoring the mayor and Serenity.

Barnes, the councilman from the wealthy district up on the hill, snorted. "'Course. I'm going to do my volunteer work every day at seven a.m., noon, and seven at night."

Serenity thought about the value of the volunteer work this crew performed at the food lines and picnic tables but bit her tongue and said, "Liberated's going to cover the tables with desserts at midnight tonight."

Barnes grunted. "I'll volunteer at midnight, too. God, I hate overtime."

The mayor hadn't touched his plate of pork barbecue and potato salad. He was wearing his top hat and coveralls, swearing he would wear nothing but coveralls until the MAD was finished.

A man with gray hair and a still strong build came up and set his tray down.

"Mr. Molcut," said Serenity. "You've been working pretty hard since before I got here."

He took a sip of coffee and gave Serenity a long look. "Important to keep your hands on your community."

"Paul's done that," said the mayor. "Since he retired as head of one of the big aerospace companies here, he's been involved behind the scenes of nearly everything."

"I like staying busy," Paul Molcut said. "Keeps me in touch with all of my old buddies in the business world. And, out in the fresh air like this." He swallowed the last of a sausage biscuit. "Serenity, you ought to get together with us. A bunch of us community-minded folks get together for our own church service early on Sunday mornings at the Catholic Church. As important as you're becoming, you ought to join us."

"Thanks," she said.

He wiped his mouth, emptied his coffee cup and stood up to go back to work.

The mayor leaned into the center of the table. "You boys ain't listening to me. I said there was a delay."

Serenity said, "Looks like it's going great. First floor went up yesterday. One crew's adding the second floor today while another finishes the first. That's the plan: one floor a day. Snap the floor in place today, volunteers and workers complete the interior of that floor tomorrow while the next floor is added. Seth says we're an hour or so ahead."

"Not a delay in the building." The mayor patted her hand. "This isn't something you need to worry your pretty little head about, Ms. Hammer. This is real . . . statesmanship . . . for statesmen." He turned to the other men who had their heads down in their plates. "Got a call first thing that said our good government money's held up."

The heads came up. One or two paused in mid-bite with their mouths full of food, which wasn't a pretty sight.

"What do you mean?" said Bentley, spitting crumbs.

"I mean that the contact called me early. Said there was a delay, and we wouldn't get our money today. Might not get it at all this time. Said there was a problem, might take them a few days to get it fixed. Might not get it fixed at all."

Barnes said, "At all?"

"I think he's just throwing his weight around. You know how he is."

Barnes put down his fork. "No, I don't. He only talks to you. I haven't talked to him since I was recruited for the job. They can't cut off my money. I've done everything they asked."

"Well, they say it's not coming."

"This is serious. I got a payment coming up on the lake house."

The mayor said, "Said we might have to get used to it."

"We need to tell him who's the boss here," Barnes said, "We run this city."

The table was silent.

Another councilman, the quiet one, said, "We knew when we started taking this money that these guys were probably crooks."

Barnes stiffened. "There is nothing illegal about this. The Good Government Fund is a dark money PAC, legal under Alabama law. Remember when the old governor got caught with his pants down, was paying his honey with money from a dark PAC so nobody could tell who the donor was, or how much he paid?"

"Still crooks, even if they're legal crooks."

"Or businessmen," Barnes muttered.

the boss wears pink

SERENITY LEFT the statesmen to their work and walked into the new MAD.

"Hey," said Burroughs. "You can't be in here without a hard hat."

Seth Burroughs was smiling, which was not something he did often or well.

"I'll get one," said Serenity.

"Wait here." He walked off.

Serenity stood in the doorway and looked around at the big empty cavern. Men were crawling over it like ants. Half the walls were already covered with wallboard while men and women spackled, taped, painted, wired and plumbed.

Serenity saw through the mess, though, and saw what it could be. Would be. Something new and powerful for the people of Maddington. Not home, not work, but a place as welcoming and productive as either, making both home and work stronger. Up front, where she was now, there would be a welcome area where a person would be greeted by a librarian who knew everyone's name, and would help people find what they needed. And, if someone didn't need help, off to the right was the coffee shop and bakery with tables to sit and read or work, or meet with friends, book clubs or business groups. To the left, a small bar and grill would be open evenings. And—if Serenity could hold on to the money—all of them would run on a pay-what-you-can basis.

A place for everyone. Help for everyone. Open spaces, inviting spaces.

A place to grow.

Maybe. Or maybe just a rusting hulk with my grave out back, Serenity thought.

Somebody bumped her from behind.

"Hey," said Doom. "Nobody should have a smile as big as yours this early."

"That's the first-floor smile. Wait until you see my seven-story smile."

Doom nodded. "I look forward to it. Six more days."

"If we can hold the fort that long."

"Fort-holding is our new job?"

"Hold the fort while we build the shining city behind it. That's why we're divvying things up."

"You want Joy to be in charge of holding the old library together and me to set up things for the new library so we're ready to transition, while you fight the war?"

"Yeah."

"Okay. I'm packing new programs into as many places as I can in the old MAD to get them up and running, ready to move into the new MAD, but we're running out of room. What do you think about renting a couple of trailers for overflow?"

"Don't rent, buy. When we're done, we'll put them around town as little pocket libraries and help centers."

"Good idea. We can put a couple of them in the poor areas."

"Rich areas, too. I want garden clubs and bank presidents to rely on the MAD, too. They need to stop feeling like libraries are something they have to pay for to help others. Keep me posted. I'll be spending most of my time here getting the MAD built. And trying to protect the money."

"Keep Bentley's hands off this."

"Bentley and anyone else. But I need to find out where the money is coming from. You and Joy keep the library running. Keep Faulkner fed, but don't give him too much rum. And, I've got one more guerrilla operation for you."

She opened her notebook and took out a slip of paper. "That account made the last deposit to the Residuals fund."

"How'd you find that? I looked for the deposit history last night, and it looks like it gets wiped after each deposit. The little Residuals account should have pennies, but instead it has millions. No record of how it gets there, it just does."

"Well, they missed a spot somewhere. Do you think your library hacker club can find out who owns that account?"

"Aye, aye, captain."

Burroughs came up. "Told you, you need a hard hat."

"Sorry. I got distracted. I'll get one now."

He pulled a pink hard hat out from behind his back. "Figured you'd be spending a lot of time underfoot here. The boys painted you a special hat." He handed it to her. "Asked me whether to put "Hammer" or "Serenity" on it. Figured this was the right title."

Serenity looked at the label of "Boss" and tried it on.

thirty-eight

mountains and mohammed

SERENITY WAS ON THE SECOND FLOOR when she heard a familiar voice behind her. "If the mountain won't come to Mohammed." She turned, and saw Joe's head was at her knee level, climbing up the ladder to the second story. He rose until his head was even with hers, then kept rising above her. Finally, he stepped off the platform.

"Then Mohammed must go to the mountain." He smiled. A little forced, a little weak-hopeful, and a little tough-defensive all at once.

He looked like the big little-boy she had fallen in love with, and she hugged him.

"Honey, I'm sorry," she said. "This is hard."

"Everything's hard when I don't have my Sweetblossom on my side. I've been going crazy imagining all the things you can't tell me."

"Don't. It's . . . complicated."

"Always is." He studied her face before she turned away.

There was nothing for her to say.

"Okay," he said. "How's this? I'll be at Stem and Stein tonight at five o'clock, if you want to talk. You don't show, I'll go stay at Rick's until we work things out. Be at Stem and Stein every night waiting for you."

"Oh, Joe, don't make such a big deal out of this."

He pulled back. "When you're married to a woman twice as good and twice as smart and twice as hot as you are, you worry every day. When she kicks you out of her bed, you worry a lot."

"Joe, you're being silly . . . wait, you see me that way?"

"I'm not blind." He waved his hands. "All of this costs a lot. Only one man in Maddington County has this kind of money, and it's from drugs. And he's also a lady's man who hates me."

"Joe, no—"

He stepped away and put his hand on the ladder. "Five o'clock. Every night until I know what's going on."

Then he was gone. But the line of men waiting to see Serenity was not.

"Boss," the IT guy said, "we haven't talked, but I'm assuming you want the same kind of internet service you had at the library before? Shared DSL?"

Serenity focused and said, "Crappy service barely good enough for a couple of people to check email at once? Hell, no."

"Bandwidth costs money."

"Spend it. And when it comes to equipment, don't rent, buy. Today. What would we need if we were a high-tech corporation?"

"T1 line. At least."

"Suppose we had twenty high-tech startups working at once? And a digital film studio?"

"Multiple scalable T1s."

"And suppose we offered free Wi-Fi satellite hotspots around town?"

He swallowed. "Then I would have to get smarter."

"Get smarter, today. Tomorrow morning, I want to see this starting. Not options, not plans. I want to see wires going in. Clear?"

"Yes, ma'am."

Seth Burroughs elbowed his way to the front of the line.

"Boss, we've got a problem."

"Then let's fix it."

Burroughs snorted. "This may be beyond your super-powers, Boss. Rain coming in Friday. We're going to lose most of that day. Nothing in your bag of tricks for that."

"We've got money. Lot you can do with that."

"Can't stop the rain."

"No." She paused. "But—what do people do when they want to cover the outside in a hurry? They put up a tent."

Burroughs said, "You think we run over to Cabela's and pick up a couple of pup tents? Maybe get umbrellas for the men?"

"No. Bigger. Like circus tents. Big circus tents. Got to be someplace that makes them. We don't need quality—we only need them for a week—just big. And fast. Your engineers can figure how to put a tent up on top and keep moving it up with each floor."

"Take time to make it and get it here."

"Not if the tent company wants more money than they've ever seen. Remember, Seth, you've got money. You don't have time."

"Maybe," he pulled on his chin. "By Friday."

"Definitely," she said, "by tomorrow."

There was a tug at her sleeve. "Ma'am," the man said, "there's someone yelling for you down below."

Serenity nodded and walked to the open edge and looked down. Doom was standing on the ground looking up.

"Ms. Hammer," she yelled, "I've got news."

thirty-nine

goddamned army desk

DOOM GAVE SERENITY THE WORD before she was off the ladder.

"Ms. Hammer, we're not going to be able to find out who tried to make that withdrawal last night."

Joy walked up and joined them. "Bahama banks are the new version of Swiss banks. Even the government, with warrants and double-naught spies, can't find out who owns what there."

Serenity jumped down the last few feet. "Yeah, but what about the deposit?"

"We've got that one, but it doesn't make a lot of sense. Baring Aerospace. Local army and NASA contractor. How could they make a deposit that big to a little nothing? Why? I mean, they're not even in Maddington, but next door in Jericho."

Serenity looked up at the second floor, yelled at a man to be careful, and turned back to Doom.

"Doesn't make sense to me either." She squinted up at the last wall of glass going up on the second floor. "Doom, I need you to come out of the library and park yourself at Seth Burroughs's side."

She put the "Boss" hard hat on Doom's head, and Doom reached up to tilt it to a hipper level.

"What do I do, other than rock the hat?"

"Write checks. I don't know why Baring Aerospace is writing their checks, but someone down there does and we've got to find out why before this whole thing blows up."

• • •

SITTING IN THE WAITING ROOM at the office of the Baring Community Affairs Manager felt like sitting in Bentley's office, except without the thermometers. The office felt just like Bentley's. That is, if Bentley had a ton of money to spend on office decor and the taste to spend it. Even the receptionist was expensive. Well, looked expensive. Everything in the room was designed to show a visitor how big Baring was and how little the visitor was. Serenity opened her notebook and wrote: MAD first floor feeling—warm, inviting. Not rich.

"It shouldn't be too much longer, Ms. Hammer," said the rich-but-not-inviting receptionist. "Mr. Franklin is such a big fan of libraries. All of us are."

"That's probably why I've been waiting out here for an hour; bet he's finishing up a book for the book club tonight."

The receptionist gave a lilting, musical ha-ha-ha sound, something she had probably practiced to harmonize with the sound of clinking champagne glasses.

Serenity looked at her watch. Four o'clock. If Franklin was quick, and if she drove fast, she could get to Stem and Stein in time to catch Joe.

That is, if she wanted to catch Joe.

She opened the book she had brought with her, a funny Florida-weird mystery titled *Engulfed* from Kathleen Cosgrove. Usually, any two sentences of Cosgrove were enough to distract her, three were enough to get her laughing. Today, she read a sentence. Then she imagined herself sitting with Joe on a beach, both smiling. Problems resolved. Partners again. She read the same sentence over, and imagined Joe putting handcuffs on her and shutting down her library.

She got very good at reading that one sentence over and over until she heard, "Ms. Hammer?"

Washington Franklin stood in front of her, smiling. He was a magnificent figure of a man, inspiring-looking with graying hair swept back like Andrew Jackson on the twenty-dollar bill. Except that this modern Jackson had perfectly white capped teeth, skin that glowed orange and features pulled back so tight she was afraid his skull would pop through.

He leaned into her. "Certainly must be a great book you're reading." He laughed and she laughed, too, hoping she'd catch the joke soon. "I had to say your name twice to get your attention."

"It is." She stood up and smiled. "Sorry for my rudeness."

Franklin chuckled and his receptionist made the tinkling-champagne sound behind him. "No need to apologize, Ms. Hammer. We all love great books here. Perhaps you can show the book to Natalie and she can order me a copy."

Serenity held up the book and Natalie snapped a picture of the cover with her phone. "Mr. Franklin reads all the time."

"Oh, that's great," said Serenity. "What are you reading now?"

Franklin's smile froze and he chuckled again, "Shall we talk in my office?"

"Lovely."

His desk was a curved piece of aluminum the size of a barn door with nothing on it. He pointed to a framed photograph from World War II on his wall. "Baring gave me this, in recognition of thirty years' service."

"They gave you a piece of scrap metal?"

He gave his booster-club chuckle. "Not just scrap metal. When the government was finally going to scrap all the old war planes from WWII, Baring bought them up and made office furniture out of them."

"Practical."

"See these holes here? I like to think they're bullet holes."

Serenity looked at a pattern of small holes the size of pencil points. Maybe the Japanese used BBs.

"Well," he smiled, taking his seat behind the wing desk. "Now I get to sit behind this fine old relic and support our community." He swiveled to a credenza behind him and took out a checkbook. "We love our libraries here at Baring. We rely on an educated population. Yes, sir." He sat the checkbook on the wing and shifted it back and forth to find a place where the slope of the wing would let him write. "Yes, ma'am, I mean." Another chuckle. "Even though we're actually in Jericho, a lot of our engineers and technicians live in Maddington." He tore off the check and stood up so he could reach across the wing to hand it to her. When he did, the checkbook slid off the wing.

He laughed and bent down to pick it up. "Happens all the time."

He straightened up, "Well, that ought to put a hundred books on the shelves of your library."

Serenity looked at the $100 check. "You really must buy a lot of books yourself."

"All the time."

She put the check in her purse and snapped it shut. "Thank you so much, Mr. Franklin. But I really came here to ask you about another matter."

He didn't chuckle. "I've heard about your new library. We at Baring wish we could help, but profit margins in the government contracting business aren't what they could be. We really have very little money. In fact, when I was awarded this desk I had to contribute a thousand dollars, just because Baring was so strapped for cash."

"I understand. It's amazing the sacrifice that companies like Baring make for our country."

He chuckled. "You do understand."

"Yes, sir. I had a question about another matter. Bookkeeping for the city is now handled through the MAD, and Baring had a deposit bounce yesterday in one of our accounts."

He chuckled and waved a hand. "That's the business side. I'll get Natalie to take you to the business office."

"Actually, it was a deposit to a specific small account made from your office. For ten thousand dollars."

The chuckle disappeared and his eyes grew wide. "Our deposit to the Good Government fund bounced?"

Play along. "Yes, sir."

"I am so sorry." He turned back to the credenza, pulled his keys out of his pocket and opened a drawer. "We will correct that right now. I am so sorry. You know that Baring supports good government. The director of the fund knows we support the fund." He paused and looked back with a begging expression.

"We know, sir." Serenity put on her best crocodile-mogul smile. She was not used to looking powerful. "We were sure Baring would want to correct it immediately."

"Yes. Yes." He pulled out another checkbook and pinned it on the wing with one hand. He looked up at her and his face was white. "You don't . . . I mean, the director doesn't think we need to make a lesson out of this, do we? We've got a bid in for the BISAC computer center, and we sure do need to win it."

Serenity played along. "So you do understand that no bribe, no contract?"

His face hardened. "Bribe? Bribes are illegal. We would never bribe anyone."

She decided to stay quiet and let him talk.

"We understand that we all need to be team players. Before the Good Government fund, we made contributions to everybody running for political office, and more to those who won. All legal. None of those contributions will win you anything. But if you don't support the movers and shakers, well, they won't support you. Your fund just made it easier for us to make one contribution and let you distribute the money."

She smiled and leaned forward. "We appreciate your community spirit. No lesson. Not as long as it's corrected. Now."

"Yes, ma'am." He scribbled furiously and pushed the check across to her. "I put next week's contribution in there, too."

Serenity kept smiling but said nothing and waited until he became uncomfortable enough to talk more.

"Unless you think that maybe this should just be a special contribution today, and we still make a payment next week."

She looked at the check. Twenty thousand dollars, with the payee blank.

She stood up and extended her hand across the wing. "What do you think?"

He reached across and shook her hand vigorously. "I'll make sure we have our contribution on time next week."

They both watched the checkbook slide off the wing and hit the floor.

Franklin glared at it. "Goddamned army desk."

forty

truckin'

SERENITY CUT THROUGH the Bridge Street shopping area, grumbling at the speed bumps and the wealth of stop signs designed to keep shoppers at least fifty-miles-an-hour slower than the speed she wanted for the trip back to the MAD.

That wasn't all she was grumbling about. "I have to beg 'til my knees are bleeding to get a hundred dollars, but hint that you're in with the big dogs and the money taps open up and drown you."

She stopped at the light that was the boundary for Bridge Street and sat there gunning the engine and tapping on the wheel. The light turned green, she stomped on the gas, and diners on the sidewalk outside the brewpub were treated to the sight of the world's fastest drag-racing minivan from hell burning rubber as it screamed as loud and fast as it could up the hill.

"I am so goddamned mad at all of this," she screamed.

The spectators had probably figured that out, and were staying out of her way.

Except for one. A scratched-up pickup truck with big wheels pulled up beside her in the turn lane of the three-lane road. She glanced over and caught a quick image of a figure in a baseball cap and a camo shirt at the wheel. He tipped the hat and grinned at her.

She screamed, "That's not a goddamned passing lane." He didn't look over. As she was holding down the button to roll down her window so he could hear her words of wisdom, the truck tapped her minivan and she had to fight for control.

She screamed, "Jesus Christ," but he ignored her even with her window down.

The truck slammed her harder and two wheels of the minivan slid off the road.

This was real. She got cold and calm fast.

She fought the urge to jerk the wheel, and instead eased off of the gas, gently turning the wheels until the minivan bumped back onto the road. She caught a quick glance down the long, steep hill to the right. Nothing to stop her until she hit bottom.

The truck separated a few feet from her van but he was just trading space to gain power. He came back hard for the knockout punch.

Serenity stood on the brakes as hard as she could and fought to keep control. As soon as the truck's bed was even with the front of her minivan, she released the brakes and swung the wheel as hard as she dared to the left and smashed the heavy front of her minivan into the lighter bed of the truck.

The truck spun as if in slow motion, dropping tail-first down the hill with the cab clawing at the edge of the road like a man clinging to a cliff, clinging until he lost his grip and the truck slid down the hill. She slowed and watched as the truck picked up speed, not quite flipping until it slammed into a small stand of pine trees next to the huge Cabela outdoor store.

Serenity pulled over and watched the truck's door, not sure whether she wanted someone to come out or not. The door opened and a man got out and ran for the store.

She sat watching for a minute, then turned around and went back down the hill to the store. She parked in the lot and examined her crumpled front fender before heading inside.

She stepped in the door and stopped, staring at a gigantic cavern of shirts, jeans, guns, fishing poles—basically, anything you might need to kill any animal.

A young man came up to her. "We have a very fine lady's deer rifle on sale today, ma'am."

"Uh, no. I'm looking for a man who just came in here. Average height, a little heavy. Kind of nondescript. Wearing jeans and a camo shirt and a ball cap."

The young man sighed. "Like everything else in here, if we've got one of them, we've got a hundred."

He waved his arm at a store full of men dressed in camo, with a flannel shirt here and there for variety.

me and mr. jones

SERENITY TOOK HER MINIVAN to Zell's Auto Repair and Discount Tobacco Store out in the woods down Stockard Road. Roger Zell looked at it and pulled on his tobacco-stained beard.

"Roger, I've got to get this fixed, fast. A day or two, no more."

Roger was a small, skinny man. He squinted up at her skeptically. "And you can't tell Joe that I . . . uh . . . hit the mailbox."

He spat a long brown stream. "Looks like you hit the whole damned post office."

She looked at him pleadingly as Doom pulled up.

"I'll do the best-est I can. Tomorrow. End of the day. But the paint will still be wet."

She kissed him on top of his head and dashed to Doom's car.

"What the hell?" said Doom.

"Drive." She told her about the Good Government fund.

"After that," Serenity said, "Franklin's answers to questions about the Good Government fund were mostly 'Yes, ma'am' and 'No, ma'am' and polite groveling evasions. No more information, but at least I didn't raise any suspicions. Maybe, at least until he realizes that the other check didn't bounce."

"And then he followed you out to the parking lot and beat the hell out of your car with a sledgehammer?"

"Of course not." Serenity told her about the rest of the morning's adventure. Doom yelped and raised her hand in a high-five. "Hero."

Serenity left the high-five hanging. "I don't know, Doom. I lost my temper. I could have killed that man."

"We're in a war, Ms. Hammer. By any means necessary."

Serenity shook her head. "I get so tired of that line. It sounds like just another excuse for more macho bullshit like guns and trucks and strutting and hurting. We ought to have something better."

"We have ass-kicking in high heels."

Serenity said, "Oh, yeah. That intimidated camo guy back there." She thought a minute. "Doom, find me a pay phone on the way back to the library."

"Pay phone? What is this, the eighteen-hundreds?"

"They didn't have . . . never mind. Try a convenience store or two."

It took a couple of tries, but they found one. Serenity dialed a number.

"Doris? Serenity, up in Maddington. Good, but listen: I've got something important and I've got to talk fast. Remember last year, when the governor was paying his mistress with state library funds? We ran down the information and fed it to the papers? I need the same librarian superpowers now, but I think it's even bigger. You'll need to get the Birmingham and Mobile libraries in, too. And keep it quiet. And when you get something, don't call me at the library, call me at home. Late at night. Now, here's what I know . . . "

Serenity and Doom drove back to the library and went to Doom's desk.

"Doom, I need you to open an off-the-books library account. With these."

She handed Doom the checks.

Doom whistled. "You're turning into a pretty good Robin Hood. A week ago, we'd have killed for this—sorry, figure of speech. But do we really need this now?"

"Not in Special Projects."

Serenity went into her office. *For Whom the Bell Tolls* was still on her desk.

She sat down and turned to the computer on her side table, but something about the book at her elbow bothered her. The title referenced John Dunne's poem, the need to stand for something more than your own little island, and focused on Hemingway's Robert Jordan's fight in a civil war against fascists in a country a thousand miles from his own safe home.

So this was her fight, such as it was. With books and dollars instead of bullets, at least for now. She looked at the computer screen. The first thing was the list of books requested by patrons and librarians. Usually, she ordered the few she could afford that had the most votes.

Serenity looked at the window with the Special Funds balance, selected all the books on the list and clicked "Order." Then she clicked all the recommended books from the *Library Journal.* After, she sat back, smiled, and felt as if she had shot a brigade of fascists.

She next took a sip of her coffee and opened her email. Scanned the list until she found the email she wanted. Mr. Andalusia Jones. She opened his email, and surprise, he told her he had made another generous contribution to the Special Projects fund. Creative writing time, she thought. She replied,

Dear Mr. Jones,

On behalf of the people of Maddington, and our library and myself personally, I thank you for yet another generous contribution. Maddington is a stronger and better city for your generosity, and I think your late wife would be extremely proud of you.

She sent the email off and saved it, along with the original email, to a file documenting contributions to the Special Projects fund.

Sitting on her desk was a cheap smartphone she'd bought for cash at a convenience store. She smiled at it and said, "Your turn, Mr. Jones."

When she came up with the idea of an imaginary Mr. Jones who made daily contributions to the library, to add some credibility she pictured an image of him: a small man with big round glasses, looking like the bank examiner in *It's a Wonderful Life*. He would be a sad, rich man who had lost his wife recently—a wife who had loved the library as much as Serenity. She opened the phone's email and typed.

Ms. Hammer,
I have made another deposit of . . .

Serenity looked at the amount Doom had rolled into the Fund yesterday and typed it in.

. . . in memory of my beautiful wife . . .

Serenity paused and remembered the name she had made up.

. . . Joanie today. I have more money than I can spend now that she is gone, and I know she would want some child to benefit from books as much as she did. Thank you for giving me the opportunity to honor her memory. You and your staff are true heroes and I thank you for your magnificent efforts.

She hit send. Boom. A bomb dropped on Franco himself and all of his fascists.

Joy and Doom drifted into her office and she glanced at her watch. Time for their staff meeting already.

"Okay, we've each got a million people waiting for us. Let's get going. Problems first."

"Yeah," Doom said. "Guy came by and said we might have a problem with our electric power, now that we're seven stories, and that it's going to be almost impossible to solve it in time. Also mentioned that he was good friends with John Henessey at the power company, who could solve it. Said that he could talk to him. Then he mentioned that Henessey needs ten thousand dollars so he can run for district attorney."

Joy said, "Let's do that through a contractor."

Serenity said, "So, we pay this 'consultant' ten grand and our problems go away?"

"Sounds like it."

Joy said, "Not that anyone's asking anymore, but as long as we pay the consultant for work done, and we don't know what he does with it, we're still on the good side of the law. Barely. Maybe."

Serenity nodded. "And Henessey will be in the pocket of the consultant." A long pause while Joy and Doom looked at her. "But if I go to Henessey directly with twenty thousand dollars, we'll have a new friend and maybe the gratitude of the next district attorney."

"And be on the other side of the law."

"The law is what people enforce."

Joy shrugged.

They finished going through the items and Joy and Doom left.

Serenity looked at the book again and thought how much fun the battle was right now. But she knew that, at the end of the book, the fascists came for Robert Jordan. And in the end, all that mattered was how hard you had fought.

She heard a tap on the door and looked up. There was a small man with big round glasses and a cheap suit standing in her doorway looking at her with no expression.

wrestling with joy

SERENITY SAID, "Mr. Jones? How can you . . ."

The man standing in Serenity's doorway blinked behind the round glasses, his eyes magnified and slightly bug-eyed. "No. Name's Kendall."

Serenity breathed easier. While she was opening her mouth to welcome him, he said, "Councilman Bentley hired me to have a look at your books."

She shut her mouth. And her computer.

"We can't . . ." she said. "Well, we can't let just anyone into the books of the city's library. Besides, without specialized training, I don't think you'd understand—"

"Well," he said. He had a way of talking where only his mouth moved. The rest of his body froze like a statue. "I used to work for the FBI, back in Texas and some here, before I retired and went out on my own. Forensic accounting. Called in when people thought there was a crime. Reckon that'll do?"

"Well, uh—"

"If not, I've got a letter from Councilman Bentley." He reached into his jacket and Serenity saw the gun on his hip.

"Mr. Kendall." She stood up and put her hands on the desk. "We do not allow firearms in our libraries."

"Told you, ma'am. I'm retired FBI."

"Retired. Only active law enforcement may bring a gun in here." She glanced over her shoulder to be sure her new-found AK-47 didn't show.

He stood staring at her for a moment. Probably. Hard to tell with those glasses.

"Guess this ain't Texas," he said.

"Guess it's not."

He turned to leave, and then turned back. "Be back soon as I lock this up."

"We'll be ready for you."

Just before Kendall got to the library front door, he turned stiffly and looked back at her like he expected to catch her at something. Serenity was standing in the door-way of her office, waiting. After a second, he turned and left. As soon as the door closed behind him, Serenity ran to find Doom, who was sitting at her desk in the open area of the library, just outside the door to the server room.

"You need to get to the server," she said.

Doom looked up from her desk.

"Can't. The late pregnancy group is meeting with a nutri-tionist in there."

"It's a beautiful morning. Tell them, as a treat, we're going to let them meet outside at the tables under the oak trees. Good for their soon-to-be babies. But you need to get to the server, now." She glanced back at the main door and saw it was still closed.

"Why?"

"Bentley has sent an auditor. He's gone to his car, but he'll be back. I'll stall him as long as I can, but you need to create a set of books for him to look at without the Special Projects fund and print it so he doesn't have to get on the computer. Make it as complicated as possible. And hurry. Call my cell phone and let it ring twice when you've got it."

She looked at the spike sitting on Doom's desk. Picked it up and put it back on the shelf where it belonged. "And keep that monstrosity out of the reach of children."

Kendall walked through the door, spotted Serenity, and aimed for her. She pretended not to see him and walked away fast, toward the back, trying to look like she was a woman on a mission and couldn't be stopped.

Ignoring the volunteer pointing at Kendall, she steamed toward the door marked PRIVATE, to the back storeroom as fast as she could, yanked the door open, slid in and slammed it behind her. There was a knock on the door and a tired voice saying, "Ms. Hammer, this really . . ."

The storage room had a door that opened to the back lot for deliveries. Stepping out the door, she looked around for something credible to do next and saw Seth Burroughs chewing out a man over something in the field next door with the now-two-and-a-half-story MAD hulking over them.

"Mr. Burroughs," she waved and trotted over. "How is your wife doing?"

Burroughs had a face that was a bitter collection of wrinkles, angles and scars. He looked up tiredly. "You mean the bitch that run off and left me high and dry?"

"I meant—uh—your kids."

"Last I heard, you can't have kids if your wife won't let you have sex when you're married."

"Oh." She thought fast. "Then, I'd like to see your updated blueprints. Review any changes."

He looked at her for a long time. "You want me to go to my truck, drag out my blueprints and go over any changes since you marked up the plans just an hour ago? Which, by the way, are no changes at all?"

He fixed her with what he seemed to think was a withering stare.

"Yes," she said. "That's exactly what I want to do." She looked down at her phone. Nothing.

He muttered something under his breath and dragged himself in the general direction of the trucks. Serenity checked her phone again.

Something in the library window flashed at her and she saw two round circles bouncing the morning sun from inside. She glanced away but out of the corner of her eye she saw Kendall turn and head for the front door.

Burroughs came grumbling back with both arms loaded with blueprints.

"Mr. Burroughs," she said. "I think you're right. We don't need to review these again."

She heard something about "women bosses" at her back as she jog-walked around the other side of the building and slipped back in the back door.

Cracking the interior door, she looked out past the checkout counter and through the windows, and saw Kendall outside, heading for Burroughs. The two men said something—probably about crazy women—and nodded their heads. Then Burroughs spread out his blueprints and reports on a worktable and he and Kendall bent over them.

This can't be good.

Joy was slouched at the checkout counter, head down so clients might ignore her.

"Joy!"

Her head came up, her eyes opened and she yawned.

"When I come back in that door, I'll have a man with me. I want you to flirt with him and take him off my hands."

"Really?"

"Really."

"Is he good looking?"

Serenity looked at Joy's pale old skin and tattoos. "Good enough."

She ran out the door and caught Kendall by the arm.

"Why, Mr. Kendall, I didn't know where you'd got off to. I was afraid I'd lost you."

He looked at her and a little smile flickered over his face.

"We have something for you," she said.

She started to pull his arm but he stayed rooted. "I'll be there in a minute. Mr. Burroughs has some interesting stuff here."

She yanked him across her body toward the door.

"Not as interesting as what we have."

She dragged him back into the library where Joy was waiting with a big smile.

"Hey, sailor," she said.

Kendall's face stayed blank but there was a small, unpleasant noise in his throat, like an unhappy animal was stuck there.

"Mr. Kendall, I'd like you to meet Ms. Quexnt, one of our librarians."

Joy put her arm through Kendall's other arm and said, "You want to see my tattoos?"

The small animal in Kendall's throat escaped with a full croak.

"I have business to attend to." He tried to pull his arm away but Joy wasn't letting go. Serenity knew this wouldn't last long. She checked her phone and looked around in desperation. Then she saw a friendly face coming in the door.

"Joe!" she screamed. She ran to the door and left Kendall to wrestle with Joy.

passionate kisses, interrupted

SERENITY THREW her arms around Joe's neck. "Babe," she said, "I'm so glad you're here."

She turned to Kendall with her arms still around Joe's neck. Serenity looked at him and smiled. "Mr. Kendall, you'll have to forgive me for just a few minutes. I need to spend time with my sweetie. I promise I'll get right back to you with your document." She locked her arm in Joe's and dragged him to her office leaving Kendall and Joy.

She closed the door behind them, and Joe wrapped his arms around her and bent her back with a deep kiss. She melted and felt everything unimportant fading away.

"Now this is better," he said.

Then she realized there were too many things that she didn't need to let fade away.

"No." She pushed away. "What are we doing?"

"Kissing. I thought I was kissing you. I thought it was what you wanted."

"No, I mean, what are you doing here?"

Joe studied her. "I know I said I wouldn't come after you, but I just thought I'd see how my wife's doing. Doesn't seem like that big a crime. To me."

"You mean you thought you'd check up on me."

"No," he studied her foe a long time, his look fading from romance to cop look. "Why? Is there something here I need to check up on?"

"Why? You have a book overdue?"

He paused. "There's sure as hell something overdue. Or just plain out of whack. Sweet—Serenity, all this just doesn't make a lot of sense to me. What am I missing?"

She looked at her cell. "Nothing." Then she looked at him and saw that wouldn't fly. "Look, we'll talk sometime. Just not right now."

"Okay." There was a pause while he studied her face. "I'll head on out, and look forward to that talk."

The phone was still silent. "No. Don't go."

He folded his arms. "We're not going to talk, and we're not going to kiss. What exactly are we going to do?"

"Just—stand here. Joe, I'm sorry. I know I'm not treating you right, and please, please know how much I want to. But I need you to take me on faith for a little bit. Just stand here for a time, with no reason."

He studied the matter a minute, then smiled just a little. "Faith doesn't come easy to a cop. But being with my Sweetblossom is reason enough. Take your time."

She put her hand on his arm and he gave her a sleepy-eyed grin. "Joe, I love this courtly-cowboy side of you, I really do. But I need something real right now. I'm scared as hell and excited as hell and I don't know when I can open up to you about it."

He took off his hat and stood up straight. "What do you need?"

"Just be here with me. Just for a moment."

There was that sleepy little-boy smile again.

They stood there for several minutes. Joe seemed to expand and fill the room with his Joe-ness. She felt her resolve—and more—fading, and needed to say something distracting.

"Joe, I need you to not worry so much about the things I can't talk to you about."

"The man out there is FBI. I've worked with him."

"Former FBI."

"Didn't know that. So what's he doing here now?"

"Research."

He stared at her with his flat, unreadable cop expression. "Joe, I—"

Her phone buzzed twice. She put her hand on his arm. "Please, Joe. I've got to go."

all the truth that's fit to print

SOMEONE SCREAMED. Joe pushed Serenity aside and ran past her. She saw heads turned toward the other side of the library and followed Joe at a run.

Doom was standing in the doorway coming out of the computer server room, face red. Kendall stood in front of her like an expressionless statue. Joe stopped in front of them and Serenity plowed into him.

"He—he was just standing there," said Doom. "I opened the door and this patron was just standing there. He startled me."

Kendall turned at an angle so he could face Doom, Serenity and Joe at the same time. At that angle, his glasses shined like two impenetrable mirrors. He paused a long second before he said, "Checking the layout here. This was the only locked door. Just happened to be standing in front of it when you burst out in such a hurry."

He pivoted his head forty-five degrees to focus on Joe and Serenity, and his bug-eyes reappeared. "Wondering why a library would feel the need for a locked door."

Serenity said, "Lots of doors here have locks. Plenty of places that aren't open to the public."

"But today you're so busy that every room is open, most of them full. The only one locked has a sign that says CHIL-DREN'S READING ROOM over it. Seems curious. Makes me wonder what the children are reading in there."

She watched him to see if it was a joke. If it was, jokes didn't come with smiles on this guy. Her mouth opened to explain, but her brain didn't supply any words, and she stood there with her mouth open.

Joe rescued her. "Don't I know you? Agent Kendall, FBI? We worked together a while back on that abduction that turned out not to be an abduction?"

Kendall took a step back and turned so the mirrors took in all three of them again. "Detective Hammer. Good to see you again." He said it flat. Hard to tell if it was real or snark. A long pause, followed by, "And there was a credible ransom note."

Joe slouched slightly and grinned, the pose of a good ole boy chatting about nothing bigger than a football game. "Credible note that we warned you was a joke. Looked like it was written by the dumb-ass the supposedly-abducted woman had been seeing on the side. Second-grade grammar, couple of his favorite catch phrases, more bragging about having taken the man's wife than threatening. And no mention of money."

"Sometimes," said Kendall, "small-town law enforcement doesn't recognize the gravity of a situation."

The wattage on Joe's smile turned up. "And sometimes the FBI likes to make a mountain out of a molehill. So what brings you down from the big-city office, Agent Kendall?"

"Former Agent. I retired and went private. And, of course, even you know I can't discuss what my client is paying me to look into."

"So it might just be another wild goose chase?"

They paused, an emotionless look facing a friendly look, and neither of them meaning what their poses promised.

"Or not," said Kendall.

Joe laughed a perfunctory laugh. "Enjoy our library, Former Agent Kendall. We always welcome a new patron." He turned to Serenity. "I'm gone. Unless you need me for some other little distraction." He spun and marched out the door and Serenity watched him go.

Behind her she heard Doom say to Kendall. "You're no patron. You're the miserable worm who wants to crawl through our books to find something to embarrass us and let Bentley close the library."

Kendal studied her. "Just looking at the books, like any citizen has a right to do. What makes you so sure I'll find something bad?"

She jabbed at him with her finger. "I'm not. But I'm sure you're going to try. That's what Philistines like you and

Bentley do. We are building a city of books here. You and Bentley are not going to stop us." She pushed her finger into his chest. "And if you try, we will stop *you*." She jabbed with each word. "By. Any. Means. Necessary."

"Ms. Doom," said Serenity. "Have you got Mr. Kendall's report?"

"It's on the printer."

"Why don't you go get it, and I'll show Mr. Kendall some place where he can work?"

Doom snorted and stomped away.

Serenity said, "She doesn't mean anything. She's just protective of her library."

"Protective of something. Are all of you that protective here?"

"Doom is an excitable girl. But, yes, we're all pretty protective. We love books, and we love our library."

"Actually, Ms. Hammer, I love libraries, too. I'm just doing a job."

"Yeah. It's who you're working for that makes Doom treat your visit like a poisonous snake rattling."

Doom returned with a stack of paper. Serenity took them and put Kendall in a carrel next to Doom's desk in the public area. An old man, a little heavy, with gray hair in a ponytail under a red Alabama Championship cap to match his red Alabama windbreaker was sitting at the next carrel and didn't look up.

"I'll be in my office if you have any questions. Don't hesitate to ask."

"I won't."

Serenity found Doom was waiting in her office. "I can't believe you caved to him like that."

"I didn't cave."

"I would have demanded a subpoena or something."

"Yeah, and he'd have made one call to Bentley and they'd be back, twice as suspicious."

"Well, there's nothing to be suspicious of in that report."

Serenity raised an eyebrow.

"I gave him the library's accounts. The library's accounts, without the Special Projects fund. Which, after all, is a private fund of donations from private citizens who support the library. Really, it belongs to them, not us."

need to check out a placenta? call your librarian

SERENITY'S PULSE POUNDED like the tell-tale heart in Poe's story of the same name. She couldn't sit, she couldn't stand. She couldn't . . . be. Finally, she thought of trying something long forgotten.

Folding herself in her chair, she heard her mother's voice.

"Everyone," the calm, strong voice floated over the years, "we begin our meditation by making a deliberate and definite change in posture. As best you can, establish now a posture that embodies a sense of dignity and wakefulness."

As soon as Serenity put her feet flat on the floor, hands resting in her lap, back slightly away from the back of the chair, head up, she was taken back to the last time she had given herself to one of her mother's morning meditations. A field, somewhere in the Florida sun, with lettuce fields behind her mother. A circle of people: several tie-dye shirts, and a couple of men in hip business suits. The defensive line from a local college, sent to her by their coach.

"Eyes closed, if you're comfortable with that."

It was automatic for Serenity. When her mother said eyes closed—even in her imagination—her eyes popped open. She remembered seeing her mom at the center of people who had travelled miles to be guided by her. Except for her daughter, who was unguidable, and like any good American daughter, wanted to be anything but her mother.

"Focus on your breathing. Be present and pay attention to the rise and fall of your diaphragm. Feel the stretching as your chest expands, the relaxation on the exhale."

Serenity listened to her mind and focused on her breath. Then she remembered the fight she had with her mom later that day. She had blamed her mother for her father leaving them—and everything else that was wrong.

The next day Serenity had run away, never to return. She spent the next couple of weeks hiding out in the Ocala library. A librarian named Heather found her reading and crying in the stacks the first day. Heather fed her, got her to school until she graduated, and—breaking every rule in the book—let Serenity sleep in the storeroom at night. When she left, Serenity began her twenty-year quest to just be normal and do whatever it took to fit in. Joe was the one who had convinced her to make up with her mother after their son Joseph was born, but she still had felt ashamed of her mother, ashamed of the years growing up in VW buses and tents while other kids grew up in McDonalds and Walmarts.

But now she heard her mother's voice again at the end of their daily meditation, and she sounded strong and admirable. It was the first time she had ever visualized her mother that way. Now in her forties, Serenity was finally ready to forgive her mother for being . . . magnificent. And she knew why her mother had fought so hard.

In her mind's eye, Serenity saw her mother rising, effortless and strong to give her followers their sendoff. "Now slowly expand your attention to the world. Open your eyes, and commit to being daring, go do something wondrous for your world."

Serenity felt strong and calm and clean. After years of pretending, she finally was an honest woman.

A knock on the door interrupted her trip to the past.

She opened the door. "Mr. Kendall."

"Ms. Hammer," he said.

"Mr. Kendall."

"I need the report."

"You have the report in your hand. Tell Councilman Bentley we have been more than cooperative. Can I bring you a cup of coffee?"

"As long as the coffee comes with the rest of this report." She looked at him and he twisted slightly so his eyes appeared out of the mirrors and focused on her. She tried to see if he was joking or not. Couldn't tell.

"There's one account that seems to be missing." He looked at the report in his hand and read off the number of the Special Projects account. "Permanent accounts with numbers preceding and following this account are here."

Serenity paused. "I'm sure it's nothing. Probably an old account that was deleted years ago. Give me the account number and I'll get Doom to go into the history files and get you an explanation while you sit back in your cubicle and go over the books you have now."

"Also," he made a long pause and Serenity wondered if he were done. But the glasses stayed on her. "That account was the one your contractor had on his invoices."

"Really."

"I look forward to your explanation." Kendall turned and walked back to the little cubicle, behind the man with the Alabama hat.

Serenity looked at Doom's desk. No Doom. Then she went around the corner to the server room. The door was locked. She pulled out her key ring, unlocked the door, and peered inside. No Doom. Serenity locked up and made the rounds without finding Doom anywhere inside the library.

When she reached Joy she mouthed, "Doom."

Joy pointed out the door. "Outside. Practicing to be a mommy."

Serenity ran out the door and found a crowd of bulging stomachs standing under the oak tree, but no Doom. She turned to look back at the door, and started to ask the group's leader if she had seen Doom. But when she turned again, Doom was walking up to the back of the crowd of pregnant women, her thinness making her look like a solitary "1" in a field of "0"s. Serenity pulled her out from the crowd. "Where were you?"

Doom smiled a conspiratorial smile. "Taking care of business. Inside."

"No, you weren't."

Doom smiled. "Then I was here."

"No, you weren't."

"I might have been. No one can tell." While she spoke she stared over Serenity's head, scanning back and forth. "I'm studying paramilitary techniques to help me patrol the library. We need a security force with some bite."

Serenity pointed two fingers at her eyes. "Doom, my eyes are here." She paused. "First time I've had to use a line like that, that way."

Doom met her eyes.

"We have security, Doom."

"We have seventeen-year-old Caleb, who is so shy about his acne that he hides in the break room. Besides, I'm not patrolling for people like that boy who takes books without checking them out just to prove he's a non-conformist. I'm taking care of real threats to our dream. The price of a library is eternal vigilance."

"God protect us all from you. Anyway, Kendall needs your help again."

Another conspiratorial smile. "Took care of Kendall. Karen here was just about to show us a real placenta. That's why I came back out here. Can't it wait?"

"No, it can't. A what?" Serenity looked around and saw the other women turning green. Doom's eyes glittered.

"I'm not afraid of a little blood."

"Jesus, Doom. Look, right now, I need you inside or it's going to be our blood. Kendall wants to know why the Special Projects account isn't on the books."

"Give me ten minutes and I'll build a trail showing Special Projects moved to the Friends of the Library, since they do most of the fund raising. Probably should have given him that in the first place."

"Good. Remember to log in as me. Anyone goes to jail, it will be me."

"I promise, but I also promise that I will not let you go to jail. Or let the library be stopped. No matter what."

"That's not what I said, but go."

They fast-walked back inside and took a right toward the server room. Kendall was coming back from the central printer with a stack of paper in his hand.

Serenity smiled. "We've got you covered, Mr. Kendall. Ms. Doom will have your information for you in just a few minutes. You can tell Councilman Bentley that's what we do here at the Maddington Library: get information to people when they need it."

"No need."

Serenity thought he was smiling this time, but she wasn't sure. "Got a copy of the report myself right here, with that fund included. Went into your computer room myself to save you the trouble."

Serenity's smile disappeared. "That room was locked. And there are passwords on that computer."

"Wasn't a problem." He was smiling now and Serenity was sure of it. "For me."

call for help

SERENITY PUT ON HER BIGGEST fake smile (so much for honest living) and said, "Oh, how very nice," and ran to her office. She picked up the phone.

"Donna, I've got to talk to him *now.*"

"He's doing a closing, Serenity. He'll call you back in half an hour."

"He's my lawyer. I need him *now.*"

"Serenity, he's a real estate lawyer. He did a closing for you and Joe like ten years ago. Do you have a real estate emergency today? What does Joe say?"

"That's just it. I can't talk to Joe."

There was a long pause, followed by, "George doesn't handle divorces."

Another long pause. Faulkner peeked out and she thought of handing the phone to him.

"How about this, Serenity? I get him to call you back as soon as he gets out, and in the meanwhile, you go talk to

Joe? Or maybe a marriage counselor? Or maybe just an individual therapist for yourself?"

"Fine."

Serenity slammed down the phone as Doom burst into the room.

"Ms. Hammer, we've got to do something. He's going to destroy the library."

"Calm down, Supergirl. Go fly around the building a couple of times to burn off some anger."

"Calm down my ass. The time for playing it safe is over. If we don't act now, he's going to take that to Bentley and in a matter of hours everything we've worked for will be shut down."

"That's what you're worried about? Being shut down? Not going to jail, your life ruined, that sort of stuff?"

Doom tossed her long black hair. "Jail doesn't scare me. Jail didn't break Martin Luther King or Gandhi or Angela Davis. They were heroes to their generations because they were passionate enough to go to jail." She raised her fist. "Power to the people! Power to the books! This generation needs a hero, and I can't back away if it needs to be me."

"You may be getting a little carried away here."

"You think King got carried away when he wrote the 'Letter from Birmingham Jail'? Or Morgan Freeman when he changed the world from a South African jail?"

"Technically, I think that was Nelson Mandela."

Doom thought about it a minute. "Whatever. That man out there has got to be stopped. By any means necessary."

"But we've got to draw a line somewhere, Doom."

Doom pointed to the front door. "You see that sidewalk out front? That's my line. Enemies of the library cross it; they get what they deserve. I am Justice."

Serenity looked at the phone, which wasn't ringing from the callback from the real estate lawyer who couldn't give her any good advice anyway. So, if she couldn't get good advice at least she could make bad promises.

"Okay," Serenity said, "get out of here and let me handle it. I promise I'll take care of this. And protect the library. And you."

Doom opened her mouth to say something but Serenity pushed her out the door.

"And Doom—switch to decaf."

Doom made an un-superheroish "mmph" sound and spun out of the room.

Serenity decided to switch to super-decaf herself and opened the left-side desk drawer. She took out the fresh bottle of Myers and broke the seal. As she was pouring, Faulkner stuck his head out of the stacks.

"Oh, hell, no," she said. "I'm not feeding you anymore."

She sat sipping and staring at the phone. Promised herself she'd call Joe after one sip. After that sip, she promised she'd call when the cup was half-empty (nothing seemed half-full right now.) Then maybe after the cup was all empty.

Then her choices were either another cup or pick up the phone and get this over with.

She picked up the phone.

"Joe, I'm ready to talk, and it's important."

"Good," he said.

Then a woman screamed somewhere in the library.

how to spike a story

SERENITY STEPPED OUT of her office with the phone still in her hand.

"Jesus, Doom, what now?" She pulled the phone up to her mouth and said, "Hold on, Joe."

The screaming grew louder and broke into a series of breathless yelps. She saw faces turned to Doom's side of the library. The closest ones had their mouths open. Serenity broke into a run.

She turned the corner and saw a screaming volunteer in front of Doom's desk. The desk sat empty, but in the cubicle next to it lay Kendall, face down.

"He's not moving, Ms. Hammer," she said. "Not moving, and the back of his neck is bleeding. I came over to see if he needed anything and saw that his head was down. I touched him on the shoulder and his arm just fell out. I think—"

Serenity put her hand on the front of his neck. Still warm, but she could find no pulse. She turned back to the crowd that was starting to gather. "Is there a nurse here?"

A blonde woman with a blue ball cap stepped forward and put her hand on Kendall's neck, then leaned down to listen to his nose with her hand on his back. She started to turn him over, but noticed blood on the back of his neck. She turned to Serenity, pointed to the hole in the back of Kendall's neck and shook her head, no.

Serenity raised the phone to her mouth. "Joe, you still there?"

"What the hell do you think? I'm going to hang up a phone with people screaming? What's going on there?"

"You need to get here," she said. "Run code. And bring backup. This is official."

She could hear him trying to say something but she hung up.

"Clarisse," she said to the volunteer.

"Ms. Hammer, he's—"

"I know. Clarisse, I need you to sit at the front desk until the police get here."

She turned to look at the gathering crowd. "Did anyone see what happened?"

No one answered.

"Okay. All of you go over to the other side of the library and take a seat until the police get here."

She saw another volunteer at the edge of the crowd. "And tell Amanda Doom I need her here right now."

Serenity looked back at the body. The desk under Kendall's head was empty. No papers, no report.

Most of the crowd was drifting away, but a woman with two young kids hung back and approached Serenity as close as she could while shielding her children.

"Ms. Hammer," she said. "I think Ms. Doom is in the back. She and this man got into a fight and she hit him in the back of the head and said something like, 'This will not stand' and took off toward the back."

"What happened then?"

"I don't know. I didn't want the kids to see anymore, so I took them to the storytelling area."

Surely not.

But this woman made Doom the prime suspect.

She said to the woman, "Why don't you take your family to my office and get them away from all this? Close the door behind you."

The woman nodded and left.

Serenity looked at Doom's desk. The library spike sat on the corner of the desk, covered in blood. Next to it was the book Doom was researching for her murder group, *Fifty Ways to Kill Your Lover, or Any Other Enemy*, with a page bookmarked.

Joy came around the corner, and Serenity heard sirens in the not-too distance.

She grabbed Joy. "Get the keys to the bookmobile. Then find Doom. Someone said she was headed to the back. Tell her to get the bookmobile, right now, and take it to New

Horizon Elementary School for the rest of the afternoon. Tell her not to come back inside for anything, not even her purse. And tell her that she left fifteen minutes ago."

Serenity picked up a book bag from the box beside Doom's desk and swept both the spike and the book into it.

good girls don't kill

SERENITY HAD NEVER IMAGINED her library as a crime scene.

She stood ten feet away from the desk and the body, watching out the front glass doors. When she saw Doom and the bookmobile leave the lot, she started counting "Mississippis" until the first black-and-white pulled in with Joe's Charger right behind.

Eighty-three Mississippis. A little over a minute. Maybe enough—if Doom turned the right way and didn't drive right past them. If, if, if.

If Doom even needed protecting. Surely not. Surely there was a simple explanation for the bloody spike . . . and the body of the man Doom had just fought with . . . and the missing report that only she and Doom knew about . . . Surely, she'd get an explanation and be able to tell Joe about the spike. And the fight. And the Special Projects fund. All without ruining the life of a youngster under her protection. Maybe one she inspired to murder.

Maybe even without putting herself in jail and shutting down her library. Or helping a killer walk free.

Jesus.

A patrolman held the door open and Joe burst through it. Serenity pointed at Kendall.

"Nobody's touched anything," she said.

You're lucky your lying tongue isn't jumping out of your head and scampering away like a big pink inchworm on speed.

Joe touched Kendall's throat and shook his head. Then he looked up and studied her. "Good to have someone here who's spent enough time around cops that we can trust them to take care of things."

"Yeah."

"Crime scene secure?"

"Should be. I was here fifteen seconds after the volunteer who found the body screamed. I checked him for a pulse, like you just did. Then I had a nurse check him and sent everybody to the other side and told them to wait for you. The volunteer who found the body is over there, waiting at the front desk. Figured you'd want to start with her."

"Good." He took his hand away from Kendall's throat. "Serenity, it's good to know that when it comes to something important like this, we can still work together."

She tried a smile, but it wouldn't come. "Yeah," was all she could say.

More blue shirts came in, followed by a man in a suit. Joe turned to them all. "You two, rope off this side of the library. Steve, can you talk to . . ." He looked at Serenity.

"Ms. Hellier."

"Ms. Hellier at the front desk. She found the body." He nodded at another blue shirt. "Can you get names and contact info for everybody who was in the library at the time?"

They all nodded and walked off.

Joe pulled out his notepad and turned back to Serenity.

"Okay, what do you know about this?"

"Not much more than you," she said. "You met this guy about the same time I did, and you seemed to know more about him than I did. He came in this morning, said he worked for Bentley, and demanded to see a copy of our books. I printed him one and parked him here. When I left him here twenty minutes ago, he was going over them and making notes."

"Bentley had him auditing your books?" He looked at her evenly. "You don't see many requests to audit the books of a library." He paused. "You don't see many murders in a library, either."

He waited. When she didn't say anything, he said. "Fortunately, we've got two experts here. You know everything there is to know about libraries—particularly this one. And I know how to catch killers."

"Lucky us," she said.

"Anybody besides you talk to him?"

"I know he talked to Seth Burroughs, the contractor outside. And he talked to Joy a little." She paused. "Nobody else I can think of."

Serenity gave her formal statement to one of the blue suits and then wandered around the still-open side of the library, randomly shelving books and trying to listen in on as many statements as she could. No one had seen the murder.

She found Joy sitting alone at the checkout counter. "What have you heard?"

Joy looked bored, "Nothing worth repeating. Somebody saw Kendall sitting up reading the report. Then Hellier saw Kendall slumped down. Couldn't get a pulse, and screamed."

"Nothing else?" Serenity took a breath. "No reports of a tall, skinny, young, black librarian stabbing anyone?"

Joy lost her boredom and studied her boss. "C'mon. You don't think our excitable girl did this?"

Serenity looked back at her for a long second and then said, "Of course not. Just a joke. You know Doom and all her by-any-means-necessary crap."

They both looked at each other for another long second before they said in unison. "Of course not."

"I just wondered how Doom seemed when you told her to high-tail it out of here," Serenity said.

Joy hesitated a beat. "Let's get this straight," she said. "From this moment on, I don't remember telling her to do any such thing. And you don't remember telling me to get her out of here. She was gone before the first scream."

"Yeah."

"But, just so you know, if I had actually gone looking for her, I might have found her with her head down in an adult coloring book, coloring furiously like she does when she's mad. And if I had told her you said to get out, she might have flown out the door like a bat out of hell, without even bothering to argue about it."

"Shit," said Serenity. "I'm going to my office. I've got to think."

Joy started to stand up. For her that was a complicated, multi-part exercise of arms unfolding in slow motion, back shoved out of the chair and into the air, with her head raised last and slowest, accompanied by stage-voiced grunts and curses. When her head was finally solidly atop her body, she gave what passed for a smile and said, "Might come with you. I need some of that thinking juice of yours."

"Not this time," Serenity said. "We don't need to be drinking now, and we don't need to talk to the cops with rum on our breath. I'm just going to sit at my desk and stare at the wall and try to make some sense of all this."

Joy gave her a nasty look that clearly said, "I stood up for nothing" and collapsed back into her chair.

"Fine," she said.

"But come find me if you hear anything."

Joy looked at her like she'd asked her to run a marathon. "Yeah. I'll do that."

As Serenity went to her office, the faces of her patrons all seemed to be begging for answers she didn't have. She felt like she needed to give them a reassuring smile, but all she could do was look away without letting anyone make eye contact. She still had her eyes high when she closed her door behind her, leaned back against it, and sighed.

As the sigh finished, she saw the woman sitting in her chair smiling weakly at her. Two very polite children were sitting in her visitor chairs, noses buried in books, pretending that they weren't sitting in a strange office and a strange woman hadn't just walked in.

"Oh," said Serenity. She now remembered sending them to her office but somehow didn't expect them to, you know, actually be there.

She put on a warm, non-threatening smile as she remembered why they were there.

"I hope you've been all right," she said.

"Thanks to you. Thank you so much for letting us use your office and for keeping the children out of the madhouse out there."

"Certainly. And what wonderfully well-behaved children they are." She smiled at them but the children didn't look up.

The two women smiled at each other for a second.

"So," said Serenity, "has anyone disturbed you?"

"No. I don't think they even know we're here."

"No reason for them to care. Not like you have any real information for them."

"No. My children and I didn't actually see the . . . unpleasantness."

"No."

"Really, we'd just as soon be left out of this."

"Of course," said Serenity. "For the children. So, no one's asked you for your name or anything?"

"Nothing."

"Where are you parked?"

"Around to the side. Away from the construction."

And away from the police cars, thought Serenity.

"Why don't I show you the back door? We can avoid the unpleasantness."

"Thank you so much."

"My pleasure."

After she closed the back door behind them, Serenity walked to the murder side of the library and wondered if that was how she would always think of that side. Joe was talking to the medical examiner. They stood front of a long black body bag lying on a gurney while two techs waited for permission to take the body away. Joe saw Serenity, nodded a curt goodbye to the ME, and the gurney was wheeled out. Joe came over to her.

"This is your fault," he said.

She caught her breath. "No, I . . ."

He smiled a small smile. "Since when do you allow people to come into your library with an ice pick?"

"An ice pick?"

"That's what the ME says it looks like the murder weapon was."

She tried to respond without a pause. "Have you found it?"

"No. Right now, it looks like a guy walked in carrying an ice pick, stabbed Kendall at just the right spot in the back of his neck, and walked out carrying the bloody pick—without anybody seeing a thing."

"Random?"

He laughed a harsh laugh and pushed his hat back. "Knowing how to kill someone that way usually means a pro, maybe a superpro. Hard to believe anyone just happened to be carrying an ice pick in their pocket and said, 'I think I'll kill that random stranger.' On the other hand, why would a pro kill someone in a place as public as this—and then take the pick with him? Right now, I've got a lot more questions than I've got answers."

"So where you going to start looking for answers?"

"Right now, I think I'm going to ride over to the FBI office in Jericho. See if they knew what Kendall was up to."

"Not Bentley?"

"No, I've got Steve on the way over to talk to him, catch him before he's heard the news. I'll follow up with him later. But my experience is that politicians are the last to know anything worthwhile, and the first to give you canned speeches."

"Okay," said Serenity, "let me get my purse."

Joe took his time looking at her. "Why do you need your purse?"

"I'm coming with you."

"Like hell. This is my case."

"Your case. My library."

forty-nine

horses' heads and horses' asses

THE RIDE TO JERICHO, the bigger city next door to Maddington, had always seemed short to Serenity.

Not today.

Mile markers were the only things breaking up the pine trees and soybean fields. It was a long, muttering ride with no intelligible words between them until Serenity said, "Three."

Joe grunted and said, "Three what?"

"Three words in a single mile. That's the first time you've said more than two words since we left the library."

"Could have been thinking."

"Could have been. Not sure what internal train of thought ends up with the words, 'Hell, no' being so important they had to come out under your breath. Over and over."

They were passing the Saturn rocket that marked the edge of Jericho, the rocket itself built in North Alabama for the Apollo program years ago but left behind when the moon program was abandoned. He cut his eyes at her.

"Wasn't so much that they had to come out, but that they needed to be heard by you. Really heard. I can let you ride along this once, but we're not going to make a habit of it."

"I understand. You're the detective. You're in charge."

Another mile marker passed in silence.

"It's just that I'd like to know what's going on in my library," Serenity said. "And because it happened in my library, I might know things that might help you. If you'll listen to me."

The glass-and-steel buildings of Research Park, home of rocket scientists, geneticists and other specialists whose titles would take a technical dictionary to decipher, had replaced the pine trees that used to separate the small town of Maddington from the city. Their architects might be proud of the buildings but they looked like high-tech prisons to Serenity.

"You're not a cop. Plain and simple."

"I'm a cop's wife, and I took the auxiliary training years ago so I could ride with you when you needed me."

"That was for little things."

"Remember when we spent the night on the stake out? Remember what I did?"

His back stiffened. "I kept my eyes on the house we were watching the whole time."

"Wasn't your eyes I was interested in," Serenity said. "And remember, I've got my own gun and my own training from Maddington's finest, and my own carry permit."

"Tell me you're not carrying a gun."

"Not today."

More buildings slid by.

Serenity said, "Just trying to help."

Joe grunted his thanks, but was silent the rest of the way downtown. He pulled into an "Official Business Only" slot in front of the old post office, which now housed the federal court and federal offices.

Serenity stepped out of the truck, waited for Joe, and tried to make small talk.

"I like these old antebellum buildings in Jericho and Maddington, back from when they were just two sleepy cotton towns."

Joe said, "Be better off if all those German rocket scientists hadn't come to Jericho in the fifties, building moon rockets and tech empires that turned Jericho and Maddington from honest little towns into corrupt feeding troughs for every kind of two-bit crook and bent politician."

She looked at him. "We're just full of sunshine and happiness today."

He had been walking fast, which made her hustle to keep up with him. Now he stopped and stared at her.

"We're here on a murder investigation, you know. A man has been killed."

"Doesn't mean you can't keep the joy of Jesus in your heart."

"You're not even religious."

"I'm a Southern woman. We invoke Jesus whenever we need to."

She elbowed past him, quick-stepped, and held the courthouse door open for him.

They made their way through the guard and metal detector in the lobby, the guard in the FBI's outer office on the third floor, and then the soldier stationed with an M15 who was guarding the inner offices. Finally, Rashad Tavana came out and gave Serenity a big hug.

"So," said Serenity, "it looks like the FBI is keeping the world safe. Or at least spending a lot of money to keep the FBI safe."

He smiled. "Got to start somewhere. Keep it safe here. We could even keep Maddington High School baseball games safe, too, if we could rein in you and my wife from threatening the refs."

"They had it coming," Serenity said. "And for the record, Pearl—your wife—was the ringleader and I was the follower."

"Not the way she tells it," Tavana said. "I kept elbowing Joe, saying 'This is local. You're going to have to be the one to arrest them if things get out of hand.'"

"And the fact that I'm here, and not in jail, is proof that Pearl and I never got out of hand."

"And now both boys are out of high school, miraculously. Joseph still playing baseball?"

Joe shrugged and Serenity said "Yes," and Tavana looked back and forth between them. After an awkward pause, he said, "So, Joe, I guess you're here to come to work for the Bureau? Brought Serenity to negotiate your salary?"

"Got too much work where I'm at to try to move up to the big leagues," said Joe.

"I keep telling you, the big leagues are where you belong."

Tavana turned to Serenity. "You may not believe this, but your big, sloppy-looking dude is a helluva good cop. Got a way of finding out anything, getting anybody to tell him anything."

"I believe it."

"He's too good to be wasting his time on small crimes in a small town."

"Think globally, act locally," said Joe. "Life in a city like Jericho—or a smaller suburb like Maddington—is where the rubber meets the road. Standing back behind federal laws and three levels of protection is not where I belong."

Tavana shrugged. "That protection may be necessary, these days. Jericho's got so much high-tech money flowing now that it's turned into one of the most corrupt cities around, with the most corrupt politicians. Maddington's turning into a dirty little city, too, although right now your politicians are too inept to be crooked. But the people who truly have the power aren't."

Tavana turned back to Serenity. "Did he tell you how his partner got hurt?"

Serenity turned to Joe. "Carl strained his back, is what he told me."

"Strained his back after an 'unknown assailant' slammed an aluminum bat into it," Tavana said. "City made him write it up as an accident, since the guy had friends at city hall."

"And that's why I can't leave Maddington PD, Rashad," said Joe. "I'm not going to let them win."

"And if the bosses in Maddington don't let you investigate the big dogs and prosecute anybody with money, how are you going to stop them? You need something bigger than what you've got to win this war."

"Wars aren't won by generals safe in a clean war room surrounded by armed guards. Wars are won by dirty grunts on the ground."

Tavana nodded, "Well, let's talk about something a little safer. Serenity, how's the library?"

"Actually," she said, "that's what we're here to talk about. Your dirty little city came into our library today."

Joe said, "You know an agent of yours named Kendall? Worked with us on the Mangum case?"

Tavana turned serious. He walked to his chair, and sat down at his big walnut desk with his nameplate between the Hammers and himself.

"Former agent," he said.

"Former everything," said Joe. "Somebody put an ice pick in his neck this morning. In the library. Wondered if you had any idea what he was doing there in the first place."

"I do not." He paused. "I hadn't heard. What do you know?"

"Not much," Joe said. "Came into Serenity's library this morning demanding to see their books. Said a local councilman named Bentley had hired him to audit the library's accounts."

"Bentley?" Tavana smiled, but just a little. "Couple of our guys call him 'Yugo.' Like, 'Named like a Bentley, performs like a Yugo.' What's his interest in the library?"

"He doesn't like me," said Serenity.

"He doesn't like anybody, from what I hear," Tavana said, "but he doesn't ask to see their books."

"He thinks libraries should shrivel up and die. He shut off most of our funding, but we found a way to press ahead with an expansion with private donations."

Tavana looked at Joe, then back to Serenity. "I can see how he might be curious. That's a pretty big expansion you've got going there. Any big fish making those donations?"

"Various people. At this point, they'd like to remain anonymous."

Tavana paused again. "So Bentley sent Kendall down to investigate the library, and the librarian killed him?"

There was a moment of silence before Tavana laughed. Once he laughed, Serenity joined in as loud as she dared.

"Okay," Joe said, "we've talked some. How about you talk some?"

"Not much to tell. Kendall was a strange bird: too private to really get to know him, but competent and stubborn as a mule when he thought he was right about something. He has—had—a small horse farm in Maddington. He had been pushing the bosses here for a long time about something he thought was going on in Maddington. The bosses view was that there was no proof, it was too political, and it was a local matter anyway. Every time they told him 'no,' he'd walk out of the meeting and schedule another meeting, tell them the same damned thing all over. I was at the last meeting. He got about ten words into a speech that they seemed to have heard a hundred times, and the big boss shut him down, told him he didn't want to hear it anymore. Kendall stood there in front of the room for a long time. Hard to read him with those Coke-bottle glasses of his. Finally, he said, 'I got my forty years in. More than all of you experts put together. Believe I'll put my papers in. Go to the horse farm, where horses' heads and horses' asses come in a one-to-one proportion.' Walked out, and I never saw him again."

Joe said, "So you don't know what he was doing with Bentley?"

"No. But that's a strange combination. A couple of years ago a local mob boss was running a protection ring on all the corporations in Jericho. Kendall was working it, but before he could bust it some mysterious giant—I'm not making this up—killed them all and broke the whole thing up."

"I remember that one," Joe said. "Always thought that was kind of a myth."

Tavana shrugged. "Something happened. Any case, the ring was pulling in a ton of money until a bunch of folks died and it stopped. But here's the thing: Kendall thought something much bigger was going on now, with ten times the money. But we could never find anything in Jericho."

"Any idea what could squeeze more money out of corporations than the mob?" Joe asked.

"No. But it doesn't sound like a library." Tavana laughed and turned to Serenity. "So he came in, asked for the books, then what?"

Serenity said, "We printed him a copy and gave him a place to work. A few minutes later, a volunteer found him face-down and couldn't wake him up."

Joe said, "Ice pick in the back of the neck. ME says whoever did it was either very smart or very lucky. You don't catch it just right, the pick'll either bounce off bone or just damage muscle."

"Huh." Tavana turned to Serenity. "So your librarians have taken to carrying ice picks?"

They all laughed. Serenity tried to study both their faces. Saw that they were studying hers.

She needed a joke. "Don't know about ice picks, but I may start carrying my Smith and Wesson if I'm going to help Joe find out who did this."

"Ain't happening," said Joe.

"Actually," Tavana said, "it might be good to keep Serenity involved. I know you're partnerless right now, Joe. Might be good to have another head to bounce ideas off of. And nobody knows more about what's going on at the library than Serenity. And nobody has more contacts in the community."

Joe grunted.

"Keep me posted, too, Joe. Kendall was a smart guy, no matter what the big boys here thought. You find anything out there, I might want to press on it." He laughed. "Even if I have to buy me a horse farm to get the parts to line up."

fifty

people's heads and people's asses

RIDING BACK TO MADDINGTON in the Charger, Joe said, "Don't know what else to say to you, Serenity, but I'm sorry about stuff between us."

They were on the west-bound interstate, crowded with Suburus and Chevys coming home to Maddington from day jobs at the Jericho tech giants. They were driving dead into a red-hot crimson sun that was hanging on the horizon, blinding them and every other driver, and turning the inside of the cars blood-red.

Serenity looked at Joe's dark sunglasses, at his hat pulled low, his head pushed forward almost to the windshield in concentration, and waited. He didn't say anything more. She knew it wasn't a good time for a serious talk, but the silence drove her to talk anyway.

"What's that supposed to be, one of those rote prayers from the Book of Male? When things go to shit, just say, 'Honey, I'm sorry.' Hope she'll know what you're sorry for because you sure as shit don't, and you sure as shit aren't sorry, you're just hoping that somehow it gets things back on track so you can get back in her pants again?"

A shapeless blue car slashed into Joe's lane, neither Joe nor the other driver seeing each other at first, due to the glare. Joe popped the brakes to let the car in, then got back to speed before anyone could hit them from behind.

He thought about Serenity's question. "Pretty much."

A few more buildings slid by.

"Let me put a better spin on that," he said. "Just wanted you to know that I feel like shit about where we are. I'm tired of trying to figure out why we're there. And I wanted you to know that I can change if I need to."

"But the law is the law and you are what you are."

They turned away from the sun and he shot her a quick glance. "Maybe. And maybe you might be surprised at what I can be."

She leaned over and kissed him on the cheek. They pulled into the parking lot of the library and Serenity said, "What's next?"

"We both go back to work. Me out here, you in there."

"You wish. You need me on this. So what are you planning to do next?"

He exhaled and looked at his watch. "May go by and see Bentley, catch him after Steve got to him earlier. Should catch him at about the end of his day, thinking he's about to get the last patient or the last errand taken care of before he gets to go home. People tend to get irritated when you catch them like that and they make mistakes."

"See, that's why you need me. Nobody can irritate Bentley like I can."

He looked out the window. "Sometimes," he said, "I can understand his point of view."

. . .

Bentley's receptionist, Sharon, put down her phone and smiled a weak apology up to Joe and Serenity. "Doctor Bentley says to come back tomorrow. He's busy with a patient and then he's going home."

"Who's the patient?" said Joe.

Sharon didn't even have to look at her computer. "The last patient was Danny O'Keefe. You know, Charlie's boy. At three o'clock."

Joe said, "To hell with that," and went through the door with Serenity a step behind.

"Madison PD, Councilman," Joe said as he stepped into Bentley's office.

Bentley looked up from the magazine he was studying, one with a beautiful deer on the cover, staring into the camera and probably thinking what an honor it was that he was about to be shot and mounted on some redneck's wall.

"Keeping up with your medical journals?" said Serenity. "The one that compares deer anatomy to children?"

Bentley put the magazine down. "Two government employees with no respect for a businessman's time. What a surprise."

"Sorry, Councilman." Joe stood in front of Bentley's desk. Serenity slid by him and took one of the visitor's chairs. "This is business. Police business. You hired a man named Kendall to look into the books of the library?"

"Told the last cop. It's my right, the right of any citizen to question public records. And I ought to be able to do it without the lie-brarian getting her husband to come down here and strong arm me."

"What did you hope to find out?"

"Find out where the money's coming from to pay for all those giant Lego blocks down at her obsolete library. Know the city didn't authorize it."

He looked at Serenity and she spat, "Donations."

"You mean like when you and the mystery writers had a Noir @ the Bar event to raise money for the library?"

"Yeah. Like that."

"You said that was the best event you ever had. Raised almost five hundred dollars for the library."

Serenity didn't say anything.

Bentley said, "Takes a lot of five-hundred-dollar-bills for that expansion."

"I explained it to you. Special projects," she said. The two men looked at her and didn't say a word. After a long beat, she added, "Lots of special projects." After another long moment she added, "Generous donors."

"You don't seriously—"

Joe interrupted. "Councilman, let me ask you about money. Mr. Kendall was a former senior agent for the FBI—and a big gun in the forensic accounting world. I doubt if he came cheap. Did you pay him personally?"

"I don't see how that's any of your business. You're just down here to harass me to protect your wife's little government fiefdom."

Joe gave Bentley his cop stare, the one that says he's trying to decide whether to kill someone and eat them like the deer on the magazine. Bentley squirmed.

"Dr. Bentley, what exactly did Steve tell you?"

"Nothing. I told him he was harassing me and I wouldn't talk without my lawyer. He smiled and told me he'd be back, and I'm about to tell you the same—"

"Before you finish that sentence, Dr. Bentley, you should know that Mr. Kendall was killed a short time ago. This is a murder investigation. Do you want to continue the conversation down at the station with your lawyer?"

Bentley turned white. "What? Murder? Don't blame me. Must have been something to do with one of his old cases."

"I honestly don't know and—at this point—I don't want to talk about what I do know," said Joe. "Can I just ask you some questions now?"

"Well, of course. I always support our police."

"Always. Back to my question: who paid Mr. Kendall?"

"I did."

"Out of your personal money?"

"Of course not. City money. The library's budget, if I find enough there."

"And what did Kendall say when you asked about the library?"

"Not much. I told him I was interested in where the mystery money was coming from. He said he might be interested in that, too."

Joe took his pad out of his jacket pocket and wrote something on it.

Bentley said, "Detective Hammer, I've been more than cooperative with you. What can you tell me about the killing?"

Joe thought about what would be public information soon enough.

"He was stabbed in the library."

Bentley turned white again and shook his finger at Serenity.

"It's that librarian," he said. "Detective, the last time I was in the library, your wife threatened to stick something in me."

"Did not," she said. Joe was looking at her. "Well, it was a joke. Doo—one of us gave him a cattle thermometer."

Joe turned to Bentley. "Why would they offer you a cattle thermometer?"

"It was a threat," said Bentley. "They were threatening to . . . to . . . well, you know. They threatened me, and now my representative has been murdered."

Joe kept looking at Bentley.

"Dr. Bentley, the last time she was in here, did you threaten to take my wife's temperature, with your own instrument?"

Bentley said, "She had it coming."

Joe slowly picked up the pad, flipped it closed and put it in his pocket while he kept his stare on Bentley.

"I believe we're done here."

Then he leaned on the desk.

"Dr. Bentley, I don't take it real well when anyone threatens to stick anything into my wife."

once you get started

THE MAD WAS TOO BUSY NOW, twenty-four hours a day, for Serenity, Doom and Joy to conduct a staff meeting without interruption. Even the restaurants and bars close by were constantly packed with overflow from the round-the-clock mission and party of the MAD.

So, they met at Buffalo Bill's a few miles away. It was supposed to be a franchise neighborhood grill like Applebee's or Ruby Tuesday, except with a western theme. But the owner of the Maddington franchise didn't give a shit if anybody other than his barfly friends ever came in, and he managed the place accordingly. "Managing" consisted of not unlocking the doors half the time or cleaning the place ever.

Which made it a perfect place for the librarians to meet.

Serenity knocked on the darkened door and got no response. Then she pounded harder 'til she heard, "Hold your damned horses, cowboy." She waited a few more minutes until the door cracked open.

"We're closed, asshole—oh, Serenity. Didn't see it was you."

The door opened wider.

"Hey, Jerry."

"Where's that overgrown Nazi you've usually got at your back?"

"Joe's watching the Braves with Rick. And he's no Nazi."

"Member of the police Gestapo. Only reason I let you in here is I'm afraid he might shoot me."

"And he's the only sane one who'll listen to your stories of how the political machine and the flying saucers exiled you here."

"It's the truth, and you and he know it. I was the best city councilman Maddington ever saw until I went up against them. They bribed me with enough money to buy this place, told me as long as I never sobered up enough to stick my nose back into civic affairs—ha! Now that's a crazy term for you—I could stay alive." He cocked his head to one side and studied her. "Not sure that letting the town librarian in won't violate my parole."

Joy appeared behind Serenity. "I'll vouch for her."

Jerry beamed at her. "Hey, wondered where you've been. Haven't seen you lately."

Joy pushed the door open all the way and pointed a finger at Serenity. "She's keeping me too busy. Tell the

Association of Obsolete Boys and Girls in the back that I
sent my regrets, and clear out a table in the front for Serenity and me."

Serenity followed her in. A couple of faces peered out
from the perennial twilight of the back room. Joy flipped a
light switch and flooded the dirty dining room in the front
with lights.

Jerry blinked. "Jesus F., Joy. Turn all the lights on and
people will come in and demand service."

She snorted. "What'd you say the motto for the Obsolete Boys and Girls was? 'Anybody desperate enough to be
here deserves to be here.' Wouldn't worry about anybody
respectable falling in here."

"I won't." He reached to lock the door.

"Leave that open," said Joy. "In a couple of minutes, a
beautiful young woman's going to walk through that door.
Don't stop her, and don't stare. Bring us a bottle of rum—
unopened—and three glasses—preferably washed. And a
pile of wings. I know you eat them yourself so I can trust
them."

"Who's paying for all this?"

Joy nodded at Serenity. "She is. Make the receipt look
like it's books. Maybe *Island Happiness* by Alfred P. Myers,
and *How to Cross the Road* by Chicken Little."

"Bossy woman."

"You got it."

He rolled his eyes.

"Like I said about bossy women."

Joy picked up a rag from one table and wiped the dust off a booth with a framed picture of William Bonney before she motioned Serenity in.

"Sure we want a booth with a baby-faced killer?" Serenity said.

Joy looked at the picture of a boy with dead eyes and a gun dangling from his hip. "Don't ask, don't tell." Then she added. "And don't let Joe find out."

Serenity slid in across from her. "I'm doing my best to keep him off track. Remember when a big day for us was deciding whether *Fifty Shades of Gray* belonged in best sellers or pornography or the trash?"

"Yeah."

The door opened and Doom came in. A couple of old men stuck their heads out of the back and stared.

"Back," Joy said to them.

They disappeared.

Doom slid in and Jerry set down rum and glasses, and a plate of red-orange wings. He paused for a minute to stare at Doom.

"You, too," Joy said.

Serenity pulled a notebook out of her bag and opened it on the rough wooden tabletop. "Let's get down to business. I'm sure we've all got other things to do."

She paused and looked at Doom. Looked at her for the dead eyes of Billy the Kid. Looked at her to see if she was scared. Or guilty.

All she saw was eagerness.

What the hell is wrong with you, child?

She put her head down and focused on the page.

"We—I—shot off my mouth and got us this seven-story monster. I keep acting like I have it under control and that we desperately need every square foot. But I don't know what the hell I'm doing."

Joy cracked open the bottle. "One floor of books, six floors of bars."

"Yeah. Believe me, I thought about it. Even I don't know if we need all of it."

Joy poured a glass, slid it across the table. Serenity took that long first taste that usually brought back white sand and hot sun and no worries.

Not tonight. "If we don't have a real need for every square foot, every librarian who ever asks for an extra dollar for a new table will have a harder struggle when people say, 'just another boondoggle like Maddington.' We have more money pouring in than we've ever imagined. But if every dollar we spend doesn't bring two dollars back to Maddington, it will all be a waste."

Doom said, "I claim one floor. My brother makes a living writing books that help people start micro-businesses. How to start a business on a hundred dollars, that sort of thing. How to set goals. How to navigate bureaucracy, and banking, and a million other things. I asked him what he's going to do when he runs out of books and he laughed. Said 'Once you get that one great idea that can change the world, there are still a million ways to fail, and nobody to help you.'

He said he could write a book a year and still be writing when he's a hundred. What you need, he said, is not books but communities.

"My brother means business incubators and help centers, but I want more. One place. A place where guys with ideas can come in and say, 'I've got an idea' or 'I've got a problem' and talk to people who know how to connect to knowledge. Call it 'Maddington Works.' The businesses we grow will pay for all seven floors by themselves."

Serenity scratched in the notebook. "You got it. Part of that floor's also going to be a jobs center. We spend enough time helping people write resumes and find jobs as it is. Now we're going to do it right, not separate from the businesses, but right there, on the same floor, people looking for jobs and businesses looking for people. Next."

Joy said, "Probably one whole floor of day care by day, with shelter for the well-behaved by night."

"Some people will say we've already got day care centers and homeless shelters," Serenity said.

"Yet there are dozens, maybe hundreds, of women in Maddington who can't hold onto jobs because they don't have day care they can count on and afford." Joy nodded at Doom. "And start-ups going out of business because they can't find people like these women."

"People already drop kids off at the library for hours at a time and hope that we and the kids don't notice," Doom said,

Joy waved a wing at Serenity. "We're already doing the job. But because we're so hit-and-miss at it, women can't count on it, and can't hold onto jobs. And, because nobody recognizes it as our job, we don't have the funding or skills to do it right. I bet that, if we do this right, the money saved by women having jobs, and businesses having workers they can count on, will pay for this one."

Serenity looked at Joy. "Okay, but how do you justify a shelter? I know we're doing that now, but how come we need to go big?"

"Because the current shelters have gaps," Joy said. "They have to handle the mentally ill, and those with drug problems. They can't really help people who have just fallen into the life and need help getting out. But we can. We'll have the resources. By night, our folks will have a bed. By day, they'll have educational opportunities—something we need to talk about next—and the best connections to jobs in the state of Alabama. Can you imagine how much the city and the state would save for every person who moves out of homelessness and becomes a tax-paying citizen?"

"All right. That's in."

Doom said, "You already hit the next one: boosting education. Portland did a study last year and found that improving a student's SAT score one hundred points gave them an average of eight thousand dollars more in scholarship money. We can do that for every student in Maddington. And that can make parents willing to pay more for houses here, and make businesses fight to locate here."

And so it went. Areas for medical/legal advice, a TV/movie studio to ensure Maddington students had the skills to compete for entertainment and communication jobs, and maybe even bring movie production to Maddington. On and on. Each idea spawned four more.

Joy said, "Once the dam of 'can't do' is broken, and we raise our vision of what a library could be, we've got a flood of ideas. Are you sure seven floors are going to be enough?"

Serenity looked at her and smiled. "Where did Miss Sunshine come from?"

Joy raised the glass in a toast. "Got cause for sunshine. To paraphrase old Ben Franklin, 'A library, sir. If you can keep it.'"

"That may be the hard part," said Serenity. "We've got somebody who wants their money back, and people who will try to stop us."

Doom said, "So let's get ahead of them. Let's take some of their money and hire a PR firm to get articles in regional press, 'Maddington: The City Built on Books.' We can feature success stories about businesses coming here because of the library. Kids getting scholarships. And, lots of pictures of local and state politicians at groundbreakings and fundraisers."

"We're also going to have to start finding quiet ways to make contributions to those same politicians," said Joy. "At the very least, we need the mayor and the district attorney in our pockets."

"I don't know if I want to get in bed with some of those guys," said Serenity.

"That's the way I saw it done when I was a cop in DC. Big dogs run together." Joy shoved her glass back at Serenity for a refill. "We're big dogs now. We may have to cross some lines we don't want to."

Doom raised her glass. "By any means necessary."

Serenity set her glass down and put her finger in Doom's face.

"I've had enough of listening to that shit. A man is dead. Dead! And now I've got to carry that to my grave, and even protect the killer, which makes me a part of this. Fine. I'll do it. But no more damned bragging and pretending."

Doom sat up straight. "I'm glad he's dead. He was a Bentley worm trying destroy our library and . . . wait! You were part of it?"

The door opened with a crack and they turned to look.

"Hello, ladies," said Joe.

fifty-two

the case of the distant librarian

"I THINK we're done here," said Serenity.

Doom hesitated, and Serenity said, "Go." Doom and Joy quickly stood up and cleared out.

Joe slid into the booth opposite Serenity and picked up a wing. "That was fast."

She looked at him. "The law can be intimidating."

He looked back at her evenly and studied her for a long second. "Only to criminals."

"See any here?"

"I'm a cop. I see criminals everywhere."

Now she studied him. "Maybe you should look somewhere else and leave people who are trying to build something good for this community alone."

There was a long pause between them.

"Let's start over," he said.

She nodded. "My turn. Let me ask you a question. I thought you were going to Rick's. You just decided to drop in here for Jerry's fine cuisine and warm atmosphere?"

"No. Stopped by Publix for a six-pack of Vapor Trail. Thought I'd drop one off for you. Nobody home, killer on the loose, thought I'd check on my partner."

He picked up the rum bottle and studied it.

Serenity said, "Want some?"

He sat the bottle down and smiled at her. First smile of the night.

"I'm on duty, ma'am. Always."

"Bullshit." She pushed Doom's mostly untouched glass at him and waited until he took a sip.

"How're the Braves doing?" she said.

He set the glass down. "They're not as interesting as the case I'm working on. 'The Case of the Murder in the Suddenly-Rich Library.'"

Serenity laughed. It was more for a release of tension, but it was something. "Did you check the Hardy Boys? That sounds like one of theirs."

"Nah, I thought I'd try talking things over with my friendly neighborhood librarian."

"Sounds like a police thing. How'd you find me?"

"I'm a detective, ma'am," he took a drink, "with the Maddington PD behind me. One call, five minutes, and a patrol car reported your car here."

"Maddington PD."

"Sees all, knows all."

"Except who did this."

"Except that. So, partner, give me a suspect."

Long pause. "Bentley."

"Bentley? You think the guy who hired Kendall sight unseen sent him down there so he could kill him? Did anyone even see Bentley in the library?"

"No."

"So we don't know his motive, he didn't have the opportunity, and—unless the coroner says he was stabbed with a rectal thermometer—he didn't have the means."

"I know. But he's involved somehow. He thinks he's on a mission from God to destroy us."

"Could be. On the other hand, I keep coming back to the advice from the book *All the President's Men*: follow the money. I'm not saying the library's doing anything wrong, but you've sure got a lot of manna falling from heaven these days."

He waited for Serenity to offer something, but got nothing. Finally, she put the top back on the bottle. "Are you investigating the library or a murder? I thought we were partners trying to solve a murder."

"Are. Sometimes you just scratch at what itches. And what itches right now is this: there's only one man in Maddington County that I know of who has the kind of cash flow the library's got right now."

"Bentley?"

Joe snorted. "Bentley is someone who's bought, not someone who does the buying. Told you, only one man with money in Maddington these days. Don Juan. North Alabama's drug czar."

"Why would he be interested in the library?"

"There's only one thing I know of in the library that might be of interest enough for him to throw his money around. And, one thing important enough for him to kill to protect if Bentley sent someone to threaten it."

Serenity said, "What? Large print books? Romance novels?"

Joe watched her eyes as he spoke. "They don't call him Don Juan because he loves books. They call him that because he loves women." He paused and watched her reaction. "The library has the hottest woman in Maddington—who has something she can't tell her husband."

Now Serenity stared at him, confused about how to act, and decided anger was the safest. "How dare you—"

He stood up.

"Yeah, I know. I've just paid you the horrible insult of telling you how you look to every man in Maddington. Including me. And that just makes you angry."

He tipped his hat. "Maybe we should call this 'The Case of the Distant Librarian.'"

the sound of one hand working

FRIDAY MORNING, three stories of MAD up, and Serenity had Joy in her office. "Cots put back, boss. Lost Boys off to their day homes. The original MAD is open for day business."

Serenity raised her head and Joy looked at her. "Jesus, Serenity, what happened to you? Last time my eyes looked that red was . . . well, just a couple of nights ago. But that's me. What happened to you?"

"Too much playing cop yesterday. Too much rum last night. Too little sleep. Too little real talking."

Joy smiled. "Celebrating?"

"Oh yeah. Trying to keep the library and Doom running from the lawman who sleeps next to me. Most nights."

Joy gave Serenity a quick head nod and a sad look.

"Cops can sense when someone's hiding something. Reason why I lost my husband. Well, the second one." She reached over and put her hand on Serenity's. "Joe seems like a keeper."

"He is. Or was. I'm not sure. Joy, I've got kind of a weird question for you. On a scale of one to ten, what am I? In hotness, I mean."

Joy tried to read Serenity's face, gave up, and answered the question straight. "I don't know. Seven. Eight on a good day. What brought that on?"

"Not the absolute hottest woman in Maddington County?"

"No. I mean, no offense. Remember a couple of years ago that reality TV show had that woman from Clift's Cove on that dating show? Flew her out there and all that. Don't think they'd do that for you." She paused. "No offense."

"None taken." Serenity exhaled. "Joe sees me as a lot hotter than I am."

"Fight for him." Joy pulled her hand back. "On the other hand, you need to find some story to keep him away from our Excitable Girl and make sure he doesn't think your library secret has anything to do with, you know, murder and actual crimes at the library."

"I don't want to lose him."

Serenity slid the *Scarface* DVD across the desk to Joy. "Let's talk about something else. This was in the drop box the other morning."

"Good movie."

Then Joy read the note.

"Good movie," said Serenity, "unless someone is pointing their 'little friend' at you. And, someone tried to run me off the road."

"Serenity, we need security here."

Serenity took a sip of her coffee. "We've got our high school kids. And for now, we've got Maddington's finest."

"Who we can't tell about the danger." Joy paused. "We need to do *something*. I've got an Israeli submachine pistol that is so cool. Give me the budget and I can have our whole staff armed with them by this afternoon."

"No. Hell, no. And if I catch you bringing any firearm on MAD property, you are fired on the spot. You got that?"

"Thought you'd say that. Choice number two. I know a guy," said Joy. "OHR."

"Is that a company? Are you sure we can trust them?"

"Not them. OHR is a guy. One Hand Ryan. And, yes, we can trust him. If he takes the job. I ran into him when I was on the force, but he wasn't a cop. He was kind of invisible security for a rock star. The star had all these people strutting around in dark suits like FBI, or maybe Secret Service. But they were just for show. OHR stayed invisible and took care of everything. He is loyal with a capital 'L.' But he only takes jobs he wants to."

Serenity nodded. "Bring him in."

• • •

A few hours later, Serenity rubbed her eyes and shut down her computer. Enough. Who would have guessed that spending money could be so tough? She had spent all morning staring at the screen and sending money everywhere she could.

She stood up and stretched. No sleep, no food. At least five trips to the coffee pot. And now she needed one more. Maybe she'd get some peanut butter crackers from the machine. That sounded as appealing as week-old cat litter, but she needed something.

Serenity opened her door and looked out through the glass wall from the old library to the new MAD. Three floors of steel frame were up. Glass was going in on the third floor and the frame was started on four.

Amazing what you could do with money.

She went to the coffee bar that was crammed into the corner of what had been the break room. Tom, the new library barista hired to set up shop in the MAD, smiled from his temporary quarters.

"You're keeping me busy today, Ms. Hammer."

"Yeah. Good thing we made this stuff free for everybody or I'd be broke."

"How about some decaf? I can make you a caramel decaf latte. Take some of that edge off."

"I wish. Even straight caffeine's not getting it done today. Give me a large Depth Bomb. Make it a double."

"You sure? Dark coffee with two shots of espresso?"

She handed him her cup. He worked on it a minute and handed it back. "When you get done drinking that, you may want to throw the cup out. But don't kill anyone in the ptocess. Aim well."

"I promise."

To keep Tom's brew from spilling and eating through the carpet, she cradled the cup in two hands as she walked back to her office. She unlocked the door, kneed the empty visitor's chair out of the way and sat down at her chair. Faulkner peeked out and stared across the room.

"Don't touch this stuff," she warned. He kept staring.

She jumped when she saw a short teen-aged boy sitting in her visitor's chair.

"Young man," she said, "where did you come from?"

He didn't say anything and she looked closer. The teen-aged boy had wrinkles around his eyes and a gymnast's build.

And one hand.

She caught herself staring. "I'm sorry. I wasn't staring."

He let her hang there for a long moment before he said, "Yes, you were."

"Well, yes, but . . . are you . . ." She realized she didn't have a full name and wasn't sure if One Hand Ryan was offensive. Just because Joy said it, didn't mean Emily Post would approve. "Are you, uh—"

"One Hand Ryan. Just call me OHR."

"I'm sorry," she stood up and reached a handshake across the desk. She was glad to see his right hand was the functioning one.

Didn't matter. He didn't take it. Her hand hung in the air for a second before she pulled it back.

"Well, Ryan," she said, "if you come to work here, what last name should we put on your paychecks?"

He shrugged and looked at the wall behind her. "How about Maddington?"

Could be worse. Could have just been Mad.

"Okay. Mr. Maddington—"

"OHR."

"OHR. How much do you know about our situation?"

"Everything. Joy told me everything she knew, and I did my own digging."

"When? We just decided to talk to you—and that's all this is, just an interview—a few hours ago."

"Plenty of time to dig. And travel."

"We're pretty secretive here these days, and our computer security features some of the best."

"Best for a library." He paused and leaned forward. "It's not good enough for a criminal enterprise."

"We're not a criminal enterprise."

"You are a civic criminal enterprise. Lots of organizations start that way, and then change. The people involved start taking a little for themselves, then a little more until there's nothing left. You appear to be the exception. You've raised the salary for your staff, but not for yourself."

"Joy tell you that?"

"She told me some. Most I found on my own. And if I can find it, others can. We need to fix that, and fast."

"We? You'd work for a—what did you call us—civic criminal enterprise?"

He stood up. He was small, and his muscles were compact.

"Everything's a civic criminal enterprise, if you think about it. Even the obvious criminal organizations like the Mafia and drug gangs don't survive because of their crime, but because of the roots they put down in the community and the needs they serve there. At the other end of the spectrum, churches are—sometimes—completely legal, but they only survive by the legalized theft of their tax-free status. In between are all the civic and business and political enterprises that write the laws to let them get away with murder.

"The problem that you've got here," he continued, "is that your library has nothing to protect it—no politicians, no tax breaks, no tough guys. And no OHR."

Serenity looked at him, a slightly wrinkled former teen-aged boy with muscles and one hand.

"It sounds as if you've talked yourself into taking the job. If we offer."

"As long as I'm on board with what you're doing, I'll be here."

"That's a little . . . arrogant. But you haven't talked me into hiring you yet."

"Ask me anything."

"First of all, I can't let you bring a gun into the library."

"Don't need one. Don't need a uniform either. Some days I'll have a blue polo with SECURITY written over the heart. Some days and nights I'll be in the big tree outside. Other days you won't know I'm here."

"How about your background? Do you have a resume?"

"Nothing I want to talk about with you."

"As I said about arrogance. Really, everything I've heard from you could just be bragging. I—"

"You need more Chris Knopf books."

"What? The writer? How do you—"

"Before I came in here, the last thing you did was order one of Chris Knopf's Hamptons mysteries. You need more. Chris is going to be the next big thing. And you need Larissa Reinhart. You're a southern library, for crying out loud."

"Okay. So maybe we can use you for computer security. I don't mean to be rude, but you only have one hand. One hand, and no gun."

"Sorry. My other hand got stuck in a Jihadist rocket launcher someplace I'd rather not name."

"That doesn't seem like a good place to put your hand."

"The American vice president who the launcher was pointed at thought it was a good idea. The guy firing the rocket, who was killed when the rocket jammed on my hand and exploded, thought it was a very bad idea. Opinions differ."

"Jesus. I mean, I admire your service, but aren't there limits to what you can do?"

He nodded, stood, opened the door and waited in the library for her. She stepped out beside him.

"How many people—patrons—do you count out here?"

Serenity looked. "Eleven."

"Twelve. You missed the kid under the table with the woman in the Rastafarian cap."

"Okay. Nice trick."

"Trick. Try to watch this. If anybody sees what I'm doing, I'll walk out of here and let you hire a rent-a-cop."

He jumped up and dug his fingers into the molding over her door. Then he pulled himself up with his one arm until his waist was even with the top of the door. Swung himself off that to the top of a book rack. Gathering speed, he flew from the rack to a rafter, and bounced rafter to rafter.

No sound. Serenity looked around. Nobody was paying attention to the man flying over their head. She looked back and couldn't find OHR.

There was a quiet thud behind her. She turned and saw OHR grinning, wearing the woman's Rastafarian cap.

"No one saw you."

"Actually, the kid did."

Serenity saw the child under the table staring at them. OHR gave him a little finger wave and the kid waved back. OHR handed the hat to Serenity.

"You'll do," she said.

it's all at the library

MID-DAY AND DOOM had all of her high school kids, college kids, hipsters, flipsters and finger-popping daddies working in the old library on programs they were shoe-horning into any space they could find, until they could move into the new MAD the next week.

Joy had her army of homeless men and derelicts working on the transition, moving anything they could find into any spaces already complete in the new MAD. They looked like two surreal ghost armies marching to two different beats, floating through the good people of Maddington who were battling to use the old library.

Mostly, the armies got along.

Right now, one of Doom's hipsters who went by Josh (not his real name; he was too cool to tell anyone his real name) and a walking skeleton of Joy's called Slim (because he couldn't remember his name), weren't getting along.

Josh was slouched against the open front of the men's room door, "Man, I saw it first. We're turning the men's room into a meeting room."

Slim shrugged. "Don't care, sonny. We need a room, too. Joy told me to box up the book store and find a place to store it. She needs the store space for something and the store has to be ready to move. I put that box down first, I got more coming and I'm too damned old to pick it up. Squatter's rights." He laughed a little he-he-he laugh. "Get it, squatter's rights in the men's room?"

Josh picked up a broom from the corner and waved it. "Mine."

Serenity heard the commotion and stepped in to find them wrestling with the broom. "Stop! Both of you, stop right now. What's going on here?"

"Joy needs this space for storage," said Slim without taking his hand from the broom.

"It's our space, for a meeting about a new drug from a Maddington startup. Meeting's scheduled for right now," said Josh, also with his hand on the broom.

A couple of geeky-looking young men pushed their way through the crowd that had gathered.

"Is this where GenTech's meeting?"

"Yes," said Josh.

"No," said Slim.

"Yes," said Serenity.

Josh tried to pull the broom away in victory but Slim pulled back. "What about my boxes?"

"Bring them in here anyway. It'll give the GenTech folks a better place to sit."

Done. One problem solved, about a million left. It felt good to make some progress towards peace and quiet. However, neither man was letting go of the broom. Serenity grabbed hold of it. "Oh, for crying out loud, you two."

She yanked the broom away and the handle punched a ceiling tile free. A handful of plastic bags with white powder fell onto Serenity's feet. Everyone froze.

Josh said, "Cocaine."

Serenity then pushed the tile aside with the broom, and bags of white powder cascaded to the floor like a white powder waterfall.

One of the GenTech guys looked at the other.

"Is that our new product?"

lucy, you got some 'splaining to do

SERENITY STEPPED BACK from the drugs, waved the crazies out of the bathroom and called the patrolman who was protecting the murder crime scene.

"You need to secure this," she said, "and call it in."

The patrolman—who looked like a twin to the library's high school security, with the exception of a blue suit and a gun—keyed his mic and spoke into it.

Serenity spread her arms and made a gesture of pushing back the crowd. "Everybody find a home on the other side of the library. Our crime scene is about to get bigger."

The crowd melted away until just one man was left: a tough-looking man who wasn't budging.

"Sir, you need to—"

He reached behind his back and pulled out a pistol.

"Actually, what I need to do is take all of this off your hands and get it back to my boss." He pointed the gun at the patrolman. "Take your gun out slowly and drop it in the toilet."

That done, the gunman said, "Now, dump that box out and fill it up with those bags. You're going to carry this out to my car for me."

Serenity took slow backward steps. She got to her office, grabbed the AK-47, and stepped back out in full Rambo pose with the rifle pointed at the gunman.

Or, rather where the gunman had been a moment ago. Now, the gunman was on the floor with OHR sitting on top of him and the gun on the floor.

Joe burst in the door and took in the whole scene.

"Jesus, Serenity. What now?"

fifty-six

a library full of inconvenient truths

JOE STOOD in the doorway of the men's room, just out-side the yellow crime scene tape, holding on to Serenity's AK-47. Serenity stood beside him, but he hadn't looked at her since he had taken her weapon away. His gaze was on the white bags scattered on the floor.

"This have something to do with why you're so excited about the library these days?"

"Of course not," she said.

He grunted.

After a long pause he said, "Well, somebody's going to be excited when the word gets out." To the patrolman who was first on the scene, he said, "Any idea how much we've got?"

"A lot," the man said. "Enough that we can't count the bags until we get the go-ahead to disturb the scene."

Joe stared at the bags in silence until Serenity got tired of waiting and said, "Joe, you don't really think—"

He turned away from her, to another patrolman waiting at the edge of the lobby with the two GenTech guys.

"Detective Hammer," the patrolmen said, "you need to talk to these two. They say they were supposed to have a meeting in the men's room to discuss a new drug."

Joe gave them his cop stare. "You had a meeting scheduled in the men's room to discuss drugs?"

One shook his head furiously, "Not those kind of drugs. Well, kind of, but no, those aren't ours. What we've got is a new approach, something that will reduce prescription drug addiction tremendously." His eyes got bright. "We're fusing drug tuning with genetic testing. If someone has a legitimate need for a painkiller, we sequence their DNA for markers to tell us what combinations will be most effective, and least addictive, for that individual. We think we can reduce prescription drug addiction by at least 50 percent."

"And get rich," said the other guy.

"Lot of people try to get rich selling drugs," Joe said. "Sure this pile isn't yours?"

"Of course not. Coke is really a very poor painkiller. It doesn't—"

Joe waved his free hand. "Good for you, Einstein. I still want to know who told you to go into the men's room and stand under a mountain of coke to plan a new drug."

The kid flopped a hand at Serenity without much enthusiasm. "She did."

Joe didn't take his eyes off the GenTech boys. "I want to talk to you two some more. Not that I don't believe you, I just want to get things straight." He made a micro-turn toward the patrolman. "Ardarius, I don't want these two bouncing around in here. Take them out and let them sit in a couple of squad cars."

Ardarius nodded. When the three of them were almost at the door, Joe said, "Separate cars."

Then Joe turned and looked evenly at Serenity. She said, "You can't seriously think that cocaine belongs to those two boy geniuses?"

"Pretty sure I know who owns this," he said. "Used to own this. But I'm a cop. I gather facts, and I follow where the facts point, even if I don't like it. So, I'll talk to those two. And mostly I'll talk to him." He nodded toward to the gunman, still on the floor, but now with handcuffs on. "And you."

Serenity said, "Chief's letting you take this case? In your wife's library? On top of the murder?"

"Of course he will." Joe's stare was still hard. "Besides, the chief likes you. He can't believe the library's involved. Said to do everything I could to help you keep the library open during this. So here's what I'm going to do for you, Serenity. We need to search the ceilings. All of them. Need to bring drug-sniffing dogs in to see what else we find. We really should shut down the whole library. As a favor to you and the chief, I'll just shut down this side, like I should have yesterday. I'll get the guys who are checking the ceiling tiles

to wear some kind of coverall, so they look like maintenance. We'll keep the dogs as quiet as we can. And, we'll get
as much done as we can tonight after you're closed."

She put her hand on his arm. "Thanks, Joe. That means
a lot."

He took her hand away. "Then it's time to trade with
me. Tell me what you know about the drugs."

"What is wrong with you? I don't know anything about
this. You think we're giving away dime bags with books?"

"I don't know what the hell you're doing here anymore,
Serenity. Every half hour, somebody comes up to me and
says, 'Joe, did you know the library's expanded its tutoring?
Offering basic medical advice and referral to clinics? Business startup support? Murder? Drugs?

"And I have to stand there like a dummy with a pasted-
on smile and say, 'No. I have no idea what my wife is doing
now. I knew her a week ago. Don't know the woman I sleep
with now. Scratch that, the woman I didn't even sleep with
last night.' So, no, don't play the 'you know me, Joe' card.
I'm going to follow the facts, Serenity."

"Yes, sir, Mr. Lawman. But I do not spend my days
cramming drugs into the ceiling of my library."

"Somebody does. Either under your nose, or—"

"For crying out loud. This bathroom is ten feet from the
front door. People come in all the time to use it and never
even come into the main area. And I don't spend my days
monitoring the men's room."

He pulled a notepad out of his jacket. "Reporting officer said that was exactly what you were doing when the drugs fell out."

"No. No. No. Well, yes, but it wasn't like that."

He gave her his long, flat emotionless look. "But you were doing exactly what you said you weren't doing. And the library's got a lot of new money suddenly. And you've got something you don't want to talk to me about."

They stood there not speaking for a full minute.

Joe finally said, "Serenity, I've got to follow the facts to make sense of the things I see."

She didn't say anything.

He took a deep breath and stiffened his back. "I told you. There's only one man in Maddington County with big money. One man with a taste for beautiful women. And only one man who could move this much dope through my city."

fools rush in

SERENITY AND JOE'S FIGHT had spilled out of the library and into the parking lot.

"Are you going to tell me again that I've got no reason to be suspicious?" he said.

She threw his hand off her arm. "Not what you're suspicious of."

"What's that supposed to mean?" She turned her back on him and he had to raise his voice to be heard. "Suspicious of what? Murders in the library? Check. Money for nothing? Check. My wife's eyes all alight with the smoke of some distant fire? Check. Now drugs. Drugs in the library. You know any other library with a drug problem?"

"It happens. One of the Birmingham libraries had a guy selling grass out of the men's room a while back."

"That's more than a dime bag in there, Serenity. And what was all that crap you gave me about suspecting Bentley of murdering his own guy? Something to throw me off the trail?"

"No." Well, yes.

She screamed, "You don't understand."

A saw whirred to a stop, followed by other equipment until the work site was deadly quiet and the men and the spectators were all watching them.

He yelled back, "Then talk to me."

She was starting to cry and she didn't want to. "I can't."

"Can't. I think you've got the right word. You can't, 'cause somebody's got their hands around your throat or around your . . . I can't even say it. And I've got to stop it."

She wanted to say something but her words just came out as sobs. One of the workers said, "Leave our boss alone." A couple of others picked up two-by-fours.

"You've got to either give me something to work with, Serenity," Joes said, "or I've got to do this on my own."

She sobbed as she looked at him.

He turned away. "Tell Steve he's got the scene here. I've got to pick up something at the house."

He walked away and she went back inside.

It was almost eight before she got away and went home that evening. No Joe. She dialed Joe's cell five times. Four maddeningly slow rings, followed by "You've reached Detective Joe Hammer of the Maddington Police Department. Leave a message." She yelled at the tone.

Joe was right. Don Juan had to be the source of the money, and the threat. And Joe was taking it personally.

Not good.

She heard a noise from the back of the house. Probably just an echo from her scream. Yeah, definitely an echo. Maybe.

But, she went to the kitchen and pulled out the biggest butcher knife she had. Then, with her left hand, she grabbed her phone and dialed the Maddington Police.

"Bernice, you know where Joe is?"

The dispatcher said, "He's your husband. Can't you keep him at home?"

"Obviously not."

"Well, we haven't called him in to work tonight. He should have been off-duty a couple of hours ago. He would have checked in with us if he wanted us to know what he was up to. You want to talk to the lieutenant, see if he knows?"

Serenity hesitated. "No." Then she hung up.

She knew Joe. Joe-the-cop always made sure the police desk knew where he was, in case something went wrong.

"Except," he had said with a grin, once, years ago, when they discussed his compulsion to make sure someone always knew where he was. "Except when I want to do something that can't be done officially."

Like go after Don Juan. Alone.

And that didn't feel good.

She tried his cell again. No answer.

There it was, that noise again. Jerking her head around, she thought she saw a blur out the window.

She didn't want to be there alone. Didn't want Joe to be wherever he was, alone, either. Long list of didn't wants came to her head.

Didn't want Joe going after a mobster alone.

Didn't want Joe getting hurt.

Didn't want to lose Joe.

Damn Joe.

Didn't want Joe talking to Don Juan and finding out he hadn't killed Kendall, which might lead to his finding out that Doom had killed Kendall.

Didn't want to cover up for Doom anymore.

Damn Doom.

Serenity went to their gun safe and opened it. She was right. Joe had come home for the illegal gun with the serial number filed off that he kept locked in the safe.

Next to where it should have been was the pearl-handled revolver Joe had bought her years ago, mostly as a joke. She had surprised him and taken basic and advanced training, and still kept in practice.

I've got to stop this.

She picked up her gun, cracked the cylinder, loaded five shells and threw the rest in her purse. She put the gun in behind them and walked, crouching, through the house to the garage. Just as she hit the garage door remote, she heard footsteps on the concrete.

She took the pistol out and pointed it at the rising door, which showed a growing slice of the outside world.

"This is what you get when you come after my family, sucker," she said under her breath.

Serenity watched a pair of legs in jeans appear. She cocked the gun, took aim, and waited until she recognized the body.

amanda knows evvvverything

SERENITY SAID. "I could have shot you."

Doom put her hands on her hips. "Why on earth would you do that? I'm helping you."

Serenity put the gun back in her purse.

"How exactly does sneaking around my house qualify as help?"

"I just wanted to see if you were all right."

Serenity sighed. "Doom, I don't need your help. And right now, I'm kind of tired of dealing with your idea of help. Go home now. Go back to being a librarian."

"Like you? I saw you take a gun out of your closet. You're not just shelving books yourself."

"Joe needs help."

"Did Joe ask for your help?"

Serenity hesitated. "He's a man. They don't ask for help. It's up to us to figure out when they're carrying a load that would be better carried by two than one."

"So hard-headed people sometimes need other hard-headed people to step in and not take no for an answer?"

"I don't need your kind of help."

Doom's eyes were wet and shining in the glow of the streetlight. "You don't know. Try me. If I can't convince you I can help, I'll go back to shelving books."

"Joe's chasing a drug dealer, and I need to find both of them."

Doom brightened. "Friday night in late August in a small Alabama city. Anyone my age knows there's only one place to find him on a night like this. If you take me along, I can show you."

Serenity waved her hand toward the car, and Doom squealed as she scrambled into the passenger seat.

"Buckle up," Serenity said. "And I don't want to know how you know about drugs."

"Librarians," she said, "know evvvverything."

the games people play

LATE SUMMER FRIDAY NIGHTS in Maddington—or anywhere in Alabama—meant crowding into uncomfortable concrete bleachers with five thousand of your best friends, some of whom you only saw on those nights. Then you screamed at your children and your neighbor's children to kill somebody, anybody. This all followed an opening prayer that asked Jesus to reward their noble efforts, hopefully with a victory. The fact that Jesus had never been seen in the stands screaming for the Maddington Rebels, or even at the concession stand waiting for a corndog, was not taken personally, nor did it prevent the same ritual from being optimistically repeated every week at the Maddington Veteran's Memorial Stadium—except for visiting weeks when everyone drove hours to try to ruin other people's Friday night prayers.

The VM, as the stadium was called, was also the place to go for drugs on a Friday night. Kind of one-stop shopping for God, violence, high-fat food, altered consciousness, and good neighborhood fellowship.

"I wish," said the ticket taker to Serenity, "that your son Joseph was here on the team. Big ole boy like that could sure put a hurt on that arrogant prick who's playing quarterback for Riverside."

"Yeah." Serenity didn't want to point out that when Joseph was in high school, big as he was, he never had played football. Instead, he had chosen to take out his aggressions by hitting a small sphere of stuffed horsehide with a baseball bat in springtime rituals. On a night like this, though, it felt like admitting that Joseph was either a conscientious objector or a socialist. "Two tickets, please, Joyce."

"Standing room only this late." She made change.

"Have you seen Joe down here tonight?"

"Didn't buy a ticket from me," she said it like that was a personal insult. "But I thought I saw that big hat of his floating in the crowd a while ago."

"Whereabouts?"

"Out there." She waved a hand at the sea of faces. "Somewhere."

Serenity looked out and saw a couple of dozen cowboy hats floating in the crowd. None of them immediately fit Joe's height or hat color.

She grabbed Doom as they walked through the gate, just before they were swallowed up by the mob.

"Okay, this was your idea. Let's split up and find Joe. Have you got your cell phone? Go over that way. Climb up to the top of the stands and if you see him anywhere, call me. I'll check the concession stand. First place Joe'll go."

"Yes, ma'am."

Serenity pushed, shoved and apologized her way through the crowd to the concrete concession stand in the south end zone. The lines stretched across the front of the open counter, winding so far back that they sometimes wound up colliding with players and officials in the end zone. She went to the edge and tried to push through.

A big hand landed on her shoulder and she was turned around to face a good ole boy in overalls towering over her.

"No cuts, lady. I come here for the hot dogs, and you ain't a'gonna get betwixt me and the last dog."

When Serenity had volunteered at the concession stand during Joseph's high school days she had spent many afternoons making a run to Walmart with other team moms. Buy as many of the cheapest hot dogs as she could, red sausages with so much gristle and so little quality control that she was horrified to carry the cooler. She always left a few in the fridge at home, but Joe refused to eat them there because they didn't taste as good as the ones at the VM.

But anytime they went to see a game, two steps past the gate he always turned, zombie-like, to join his buddies in the packed crowd waiting for dogs. Somehow, on warm fall nights in a concrete stadium, a combination of boiled gristle, fat, rat excrement and less than 2 percent of something called "other" wrapped in a plastic casing that had probably been banned by the FDA for ten years would transubstantiate into a substance that was irresistible to American males. Catholics had their communion miracle, and worshipers of the southern football religion had theirs. Maybe Jesus did answer their prayers.

Serenity should have known better than to try to interfere.

"Sorry," she said. She went around to the side door of the concession stand; it was propped open to let at least some of the steam escape. She wedged her way in.

The inside looked like any other sweatshop, which technically it was since the women and one poor man inside were packed cheek-to-jowl, sweating through their clothes, with customers screaming through the window and order runners trying to wedge past scrambling workers to put orders together.

"Serenity! Thank God you're here. Get on the shake machine."

"Dottie, I need to talk to you, just for a minute."

"And I need someone on the shake machine."

"I'm not here to volunteer."

"And I'm not here to talk. Give me ten minutes on the shake machine and I'll talk to you. At the counter."

Serenity picked up an apron that was crumpled next to the shake machine and went to work. Chocolate shakes came out as fast as she could make them and were snatched out of her hand before she could set them down. After what seemed like a few hundred shakes, a skinny teenaged boy walked by the door with his head consciously turned away.

Didn't work. "Harry!" Dottie yelled. "Get your ass in here and take over the shake machine from Ms. Hammer."

Dottie glanced back and a runner nodded and started filling a sack. Dottie turned to Serenity while the sack was being filled.

"Okay, what you need?"

"You seen Joe tonight?"

"Twicet." Dottie reached back without looking, took the bag, and handed it to a man at the counter. Money was passed, change was made. "He came in about fifteen minutes before kickoff, when it was just getting crowded. Got two dogs. Came back to the side door and got two more dogs about ten minutes before you showed up."

Serenity nodded and said, "Last two would have been to go. He always gets a few for the road."

Dottie said, "What'll you have?" to the next woman in line, and Serenity slipped back out the side door.

So Joe had already left. She pulled out her phone and tried his cell again. No answer, again. If Joe were heading home, he'd answer his phone. She called Doom.

"Plan B. Joe's already left. Meet me on the right side of the concession stand and we'll figure something out."

She hung up and tried to think. Maybe the drug lord was still here.

She looked around and realized the futility of looking for someone in a crowd of five thousand. It wasn't like he'd wear a sign saying, BUY DRUGS HERE.

Maybe not so futile. She saw a dark-skinned, white twenty-something boy slouched by himself against the fence behind the concession stand. He had a hipster hat pulled over his eyes, and baggy black jeans hanging halfway to his knees. She tried to approach him with as cool a walk as she could manage. Cool for a librarian, anyway.

"Hey, bro," she said.

He didn't look up. "Get lost, old lady."

"I got a hankering. And I got money."

The boy could have been a statue. "I don't know you, and I don't waste time on anybody who uses words like 'hankering.'"

"Don't you lecture me on words, young man. 'Hanker' is a perfectly legitimate word, dating back to seventeenth century Flemish."

So much for Serenity's cool drug addict act.

She heard a voice at her back. "Uh, Ms. Hammer."

She ignored the voice and pushed into the kid's face. "Okay. I don't care about drugs. But I want to you to tell me where Don Juan is."

The boy looked at her in horror.

Someone pulled her back and turned her around.

Doom said, "Ms. Hammer, that's not a drug dealer. That's Billy Zant. He's in our young writers group at the library. He thinks he has to be a disaffected young writer, kind of a cross between Raymond Chandler and James Dean. Not a drug dealer. Ms. Hammer, I'm sorry, but you don't know what drug dealers look like at Mad High."

"Then you do it. But I want to know where Don Juan is. Hopefully Joe's gone to him."

"Done."

Doom walked off through the crowd and Serenity followed her to the fifty-yard line on the home side. All the seats were packed except for a little knot of high school boys in preppy clothes who had a small ring of empty seats surrounding them. Doom crooked a finger at the boy in the middle and motioned him down.

"We need to talk to you about drugs," she said.

He smiled a crocodile smile. "You're cute, but I don't know you, and I don't sell drugs."

"You'll never see me again, and I don't want drugs."

He kept smiling a smug little smile.

"What I want is to know is where I can find Don Juan."

He leered and Doom said, "Not a Don Juan, and certainly not you, for Christ's sake. The real Don Juan."

He tried to look tough. "Why should I tell you?"

Doom reached into the big bag she carried for a purse and pulled out a card.

"Abercrombie and Fitch discount card. Forty percent off."

follow the bigfoot

"THIS HAS GOT TO BE A JOKE," said Serenity as she backed her car out of its spot, the high school band still loud even here in the parking lot. "You got played, and now we're on a wild goose chase."

"Maybe." Doom fiddled with the radio until she found something that sounded like a monkey banging on trash cans and a hound dog howling the same angry curse over and over. Serenity wanted to ask what the words were, but she wasn't sure she wanted to know.

Didn't matter.

"Hard country rap," Doom said without being asked. "The band is called Quarter Horse Cock; song is 'Kill the Goddamned Game Wardens.' You like it?"

"Uplifting. Didn't Johnny Mathis do the original?"

"Don't know who Johnny Mathis was. One of the old guys like the Beatles? But I do know that you're the one who got us out here on a wild goose chase. We're out here to protect your husband, who's like eight feet tall and carries so many guns he clanks when he walks. Seriously? He needs our help?"

"He's mad enough to do something crazy, and he's alone, against an organization that has wanted him dead for so long that he never goes up against them alone. Until now, maybe. So, yes, he does. Whether he knows it or not."

"And this helps the library how?"

"There's more to my life than a library. Besides, Don Juan may be the key to our money and to the threats against us."

Doom said, "You're so lucky. Joe's a good man."

"Better than I deserve right now, and most people don't know how good he is. He's kind of like a woman who's so pretty that nobody gives her credit for being smart. Most people look at Joe and see a big stud, party boy, which of course, he encourages with all his jokes. But when we're alone, he talks about right and wrong more than anybody I've ever met. The core of Joe Hammer is doing what he thinks is right." She paused. Her eyes were wet but then she giggled. "Well, he does talk about other things. Another reason to keep him alive."

"So are you going to write a hot bestseller about romantic life with a cop, call it *Fifty Shades of Blue?*"

"There's a lot more than fifty shades in that book."

"Good to see you joke," Doom said. "The dealer said we could find Don Juan at his restaurant, but really, if he's holding court at the Maddington Harbor Restaurant, Joe's in no danger of being killed there. They wouldn't hurt anyone in a public place like that."

"Maybe." Serenity laughed. It felt good. "Not unless he gets overcharged to death. The only time we were there, the snooty server finally came over after ignoring us for twenty minutes. He asked if we wanted a bottle of wine. Joe said sure. Joe took more time studying the wine list than the server liked, so the waiter called over the sommelier, a guy with a little silver tasting cup on a string around his neck. Sommelier studies Joe's cowboy hat and boots and says, 'Could I recommend something in the fifty-dollar range, sir?' Joe figures, why not, let's splurge. After the guy leaves, Joe looks at the wine list, and sees that the cheapest wine there is a fifty-dollar wine, a basic Tennessee red blend. The guy could tell we didn't belong."

"I'm not sure I'd want to belong to that crowd of elitist snobs."

"The worst thing was that when we got home," said Serenity, "we saw the same bottle sitting in our wine rack. Ten dollars at Publix."

She turned into the parking lot behind a Bigfoot truck that was throwing mud off of its huge tires.

"There." Serenity pointed to the edge of the lot. "Joe's pickup. We've found him." She sighed. "Hope they're not trying to kill him by making him drink himself to death. We can't afford that. Let's go get him out of there before he or they do something I'll regret."

The Bigfoot truck pulled up to the valet parking area and a guy wearing work boots and a camo jumpsuit got out and threw the keys to the attendant. Serenity ignored the valet and parked herself in an empty slot while someone from the parking stand yelled at her.

"Oh, get over it," she said. Then to Doom, "Hurry."

Serenity pointed at Camo Guy. "Something's up with him." He walked past the maître d' with a curt nod.

The maître d' let him pass, but stepped out from behind his stand and blocked Serenity and Doom, all the while wearing a big smile.

Serenity pushed past him.

"We're joining our party."

Doom gave the maître d' a little shove as she went by and said, "Get over it."

It was easy to follow Camo Guy. He was leaving muddy boot prints across the expensive carpet. Serenity thought the staff would be horrified, but they were all carefully looking away, as if the guy wasn't there.

He went to a back alcove, to a door in the back marked PRIVATE, and pulled the door open. Serenity quick-stepped the last couple of steps, caught the door as it was closing, and stepped into a darkened room.

Then three guns came out, pointed at Serenity and Doom.

size matters, sometimes

THREE GUNS. One was in in the hands of Camo Guy, three feet ahead of them with his feet still pointing into the room but his body and gun twisted around to face Serenity. The half of the room closest to the door had two black couches facing a TV that covered most of the wall—and another guy holding a gun. The back half of the room looked like a cute yuppie café. Three small bistro tables with expensive teak tabletops and intricate cast iron chairs. Two men sat at the table in the back corner, near another door. One man looked like a 1950s B-movie star with jet-black hair brushed straight back, gray temples, and a black Armani suit. His fork was poised over a dinner plate and his face carried a bored expression. The little guy next to him had his gun out and didn't look bored at all.

Armani Suit said, "Ms. Hammer. You just missed your husband."

"So he was here?"

"Here. Left. Any of you boys know where he went?"

Camo Guy snickered "Uncle Ernie," while the other two revealed no expression.

Armani Suit/Don Juan played with a forkful of food and looked across it at Serenity.

"Maybe he's home watching a movie. Say, *Scarface*."

"So, you sent that? And planted the drugs in my library to incriminate us?"

He put the food in his mouth and chewed for a few seconds while he looked at Serenity. Then he swallowed and said, "No. The public—emphasis on public—library has been our distribution center for years. And, no, I didn't send you the movie. Believe it, or don't. I've got no need to lie to Hammers anymore."

She waited.

"The people you pissed off sent it, and told me," he said, "which is good for me. Your husband has always been a pain in my . . . neck. Couldn't do anything about it. But you messed with somebody with a lot more juice than me. If—," He smiled. "If Joe were to disappear now, the police would be told by those people to not bother looking too hard. And the DVD supplier would be very grateful to anyone who helped Serenity Hammer's husband disappear.

"So." He stabbed something with a fork. "No one could touch your husband." He raised the fork. "'Til you came along. Thank you, Mrs. Hammer."

He tipped the fork in a toast and snapped at the bite like an alligator. Camo Guy giggled.

Serenity took a step toward him.

"Tell me where Joe is or that fork goes in you."

She felt hands clamp her biceps and pin them to her side while Camo Guy chuckled behind her.

"I demand to know where my husband is. Now," Serenity said, "or I'm going to the police."

"Go for it. And tell them about the DVD. See their reaction. You're too late to do anything but get yourself in trouble. We're done here," Don Juan said. "Throw them out."

There's an old saying about it not being the size of the dog in the fight, but the size of fight in the dog. The man who stood up from the couch was big, but Doom had the fight. She jumped into a karate stance in front of him and yelled an earsplitting "Hiiaa."

He punched her in the stomach and put her under one arm. Then Camo Guy rotated Serenity and tucked her under his arm. They carried the women out through a side door and threw them into the parking lot.

Sometimes the size of the dog matters.

alligator alley

SERENITY LAY on the asphalt looking up at the stars, counting aches and pains until she got tired of counting. She sat up gently. Nothing seemed broken, but everything seemed bruised. She looked at Doom, who was getting to her feet.

"You okay?" said Serenity.

"I'm sure some part of me's okay," Doom said. "Most parts feel like one of those animated anatomy texts that shows every muscle flashing red."

"That was really—"

Serenity said, "brave" at the same time that Doom said "dumb."

The valet, who had been watching, looked down at them and said, "You should have taken the valet parking."

"Thanks." Serenity got to her feet and pulled her phone out.

"What are you doing?" said Doom.

"Calling the police."

"No."

Doom put her hand on the phone.

"Doom, Joe's in trouble. It's time for the cavalry, even if that leads to you and me and the library paying the price when everything comes out. I can't play games with this."

"You're not playing games. Look, if you call the police, what will they do?"

"They will jump on this with both feet. And a lot of guns. Which is good."

"Unless Don Juan was telling the truth about things being fixed. Even if he wasn't, they'll send a swarm of cops down here. You think those guys in there will tell them anything?"

"No."

"Damned right. And, if Joe is still alive, they will send orders to kill him and hide the body as soon as the police get here."

"Joe's got friends on the MPD. People we can trust. And there's an FBI guy I can trust."

"What if you're wrong? Say one of them says or does something to make his boss suspicious. Don Juan says we're messing with something bigger than him. You don't have any idea where their tentacles reach. You'd be signing his death warrant—if he's still alive."

"Don't say 'if.' He's got to be alive."

"Then let's keep him that way. We can't wait on other people, certainly not for bureaucracies. You and me. They don't expect us," Doom said.

"With good reason. Don't you remember how we wound up on the pavement?"

"Yes, they sucker punched me and I fell on the muddy boots of the guy who was holding you. I could have taken him."

"You missed the point. Why did he have muddy boots? Think about it. Imagine you're the muddy boots guy. You work in the middle of your boss's hoity-toity restaurant. When you come to work every day, do you come in looking like you've been wrestling with hogs and track mud on your boss's carpet? Of course not."

"So?"

"The only way you do that is if your boss knows why you're muddy. Approves it. Ordered it. Muddy Boots was there when Joe got there, then he took Joe somewhere."

"Great. Now all we have to do is go back and ask them where he took Joe."

"No." Serenity marched over to the Bigfoot truck. "Look at that. Mud. Wet mud. Hasn't rained here in days." She reached up and pulled off something that looked like a corndog. "Cattail. This truck's been down by the river."

"The river, with all that yucky swamp grass? And rumors of alligators?"

"More than rumors. Before your time, the river authority decided that the way to get rid of all of that swamp grass was to bring two hundred alligators up from Florida to eat it all. When it turned out, after a few years, that the alligators didn't like to eat the grass, the river authority gave up. They trapped two hundred alligators and took them back to Florida. See anything wrong with that logic?"

"Not as long as the alligators didn't get jiggy and have any alligator babies."

"Exactly. So every now and then there are stories about alligator sightings. The biggest one keeps getting reported around Beaver Dam Creek. Know what they call him?"

"The alligator has a name?"

"Uncle Ernie."

sixty-three

the swamper

SERENITY AND DOOM sat in the parking lot of the Shell convenience store.

"There's only one way into this swamp," said Serenity.

"And one way out. They'll be watching that one way."

Doom fiddled with a black ski mask. "Lead the way," she said.

"Don't put that thing on yet, sitting here at a convenience store. We're going into the swamp down that torn-up road we just passed. It's actually called Space Age Boulevard, or was. Forty years ago a flim-flam man announced that he was going to build an amusement park named Space City in the swamp there. It was going to be bigger than Disney, and he sucked in half of North Alabama as investors."

"What happened?"

"What happens to most folks who put their hopes in swamp land? They lost everything." She paused. "Pray that's not us."

"Wonder if Shell has an AK-47 for sale?"

"Probably not. But in Alabama, you never know." She hesitated. "They might have a couple of flashlights, though. Why don't you go get us a couple? Maybe some bug spray, too."

"Couple of superhero capes wouldn't hurt either."

"Yeah. I'll wait here."

Serenity watched Doom walk away. When Doom opened the store door, Serenity reached up and switched off the dome light and slid out the door. Then she crouch-walked to the road, keeping the car between Doom and herself. When there was a gap in the headlights, she ran across the road and disappeared into the swamp. She patted her purse to feel the gun inside, and put as much distance as she could between herself and Doom.

This was no place for a superhero.

dinner for a favorite uncle

THERE'S A REASON why people don't go on romantic walks in a swamp, thought Serenity. At the moment, she was pulling herself out of a pool of foul-smelling water that a tree root had propelled her into. As she sat up and brushed the mud away from her face, she heard the buzzing of a swarm of mosquitos happy to have found a fresh meal. Great, just great.

She heard noise behind her, turned, and saw Doom's light bouncing around. Getting closer, but coming from the road off to her right, while Serenity stayed in the swamp.

She looked ahead and saw something blink. It looked like Doom's light glinting off something in the swamp.

No. She stepped to the side—avoiding the tree root this time—and the flickering light didn't change. Orange, not white like a flashlight.

Someone had a fire up ahead.

Serenity stepped deeper into the woods as something slithered away from her.

Snakes, she thought. Snakes and spiders and . . . She put the thought aside and focused.

Making quiet progress through the edge of a swamp was slow. Much slower than the crashing of Doom and her light. By the time Serenity got close enough to see the fire clearly, Doom's light was also clear, but through the woods behind her and off to the side.

At first, Serenity only saw the fire, which was in a small clearing on the edge of a watery part of the swamp. Two more steps, and she saw a figure slumped against a cypress root ten feet from the fire.

Joe. Head down. Dark spots on his shirt in the eerie orange-and-black firelight. Dark spots on his face. No movement.

She bit her lip to keep quiet and hold back her tears.

Then she heard Doom yelp somewhere behind her, and she jumped. More yelling from Doom, but Serenity waited. It was easy to follow the sounds and the light now as Doom was dragged into the firelight by a man in camo with a rifle in one hand and Doom in the other.

He threw her down at the fire. "Oh, shut the hell up."

Doom kept yelling demands at him and Serenity silently agreed with him.

"Mr. Hammer," Doom yelled when she saw Joe.

"Yep. For now. Gator food once I get done tenderizing him." He hit Joe in the face with the butt of the rifle and Joe groaned.

Joe groaned! He was alive.

"Reckon he's tender enough for ol' Uncle Ernie. In any case, if there's hikers like you out here, it's time I let Ernie take care of him, and you, and get the hell out of Dodge."

He walked to the edge of the water, to a log that extended from the bank out into the water. Then he picked up a stick the size of a baseball bat and began to hit the log in a slow rhythm.

"You ever see a trained gator, honey? He knows we don't call him unless we've got something good for him. Two course meal tonight. He'll take you both and tuck you under some tree root down in the deep, and let you age along with all your brothers and sisters he's got out there. Or I guess, from his viewpoint, entrees and side dishes."

He laughed while Serenity eased her gun out and worked as close as she could get.

Before long two glowing eyes appeared, and the man leaned his rifle on the log and walked to Joe, keeping himself between Doom and the rifle.

"Don't get cute." He grabbed Joe by his lapels and grunted as he pulled.

Serenity stepped into the light. "Leave him alone."

The man jumped, dropped Joe, and faced Serenity.

"Jesus Christ. This swamp has turned into a shopping mall full of females. Must be a sale on tampons."

"Yeah." Serenity motioned at Joe. "You're going to carry him back for us, and pray that he's all right."

"Yes, ma'am." The man turned toward Joe, half of his body in darkness. Then his hand reappeared in the light with a Glock.

Serenity's mind slipped out of gear and lurched into helplessness. She felt like the Civil War soldier in the Ambrose Bierce story about a man about to be hung, when time suddenly stands still and the man slips away to his former life. Time stood still now, and Serenity felt herself slip back into the comfort of her books, with Joe, and with her son.

The Glock came around, pointed at her. Slowly, slowly. Plenty of time.

In her mind, the books were calmly discussing life and death, and right and wrong. She was sipping wine, secure and happy, listening to the arguments like she was back in a book club with no more consequence to her actions than selecting the next book. All the listening and talking seemed like the most important thing on earth and, at the same time, a waste of life.

A waste of life. She heard that phrase ringing in her ears like an alarm clock.

In what felt like slow motion, Serenity aimed, shot and kept pulling the trigger until the gun made clicking sounds on an empty chamber.

The man fell back into the water. There was a furious splash as the gator grabbed him and shook him, and then

they both disappeared under the water. Then there was silence.

good advice from a bad mother

DOOM SCREAMED. "Oh, my God. You killed him, Ms. Hammer."

Serenity had her head on Joe's chest, listening. "And maybe saved Joe." She straightened up. "He's breathing. Thank God."

She looked at Doom. "And saved your ass, missy. Again."

Doom opened her mouth in shock. "Saved me? I would have wrestled the gun from him and marched him out, if you hadn't interfered."

"Jesus H. Christ," said Serenity. "What is wrong with you? Here, give me a hand. We've got to carry Joe out of here. And no, you can't just pick him up and fly out with him by yourself."

Doom bent down and took Joe's feet. Serenity felt his torso and head for broken bones, then bent down and grabbed his shoulders and grunted as they lifted him up.

"Jesus, he's heavy," said Doom. "What has got you so wound up?"

"Wound up? So wound up? Is your head so far up your comic book ass that you can't see reality? The man I love is unconscious, almost dead, and still may be in trouble. I just killed a man. Killed. A. Man. And that just adds to the long list of crimes and other things I swore I'd never do."

Serenity took a step backwards and gestured at Doom to keep up.

"I know," said Doom. "You're upset because you're afraid I won't cover up for you. You don't know me, Ms. Hammer. I am far stronger than you. I can take your secret to my grave, and never let the world know that you killed a man rather than let me save you."

Serenity stopped and they folded Joe up a little between them.

"Save me?" Serenity bit her tongue. Not now. They had work to do. She nodded Doom in the direction of the road and they started crab-walking Joe out of the firelight.

She couldn't keep her tongue still for long, though. "I am the one who saved you. Twice now. And I'm the one who's kept your secret. I distracted Joe so he wouldn't find out that you killed Kendall. I killed a man in self-defense. Yours was a despicable and pointless murder."

Doom dropped Joe's legs and straightened up. Serenity could see the shock on her face in the dim firelight.

"Ms. Hammer, how could you?"

"How could I what?"

"How could you think I killed that man? I am a force for truth, justice, and the American Way. Not a killer. You're like a mother to me. How could you?"

"You didn't kill him? Really?"

"Of course not. How could you think that?"

"Your spike. Your temper. Your . . . lack of reality." Serenity sighed. "Pick Joe's feet up. Let's get out of here. I've got bigger fish to fry. Although it is good to see that you're just full of words and no action."

Doom picked up Joe's feet and they trudged on. In the darkness, Doom said again, "Ms. Hammer, how could you?"

Serenity focused on not tripping on the dark path.

"Doom, I love your fire and your passion and your unlimited capacity for hard work. But there is something I've wanted to say to you at least a thousand times."

"What's that?"

"Just shut the hell up."

sleep with a librarian and learn something

"NO," SAID SERENITY. She was sitting on Joe as he lay on the bed, with her knees holding his face and pinning his shoulders down.

"I wasn't asking," said Joe. "I'm going back to work now."

She smiled at him. "It appears that asking is all that you can do right now."

He tried not to smile. "You're hurting my sore shoulder. You're sure this is what the doctor recommended?"

"How would we know? I wanted to take you to a hospital or a doctor last night. But once you woke up and Doom told you what happened in the woods, you insisted we bring you home."

"Righteous killing. Don't want MPD getting involved and making a mess of it. I'll settle this all myself," he said.

"I don't know. For a while back there, I was ready to call the police and take my chances on everything else, just to get you back."

"We're Hammers. We take care of our own."

"Yeah." She leaned back and put one hand on him. "Besides, doctors don't know everything about healing."

He smiled. "You know, I really do need to go to work. Sometime."

"Yes. Yes, you do. You and I have some real work to do between us. Healing work. Remember when Joseph Junior was first getting into his teens, and we were fighting with him and each other so much that we went to a counselor?"

He smiled. Smiled and groaned as Serenity rocked back and forth on his chest.

"If I recall . . ." He paused and let out a long breath.

Serenity took her hand away and stayed still. "We're not going to do this if you can't stay on-topic."

"I'll concentrate." She leaned forward until she was an inch above his face.

"Keep talking," she said.

"If I recall," Joe said, "she was a nice little old church lady who was horrified at the way we fought in the sessions. We wouldn't let her get a word in edgewise."

Serenity rocked back and put her hand back behind her again. "But she had one good idea."

"It also involved your hands."

She gave him encouragement and said, "Keep talking."

"She finally said, 'You two are just going to do things your own way no matter what I say. You two have no trouble talking, just trouble keeping it from turning into fighting. Why don't you come up with a rule that says any time you want to have a serious talk about anything, you have to sit on the couch and hold hands?'"

"It really was a good idea." Serenity used her hand a different way and Joe groaned again. "The only problem was that fighting with you made me horny, so I said, 'Better than that. We can only have a serious talk if you're in me.'"

"When we told her about our rule, she threw us out, but we didn't care."

Serenity released him, leaned forward and cradled his face in her hands. Then she kissed him and said, "So, do you want to go back to work, or do you want to have that serious talk we've been putting off all week?"

"Who am I," he said, "to argue with a determined woman?"

She stripped her t-shirt over her head and swung one leg off of him. Next, she eased his shorts off and stepped out of her panties.

"Now then," she climbed back aboard, "let's get . . . talking."

"You have my un-di-vi-ded attention," gasped Joe.

"Good. God, I didn't know how badly I needed—" she shifted and found a rhythm, "to talk."

Joe was out of rhythm with her. She couldn't tell if that was all, or if he was holding back for the talk.

"First," she said. "About Doom."

"Cute girl."

"Get your mind off that and back here. You know how sometimes I point to my eyes and tell you to focus up here?" She made the two-finger sign that said, look here, and pointed at her breasts. "Focus."

"Focused. Now, what about Doom?"

"She didn't kill Kendall."

The good tension went out of his face, and was replaced by bad tension. "Never thought she did."

"You also never knew the murder weapon was the library spike Doom kept on her desk."

She twisted a little to distract him, or to distract herself. It worked with Joe for only a few seconds.

"Her desk?" He paused, caught his breath and groaned. "The one next to the desk where Kendall was killed? We didn't find any kind of spike there."

"I took it. But I can give it back to you now that I know Doom is innocent."

"And how do you know that?"

"She told me."

He was silent and she seized the needed moment to bear down hard and concentrate. She shook, moaned, and said, "That's one."

She opened her eyes and saw that he was back to focusing on her eyes. "You mean one O, or one major felony, Serenity?"

He put his hands on her hips to join her and said, "How many other major felonies do I have to cover up for this? And I'll reach my own conclusion about Miss Doom."

She leaned forward and dragged her nipples one by one across his lips. She said, "I'll make it worth it."

His eyes were half-closed and he was smiling in agreement. Then they fluttered open and he said, "Wait. What about the library money?"

"I think you're right about it coming from Don Juan, but not directly. I found a little municipal fund that nobody much uses, but that gets millions of dollars every week. It has to come from him, so it's just like I'm robbing the robber."

Joe's face had the twist of a man trying to do two things at once, which he was.

"That's not . . ." He paused and moved with her. "That's not Don Juan. Even he doesn't generate that kind of money. Nobody generates that kind of money."

He started to say something else, couldn't, and breathed for a moment. Finally, he said, "As long as it's all in the past and you're done with stealing, I'm not going to play cop for something that's over with."

One matter settled, he turned his focus to the other. By this time they were panting together. She could feel what he needed and she gave it to him, got what she needed at the same time and then collapsed on his chest.

"Two," she said. "Two to one."

"Oh, my sweet, sweet Sweetblossom. I'm so glad to be done with lawbreaking and secrets."

He wrapped his arms around her and rotated her down beside him, tucked her head into his throat and let out a long, sliding-into-sleep breath.

Serenity, however, was wide awake. "We may have to talk a lot more like this, Joe. The MAD and Maddington still need that money to keep coming in."

She started to say more, but her cell rang.

confession is good for the soul

SERENITY FELT GUILTY. She had given Joe two sleeping pills along with his pain pill and slipped out of the house as the Sunday morning sun came up.

All this guilt just to go to church.

She thought about what Joe had said.

Nobody has that kind of money, he'd said. Nobody has that kind of money.

That had to be it.

She pulled into the parking lot of the sprawling Queen of the Universe Catholic Church with its gigantic mural of Mary smiling over the solar system. It was empty except for a little knot of Beemers, Mercedes, and one mere Cadillac, which looked like the poor stepsister. All were parked at the small private chapel down the hill from the main sanctuary on top. Serenity pulled around the corner and found a hidden spot between two lilac bushes.

Just in case she needed privacy when she came out. If she came out running.

She slipped into the chapel and took a seat in the back row and studied the small crowd up front.

Every local businessman was in the second and third pew. Sunday morning, very early, was a command performance for a private mass before the regular church opened.

And in the front pew, Paul Molcut sat alone. When the heads all bowed for prayer, she walked to the front and slid in next to him. An usher, big but nondescript, appeared from nowhere and put his hand on her shoulder. Molcut opened his eyes and waved him away.

"Good to see you here, Ms. Hammer," he said to her. "When I invited you to join my church, when I was at your library, I didn't expect you to join us, at least not so easily." He paused. "I'm glad that you respect the way things are."

"I respect the way things are going to be."

"So do I. But we may worship at two different churches."

The priest had paused while they whispered. Molcut stood up.

"I think we're done here for today, Padre. Thank you."

The priest opened his mouth to say something, thought better of it, and faded out through a door behind the altar. The other men stood up and walked out, shooting glances at Serenity as they left.

Serenity said, "I know where the money comes from."

Molcut put a finger to his lips. "Not here."

He looked around and motioned to two elaborately-carved wooden closets at the back. Confessionals. He stood and walked to them, slow and tired, and Serenity followed. He took the one on the left and she opened the door to the one on the right. She went in and sat down on the cushioned bench that filled the darkened space, closing the door behind her. A screen slid open between them and she saw the dim outline of his head.

"There is too much chance," he said, "of far-away people out there prying into our business."

"Like Bentley's auditor was prying at the library? I'm surprised that you don't use your same silent companion to stop them, too."

"He works for them, not me. But he does what he has to do."

"Even at the library."

He exhaled. "By any means necessary."

Hearing one of Doom's standard phrases come out of Molcut's mouth took her by surprise. She didn't say anything and he took that as a sign to continue.

"We were not willing to let Councilman Bentley find out where his money was coming from." He paused. "Although I do think our 'representative' may have overreacted. He saw a convenient weapon and a means to deflect blame, and acted." He paused again. "Ms. Hammer, I do not have complete control over this organization. Many people have tried to stop us, and many people have gotten hurt. Please don't be one of them."

"I'll be careful. You've already killed at least one man."

"According to Don Juan, so have you. At least we left the family a body to bury."

"Maybe that's your mistake, burying too many things in too many places. That's why it's going to be different this time," she said. "In the past, you've had to deal with one guy, or maybe one organization, who knew a thing or two, and might dig and find a little more. It was easy for you to hide things from them and easy to control the damage.

"But we're librarians. Finding out information and sharing knowledge is our business, our profession and, for some of us, even our calling. My librarians, and some librarians at other libraries, have been digging. They know how to dig in ways you can't even imagine.

"We know it all. Dark money PACs have been around, legally, for ten years, and have been used to blackmail businesses for contributions and, at the same time, blackmail politicians who are dependent on them for reelection. But I was surprised to learn that you've united all the Dark PACs, and all the illegal drug money in the state of Alabama. That's way past legal. We can prove it all, and you can't kill every one of us."

He said nothing, and she went on.

"My husband was right about something he said: nobody has this much money. But all of us in Maddington and in the whole state of Alabama together, do. You, and people like you, have quietly blackmailed every company, every business, every mobster—and ultimately all of us for what you call 'political contributions' for so long that we just shrug and take it without even asking how big it is."

Through the darkness, his voice said, "People want us to do this for them, but they would be surprised at how big it is. That's why we don't keep the money in a bank, even one under our control, as it could still be monitored. But a neglected municipal fund in Maddington? No one cares. And it's all legal. At least the parts I oversee are: making sure that businesses of every kind know the importance of political contributions, and making sure that politicians are controlled by those contributions. It's simple, Ms. Hammer. Everything gets organized, and when it gets organized, it gets bigger and more efficient. Think of the guy who took a little hamburger stand, organized it into McDonald's, and gave America a billion hamburgers."

"So you just organize hamburger stands?"

She saw a little bit of a shrug through the panel. "We don't worry about what our companies produce. Satellites, t-shirts, hamburgers, politicians, laws—everyone pays us a little, and benefits a lot."

"Drug dealers?"

Another shrug. "McDonald's isn't responsible for the cholesterol in their hamburgers. We're not responsible for what our subsidiaries do."

"And your enforcer out there?" she asked.

He laughed. "That's a little harsh. He's more of a persuader than an enforcer. Usually, a conversation is sufficient but, by any means necessary. We don't tell him how to run his part of our operation, nor are we responsible for what he does. Although, as I've said, I regret his last choice. I'm not a bad guy."

"Debatable. But none of that matters if people find out about all this. They won't put up with it."

He said, "They won't care. They just want someone to keep the world running."

"That may be true. But we can do a hell of a lot better job than you can."

He sighed. "You want us to cut you in? Fair enough. We've already got plans to invite you in. We're going to take over your building and let the chamber of commerce run it. We'll let you have two floors for your library, which is twice as big as it is now."

Serenity took a deep breath and hoped he didn't hear the shaking in her voice.

"No. Here's what we're going to do. Contributions stay the same. We'll let you keep half for your politicians. It's more than they deserve. We take the other half, expand the MAD, and build other MADs throughout the state. We know the money you control isn't just from Maddington, but from the whole damned state. Once we've turned the state MAD, we'll go after your brothers in other states. Try to stop us and every librarian in the country will start shining a light on you."

There was a short laugh like a cough. "I wish I'd given you a scrap when you came begging earlier. That would probably have been enough, then."

"Probably. But not now. And I honestly thank you for pushing me to fight for more than scraps for our library and for our city."

There was a long silence. "Your library is still going to join us, one way or the other, eventually. You think this is like one of the games on your library play days. But this is far more dangerous, Serenity, than you can possibly know. We can take your library with or without you—even without your life—if we have to."

"I am scared, honestly. You have power and you have guns." She opened the confessional door, stepped out to open his door, and spoke to him directly. "But we have books. I know how weak that sounds to you, but it's not. We can do this, and we will do this."

"Perhaps you can, but only for a time," he said. "Nothing lasts forever. You can hold on for a while, but every day will be a battle. You have already seen what happens to people who threaten us. You will pay prices, and you will pay them in ways you can neither predict nor comprehend, and in the end, you will pay the ultimate price. "

Serenity was tired. "Yeah. But when you don't do the things you know need doing, you pay a price there, too. We're done paying that price. I'm going to fight for this as long and as hard as I can, regardless of the price."

"That's madness."

The smile came unbidden out of somewhere inside her and bubbled up bigger than she meant. "Hell, yeah."

shout your madness to the sky

NONE OF IT FELT REAL to Serenity.

After her meeting with Molcut, she'd spent Sunday at the MAD, attending to details, looking over her shoulder, and wondering if her pink hard hat would stop bullets. Her meeting with Molcut just felt like big talk now, and when she called Joe in the afternoon he seemed distant.

"Feel like somebody hit me over the head with a sledgehammer and then stuffed the inside of my head with cotton," he said.

"Probably just the effect of the drugs from the doctor." She looked at her watch and calculated how much of the sleeping pills should still be in his system.

"Hope so."

She tried being upbeat. "Maybe you're still recovering from that awesome performance of yours last night."

Silence. Were the drugs fogging his memory? Or was there more?

After a pause, he said, "I'm going back to bed" and then hung up on her.

She sat out at the picnic tables for a long time, staring in the direction of her MAD, but really staring at nothing. How many people had she put at risk? All for a dream that might—probably would—just be gobbled up by Molcut and the great machinery of Things As They Are. After she was dead. Maybe Joe. Maybe Doom. Maybe Joy. Maybe . . . How long would the list be?

She shook herself out of her funk and saw that darkness had fallen. She couldn't face Joe like this. She went inside to the cot in her old office and made the transition from frightening waking dreams to terrifying real dreams.

She woke up with Joy shaking her, "They're here, boss."

"Who's here?"

"*Forbes.* And *Good Morning America.* Today's Monday, the day they're doing a profile on the MAD."

"Oh God." Serenity sat up. "Where's a mirror? I thought we were going to add a mirror in here?"

"You decided to put it in your new office. A supermirror, remember? But not here."

"Just as well. I'm not sure I want to see myself right now. Hold them off while I run home and get a shower."

A young woman with purple hair elbowed past Joy. "No time. We're on deadline."

"Who are you?"

She pushed up to Serenity and kneaded her face like it was a clay statue. "GMA hair and makeup. We can fix this."

"Five minutes," she yelled. "Jake!" A young man with hair like a rooster's comb slid into the room with a makeup case, clucking disapproval. They poked and prodded at her face for four minutes and fifty-nine seconds until someone yelled, "Time," and the woman said, "It'll do." The boy said, "Glad it's not my face," and Serenity was herded out the door and across to the new MAD.

The *Forbes* reporter met her at the entrance and shook her hand enthusiastically. "Thanks for doing this so early. Our photographer wanted to capture this early shot with you in front with the sun coming up."

Through the grogginess, Serenity said, "Sure." She shook her head hard enough to shake as much clarity as she was going to get into it today. "But no. Not me. Don't make me the story. Back up and get the full MAD gleaming in the sun with workers still climbing around the top floor and that line of people fighting to get in early. We're not even formally opening today, just letting a limited number into the first two floors. Despite that, it looks like half of North Alabama wants to get in. That's the story."

The *Forbes* photographer faded and a tall black woman stepped in.

"You're Robin Roberts," said Serenity.

"Yes, ma'am," she said. "I'm an Alabama girl just like you. It's good to see a story like this in my home state. Here's what we've planned to do: A quick intro with you out front, talking about the library. Then we'll follow you in and get you to show us the first floor. We'll throw it back to

New York while we go up to the second floor. We'll break the story into seven quick pieces spread out over the hour."

"They're still working on the top floor today, so it'll be a mess."

"Perfect ending."

"And until tomorrow, nothing's functional—except the first floor."

"Even better. Chaos sells."

Serenity smiled. "Then you're going to get rich here. Let me suggest two things. Focus on the MAD, not me. And do your intro out here, without me. Come inside, I'll greet you and we'll do the first floor."

"That's what we had planned on. We have a camera set-up on each floor. And thing two?"

"It's not 'the library' anymore. This is the MAD."

Serenity went inside and scampered to the coffee bar. "Depth Bomb, Tom. Fast, and in a MAD mug."

She took the mug and walked over to the door where she practiced a smile that made her feel like her face was cracking. She took as big a sip as she could and turned it into a cracked smile with a scalded windpipe.

The entourage came in and she held the smile.

"Welcome to the MAD," she said after Roberts introduced her. "This is our welcome floor. This desk is where a patron can bring any question to our help desk librarian like Ms. Doom here and she'll have a librarian—a MADman or a MADwoman—take them to the right floor to get started. People can bring us anything they need help with—

educational, business, medical, life. We won't solve it, but we'll make sure they get hooked up with whatever knowledge they need."

She laughed. "And, also here on the first floor, we've got community spaces. You can ask Ms. Doom where to get a good grouper sandwich . . ." Doom pointed to the cafe door, and Serenity hoisted her cup into the shot. ". . . or MAD coffee . . ." Doom pointed to the coffee shop. ". . . or just a good place to hang out with friends or business colleagues. Years ago, coffee shops in the Northwest hit on the idea of making their stores a kind of third place, something different from both home and work, but with characteristics that include a little of both. Our MAD will be a third place on a grand scale."

She smiled and motioned the *Forbes* guy into the frame. "This is Bruce Bowden from *Forbes* magazine. We wanted to get his take on the MAD from a business angle."

Bowden said, "Ms. Hammer has her take on the value of all of this, but we at *Forbes* have a different reason why we're excited: we see this as the next stage in American business. Business is often done away from work at parties and bars. This unites all that: work, family, and community, with more knowledge power than ever before. If two guys are having a beer in the brewpub and wonder if the idea they've just come up with is feasible, they can walk up a flight of stairs to the business center before they even finish the first beer. There's nothing like this anywhere else."

The director signaled cut and they all took the elevator up a floor.

"Second floor," said Serenity when the cameras were rolling. "This is our semi-traditional library itself. Books and knowledge technicians and who knows what else."

Roberts said, "This doesn't seem that much bigger than your old library."

"It's not. Yes, we have a few more paper books here than we had in the old library—or will, when we get them all moved in. Books will still be around for a long, long time. But we've got connections to everything else: the internet, databases, even video connections to experts across the world. And, knowledge technicians of every specialty, and no specialty at all."

"That might be a future show," Roberts said. "We might come back here one morning to take questions on-line and see what MAD can do for our viewers."

"Anytime."

"The first floor seemed to have customers—"

"Patrons. Customers are people who shop at someone else's store. This is their MAD, and we are grateful every time they come here. Yes, we have a few patrons downstairs. The MAD doesn't open until tomorrow morning—but we're doing a soft launch today. We're letting a few people in at a time to the first floor now. That's what the line is outside. At noon, we're going to open up the second floor on a limited basis."

Third floor. Serenity showed the business and employment center with mostly open desks and computers with plastic still on them. She gave a run-through and turned to Bowden.

"See, this is what is new and—we hope—revolutionary. We've tried business incubators before, and they tied corporations and entrepreneurs together. But this ties it all together: businesses, potential employees, and the services needed to make it work, all together. Maker spaces with three-D printers and other tools so people can prove their concepts without spending a ton of start-up cash. When the businesses get big enough, they'll move out on their own."

"And we'll be there with them even then," Serenity said, "helping them find or build space, and making sure that they stay connected. Once they're up and running, every business will have a librarian assigned as their contact, with an office here at the MAD and, if the business chooses, an office at their business making sure that they have all the knowledge they need. And, all the data connectivity they need will be free, coming through the MAD."

Bowden said, "We've had models where we offered free utilities and such in a business zone, but never a city built on free knowledge, of every kind."

Fourth floor. Serenity showed them the education center, with college prep and early learning centers. A man was testing a camera in the media center and Serenity motioned Roberts into the chair behind the news desk. "And this, Robin, is where we'll train your replacement."

Roberts smiled into the MAD camera and looked at her ten-foot image on the big screen across the room. The GMA camera swiveled to her image on the big screen as she said, "This is Robin Roberts, signing off from the future."

The fifth floor was mostly a mess of men who were assembling furniture.

"This will be a drop-in day care by day and a homeless shelter by night."

Forbes said, "Single moms can work one floor below their kids, and people trying to get back on their feet won't lose jobs because they don't have beds and showers."

The sixth floor was empty.

"Libraries have always been the only place where anyone can consult with a professional for free, and we've done the best we could," said Serenity. "This will be our medical, legal, and mental health knowledge center. Not a clinic, except in a very basic sense, but a link to professionals who can get people connected."

Roberts said, "If I were lucky enough to live in Maddington and didn't have a doctor, but had a strange pain, or if I had a scary legal situation, but didn't know a lawyer—"

"Come to the MAD. We'll get you started."

The seventh floor was a mess with the breeze still blowing through open holes and men climbing around and yelling at each other.

"Our administrative offices will be housed here," Serenity said, "and, appropriately, it's just a mess."

"Perfect." Roberts turned to the camera and did her closing.

When the camera was off, she came to Serenity with a serious look. "As we were moving up, it occurred to me that there are two reasons why this hasn't been done before. The first, and most important, is that each of those floors, in their own way, represents a powerful lobby that fights for its own turf. You're going to have a hard time keeping this from being pulled apart. You've got a tough fight ahead of you to keep this, maybe just to survive. Let me know if I can help."

"Thanks. I hope those are not just polite words. I may call on you," Serenity said.

"I meant it. Anytime."

"And the other reason?"

Roberts laughed. "We've all put up with these problems too long. No one's been mad enough before. Pun intended."

The *Forbes* guy came up carrying a tablet.

"I thought you might want to see a rough draft of what our cover might look like."

He turned the tablet around and showed them the screen. The shot was the outside of the MAD with men working on the top floor and a line of people waiting to get in. The *Forbes* logo was across the top and plastered across the building was, A CITY OF BOOKS.

the power of the book

DEDICATION MORNING: MAD DAY 1. Tuesday, August 19th if you paid attention to the old calendar, which no one in Maddington had for—oh, seven days.

Serenity sat on the podium and looked out over the crowd. Most who lived in the city were there, and it looked like half the people in the state were there, too. Camera crews, bloggers, tweeters, and high-school journalists, along with the *Library Journal* and other trade publications that were covering the seven-stories-in-seven-days building story were all there. Someone said Matt Drudge of *The Drudge Report* was there, reporting that Elvis was at the MAD, and threatening to turn Democrat.

In the front row sat Paul Molcut. Serenity had invited him to be on the stage with her, but he demurred and insisted that she should be on stage alone to claim the glory. Other local politicians decided not to be on the stage, either. In the back, she saw an Auburn jacket under a straw hat on a large and nondescript man and recognized him as Molcut's enforcer. She saw him make head nods to men scattered here and there throughout the crowd.

Americana singer/songwriter Amy McCarley was singing on stage, donating her time to support MAD. She came to the end of "Everything Changed," which was Serenity's cue. She stood up with a book in her hand and took the stage as Amy stepped down.

"Ladies and gentlemen, fellow citizens of the MAD, welcome to a new day," said Serenity, who paused for a scream from the crowd. "I'm not going to talk long because I'm as excited as you are to get inside." More cheers. She saw Molcut's enforcer make a "get ready" signal to his men and knew something big was coming.

She took a deep breath and savored the smell of paint and sawdust. She realized that there was book dust in it, too, and smiled.

Scanning the crowd, she realized that Joe was nowhere to be seen. Just as well. She didn't want him caught up in this. She smiled again, thinking of what their last memory of each other might be.

She knew what she wanted her last moment to be, if this was it. She took a deep breath.

"For years, here at the MAD we've done our best living on scraps and crumbs, afraid to ask for more. Despite that, we've always had a library that was a shining beacon for 'what' and sometimes 'why.' Throughout cutbacks and policy shifts, patrons always knew they could go to the library and our overworked librarians would do their best.

"But our best often wasn't good enough because we didn't have the time, the money, or the tools. Worse, if someone needed an answer to a 'how' question—how do I find a job, how do I start a business, how do I heal my broken family, they had nowhere to turn. Our librarians had one heartbroken day after another filled with people asking for help that we didn't have the tools to provide.

"And all of us paid the price." She paused, looked up from her notes, and then directly at Molcut. "We paid the price as a community, because none of us could face the price we might have to pay to do better." She looked back at the crowd. "Because we were afraid to face our own suffering, our children suffered, people who wanted to work suffered, businesses suffered, and teachers suffered.

"No more. The city of Maddington has stood up, led by civic leaders such as Ron Powell, and businessmen like Seth Burroughs and a thousand other citizens who went from saying this couldn't be done, to finding the courage to make the impossible real. That shining building in front of us, waiting for us, is an enormous toolshed for us all: Tools to build, tools to learn, tools to heal, and tools to grow a future beyond our wildest dreams."

She locked eyes with Molcut. The crowd cheered and she wound up for her finish. Molcut's enforcer saw the end coming and signaled his men. Serenity saw them shift so each had a clear line of fire toward the stage.

She raised her book over her head with two hands and shook it at them.

"Other cities are built on councils, and chambers, and committees of the absurd. But Maddington is built on books." She caught the eye of the enforcer and jerked her head up to the sky. He and his men followed her eyes up and saw OHR and his men appearing in the trees, watching and ready. Molcut's men sat down. For now.

Except for one. The enforcer himself got up quietly and edged through the crowd to a small notch in the building that held the side courtyard. Early in the morning, the courtyard was dark, and out of sight of OHR's men. A couple of them were scrambling, but it would take them time to follow him.

Serenity saw the enforcer lean against a wall, just a shadow to anyone not watching him. She saw a gleam of metal as he raised a long-barreled pistol.

Fine. But they'll never kill my books.

At the top of her lungs, she screamed, "Books. Books and courage and strength. Citizens of Maddington, welcome to your MAD."

The crowd leaped to their feet, cheering. Serenity was listening for another sound over the crowd, and she heard it. A gun boomed but she felt nothing. *He must have missed.* Then the long-barreled gun dropped, and the shadowy man collapsed into a heap. Joe stepped out into the sunlight, putting his gun away, and was swept away with the crowd.

seventy

meet the new boss

TUESDAY MORNING, seven days after Serenity had promised the MAD, a workman on the seventh floor said, "We'll put the real desk in tomorrow, ma'am."

Serenity smiled. "We're good. Leave it."

The man looked at the two sheets of interior plywood on sawhorses they had sat in an "L" as a makeshift desk for her. "You sure? They've got a desk coming in tomorrow that they say is really fancy."

"Put it somewhere on the first floor, where people can see it. There's plenty of room on this for me to work."

"Yes, ma'am." He took his toolbox and walked out.

Serenity sat Faulkner's habitat down on the side of the 'L' and opened his door. "Go explore your new home." He stuck his nose out and sniffed the air. "Sorry," she said. "No rum. I'm done with those days." She paused. "Maybe."

She looked around her new office, set in the corner with a view of the city through two large glass panes. Although smaller than most corporate offices, it was still palatial for a librarian. She walked to the big video screen that took up most of the wall facing her desk and picked up the remote control to flick through the views. Floor by floor, she watched crowds exploring their new home. She came to one that showed a twice-as-big-as-life view of herself, a high-tech supermirror, one she could adjust lighting and backgrounds as she prepared for future interviews.

The face she saw seemed to sag with tired grayness. She thought it looked like an aging amateur prizefighter wearing a bright red wig as a joke. No chance of running away to the beach and getting a job as a cocktail waitress with that face.

She punched a button and the screen filled with an external shot of the MAD and the big American flag flapping proudly in the breeze. Workmen were climbing on the roof as patrons crowded the doors downstairs and families played in the park that surrounded the building.

Her building. Her life. More than the sad flesh she had just seen, this was her real face and her future now.

A shadow crossed the monitor and she jumped and turned. A figure was at the door.

"Joe," she said, "you scared me."

"I understand there's a lot for you to be scared of these days."

She tried to read his face. "Maybe not, as long as I've got my cowboy."

He ignored her and waved his hand at the screen. "You did it. You got your dream."

She looked at him. "There's a lot to my dream, babe. You know that."

She looked at him.

He looked down, then looked up at her, squarely. "We've made a lot of dreams come true ourselves, haven't we? But this is that core for just you, even when neither of us knew it. This is what you were born for."

He crossed over and stood beside her, looking at the library on the screen, at the men and women and children drifting in. He started to say something, couldn't, and just pointed. Finally, he said it. "Looks like there's a place for everybody in your library."

She put a hand on his arm and looked up at him. "A place for everybody, Joe." Her eyes filled with hope and tears.

"No." There was a long pause. "Almost everybody. You know me, babe. I know where all this is coming from, or I at least know enough to know I can't be a part of it." His mouth moved but nothing more came out.

Serenity said, "I saw you at the dedication."

"Let's hope you were the only one."

She nodded. "I know how much it hurts you to do something that has to be kept a secret."

"Not as much as it would hurt me to see something happen to my Sweet..." He took a breath.

She reached up to wipe his eyes and that seemed to trigger the flood.

"I'm sorry, Serenity." His voice was breaking and fighting through the sobs. "Sorry as hell for both of us. Mostly for me. I'll always love you, but I can't be a part of this. I know I just said that twice now, but it feels like a song stuck in my head and it's a sad, bitter song for me, but it's the only one I hear, over and over. I'll move my stuff out today. I can't do this anymore."

She looked at him and wanted to argue. "I don't know if I would love you if you could. And part of me—a big part of me—wishes I could be different."

"I don't. This is the Serenity I fell in love with, written in a big, big book."

She could barely see as he walked away. Twenty years gone and only one thing left to say one last time. "I will always love me my cowboy."

He turned partway and looked at the floor. "And I'll always love me my Sweetblossom."

"Maybe someday—"

There was a knock on the door and Joy, Doom and OHR came in without waiting. Joe slipped past them and out the door. Joy said, "First staff meeting in the palace," and they pulled folding chairs up to the plywood.

Oddly, it felt like an ordinary day to Serenity. No rum, no crisis, just details of running the MAD: Life and death, and all that.

"We're wasting the roof," said Doom.

"Jesus, Doom," said Joy. "We expanded times seven in every direction already. Give us a break."

"No, listen to me. They've got these drones to deliver small packages. We could put a fleet of them on the roof and deliver books to homes and schools."

"So we could," said Serenity.

"We can use the roof for security, too," said OHR. He gave the security status and talked about various weapons and their placements and backups.

"This feels like Eisenhower planning for D-Day," Joy said.

"Just business," said Serenity.

Joy closed her notebook and Doom smiled a slight smile as she held up a book.

"We're not done with enemies," she said.

"No," said Serenity.

"So we need a weapon they won't expect. A library weapon."

She sat the book in her lap, opened it, and a white powder floated out in a cloud.

"Talcum powder," she said. "But I've got a source that can make ricin—a powerful poison from beans of castor plants—in the back of her farm. We can send someone a book. After they open it, we carefully retrieve the book. And fade away."

Joy and OHR exchanged shocked looks but Serenity just shook her head.

"There's a line we're not going to cross, Doom," she said. "Somewhere."

They all looked as Faulkner jumped into his wheel and started spinning faster and faster.

Turn the page

for a bonus chapter

from Michael Guillebeau's
next book

ONCE A COP

one

SOMETIMES IT FEELS like you're drawn by a Looney Tunes cartoonist on a bad day.

Picture this: a second-grade classroom full of tiny human beings, each with ten times the frenetic energy packed in one-quarter of the size of the full grown models. Running and bouncing for no reason other than that they can.

I sat at the front of the class, three-hundred-fifty pounds of obsolete cop teetering on a second-grader's chair; the wood creaking and moaning, threatening to go at any moment. The buttons on my too-small blue uniform threatening to join in, too.

Looney Tunes.

But I sat here, again, today, in front of a class of rug rats not much bigger than my hands, praying my chair won't break, or my buttons won't fly off like cartoon bullets, and the kids won't all run screaming for the door.

It didn't seem to bother the spiky-haired little girl hugging my leg as far as her arms could reach around it.

"He's my huggy bear," she said.

The teacher was a mournful-faced middle-aged woman. Probably sad-faced because of the way the years had pulled her body down until she looked like a pyramid on top of tiny scurrying feet. Or maybe because someone had shoved it all into a purple mu-mu like some kind of a bad cosmic joke.

Looney Tunes, on a bad day. But here she was, too.

I reached down to pat the girl on the head and the teacher pulled the girl away, "Jessi, today your huggy bear is a cop—police officer." The girl gave me a finger wave and a farewell smile.

I tried to return the smile. My smiles never come out right.

"Please don't make that face around the children," said Ms. Purple Tent.

Even the last woman who ever loved me had described my face as looking like an old-school prize fighter who had just lost a bad fight, and was sad about it. And that was a hundred pounds and several chins ago.

I did my best to look serious and presentable. I put on a blank face and sat completely still and completely expressionless with just my eyes flitting back and forth as I searched the little faces.

Purple Tent rapped a ruler on her desk and the faces all got quiet. Her mouth had the tight lines of someone who fought a losing battle every day to impose authority amid the rampant anarchy of the world. "OK, everybody, let's get quiet for— I'm sorry, what was your name?"

"Officer Joe. What's yours?"

I was trying to be friendly. The class giggled anyway.

The teacher had those angry lines again. "My name is Ms. Capulet. You need to give the class your proper rank and—"

"Just Officer Joe."

A huff. "Very well. Officer Joe." She turned back to the mob-in-training. "Class!"

There was silence again.

"Officer Joe has been sent here to tell you why you shouldn't do drugs."

She hissed at me. "As if we need this kind of fascist government crap in the second grade."

Out loud, she said. "They're all yours. I assume you have a presentation."

"I do." I started to stand up. Decided there was too much risk of winding up with a chair leg up my ass so I carefully and slowly reached over and picked up the spiral-bound poster boards our community outreach people had given me.

Jessi giggled. "You're funny." The class laughed with her.

"I try to please." More giggles.

I flipped to the first page. "This is Henry. He ate some drugs that the bad man there, named Alphonse, gave him, and now Henry doesn't feel good."

Ms. Capulet said, "Alphonse looks very dark-skinned. It's important to tell the children that the bad man could be any color."

Here in Birmingham, Alabama, most of the faces were what the white teacher politely called "dark-skinned." So was mine. But I didn't want to fight. Or digress.

"He certainly could. In fact, he could be a man or a woman, young or old, even a neighbor or a teacher."

The tent had sat down but now it stood up. "What's that supposed to mean?"

"Nothing. Just—look, I'm agreeing with you. I try to be honest with kids."

She snorted. "Go on."

I tried. Jessi waved her hand furiously. I felt like thanking her for the interruption, but I just nodded.

"Henry looks sick, like I look after my mom gives me medicine. Are drugs like medicine?"

"No. Well, yes, but not good medicine."

A boy slouched in the front jerked his chin at me, seven-year-old with teenaged attitude. "Medicine tastes bad. I won't take drugs if they taste bad."

I didn't want to lie.

"Well, sometimes people make them taste like candy."

"I like candy." He hesitated. "But they make you feel bad like Henry?"

I paused. "Well, yeah, eventually." I sighed. "But sometimes they make you feel good at first."

This wasn't going the way community affairs planned. It rarely did.

"Maybe," I said, "we should put off talking about drugs for right now. Let's talk about Henry being safe. If Alphonse tries to talk to you, what should you do?"

Tough Kid tilted his head to one side. "I'm going to ask him for drugs, if they taste like candy."

Ms. Capulet gave a harsh laugh, "Good work, Officer Joe." She turned to the boy. "Trey, you should tell your teacher if a strange man tries to talk to you."

I looked at Trey and tried to hold his eyes. "No. You should tell a police officer. Like me."

She said, "Teacher."

I said, "Cop."

She opened her mouth, but Jessi got the last word in. "What if Alphonse tries to grab me?"

I thought about what I would have told my own daughter. "Kick him in the balls as hard as you can and run away."

The class all giggled and Ms. Capulet rapped the table with her ruler. "Enough. I think we're going to lunch now."

Jessi said, "The bell hasn't rung. I want to talk to Huggy Bear."

"We're going to lunch early. Line up out in the hall and wait for me."

While the kids were filing out, I stood up as carefully as I could. I towered over Ms. Capulet and she seemed to take affront at my size and stepped into my space.

"Some job."

"Believe it or not, I'm trying."

She softened, a little. "The kids seem to love you, though."

"Younger ones, anyway," I said. "Older ones get suspicious of the uniform. I try to catch them before they reach that point. While I'm still a big huggy bear."

"Yeah. Kids are naïve and will trust anyone." She waited for an argument and didn't get one. "You really think kids should go to the police first, tell on their parents and teachers? Beat people up if they need to?"

"Yes."

"You really think the police can always help?"

"No."

She put her hands on her hips. "You can't teach them self-defense yet. I don't think giving every second grader an AK-47 or teaching them to kick people in the balls will help."

"Kids are getting hurt every day. So-called grownups aren't taking it seriously enough. AK-47s might not be a bad idea."

She said, "You're not the one who has to supervise recess."

I laughed and looked at her to see if she thought it was funny. Hard to tell.

She reached up and poked her finger into my shoulder. "That's a detective rank, pretty high to be doing community relations. Is this just a day of volunteer work for you? Acting like you know something about kids?"

"No."

"This is your full-time assignment? Basically a clown in a cop suit?"

I thought about it. "Yes."

"Quiet a comedown, wouldn't you say?"

"Probably."

"You weren't always called 'Officer Joe.'"

"No." She was waiting for more. "Detective Third Markowitz. Hard for kids to say."

"Hard for adults to believe."

"Yeah. People don't expect a guy who looks like a bad version of Sonny Liston to be named Markowitz. Blame my parents." It dawned on me that the name wasn't what she doubted. "Yeah, I know I don't look like a detective. Anymore." I wanted to change the subject entirely. "You know your police ranks."

"My dad was on the job. Brothers, too. We don't get many detectives in here for school officers."

"No." I didn't elaborate even when she waited. Finally, she won and I spoke first. "You seem to be older than the suspicious teenagers I talk to in the high schools. Not sure why you're so suspicious."

"Like I said, my father and brothers were and are cops. I know how you guys think."

We were both silent for a minute.

She broke first this time. "And, when I said the young kids love you, I'm not sure that's all good. You do seem to take an unusual amount of interest in kids."

I thought about it a long time.

"Yes."

I picked up my props and walked out the door.

acknowledgements

THIS BOOK was overwhelmingly the result of four remarkable librarians who inspired the birth of this book, guided it as it grew, and pointed the way to use it to help mad librarians everywhere. The librarians in this book are pale shadows of these four remarkable women who make their communities and libraries better every day. Thank you all, my librarian goddesses:

Sarah Sledge
Amanda Campbell
Anne Wood
Heather Ogilvie

Anyone who's ever read an early draft of mine will tell you that this book would be unreadable without the work of my two fine editors, Lisa Wysocky and Stacy Pethel. And you might not have bought it without the great cover that Artrocity produced.

Chris Guillebeau and Cheryl Rydbom contributed a lot of time and useful comments.

Despite all of this help, I am sure that there are mistakes, and I am sure that they are all mine.

Most importantly, I always have to thank the best partner, first reader, and co-conspirator any man ever had: Pat Leary Guillebeau.

about the author

MICHAEL GUILLEBEAU is the author of three novels and two short story anthologies. His first book, *Josh Whoever*, was named the February 2013 Mystery Debut of the Month by *Library Journal*. Guillebeau has published over twenty short stories, including three in *Ellery Queen's Mystery Magazine*. He lives in Madison, Alabama.